Lisa B. Kamps

playing HARD

Chesapeake Blades
Book 3

Lisa B. Kamps

Lisa B. Kamps

For Cat Parisi

I can never thank you enough for everything you do!

I was so lucky the day I met you, and will always treasure your guidance, your advice, and—above all—your friendship!

Lisa B. Kamps

Playing Hard
Copyright © 2018 by Elizabeth Belbot Kamps

All rights reserved. Except for use in any review, the reproduction or utilization of this work in whole or in part in any form by any electronic, mechanical or other means, now known or hereafter invented, including xerography, photocopying and recording, or in any information storage or retrieval system, is forbidden without the express written permission of the author.

The Chesapeake Blades™ is a fictional semi-professional ice hockey team, its name and logo created for the sole use of the author and covered under protection of trademark.

All characters in this book have no existence outside the imagination of the author and have no relation to anyone bearing the same name or names, living or dead. This book is a work of fiction and any resemblance to any individual, place, business, or event is purely coincidental.

Cover and logo design by Jay Aheer of Simply Defined Art
http://www.simplydefinedart.com/

All rights reserved.

contents

title **PAGE** iii

dedication v

copyright vi

other titles by this **AUTHOR** ix

Dear Reader xi

chapter **ONE** 13

chapter **TWO** 21

chapter **THREE** 33

chapter **FOUR** 40

chapter **FIVE** 54

chapter **SIX** 65

chapter **SEVEN** 74

chapter **EIGHT** 83

chapter **NINE** 92

chapter **TEN** 99

chapter **ELEVEN** 109

chapter **TWELVE** 115

chapter **THIRTEEN** 124

chapter **FOURTEEN** 136

chapter **FIFTEEN** 148

chapter **SIXTEEN** 156

chapter **SEVENTEEN** 168

chapter **EIGHTEEN**	179
chapter **NINETEEN**	189
chapter **TWENTY**	198
chapter **TWENTY-ONE**	206
chapter **TWENTY-TWO**	213
chapter **TWENTY-THREE**	226
chapter **TWENTY-FOUR**	233
chapter **TWENTY-FIVE**	244
chapter **TWENTY-SIX**	252
chapter **TWENTY-SEVEN**	262
chapter **TWENTY-EIGHT**	268
epilogue	280
about the **AUTHOR**	285
game misconduct **PREVIEW**	287
playing the game **PREVIEW**	295

Other titles by this author

THE BALTIMORE BANNERS

Crossing The Line, Book 1
Game Over, Book 2
Blue Ribbon Summer, Book 3
Body Check, Book 4
Break Away, Book 5
Playmaker (A Baltimore Banners Intermission novella)
Delay of Game, Book 6
Shoot Out, Book 7
The Baltimore Banners 1st Period Trilogy (Books 1-3)
The Baltimore Banners 2nd Period Trilogy (Books 4-6)
On Thin Ice, Book 8
Coach's Challenge (A Baltimore Banners Intermission Novella)
One-Timer, Book 9
Face Off, Book 10
Game Misconduct, Book 11
Fighting To Score, Book 12
Matching Penalties, Book 13

THE YORK BOMBERS

Playing The Game, Book 1
Playing To Win, Book 2
Playing For Keeps, Book 3
Playing It Up, Book 4
Playing It Safe, Book 5
Playing For Love, Book 6
Playing His Part, Book 7

THE CHESAPEAKE BLADES

Winning Hard, Book 1
Loving Hard, Book 2
Playing Hard, Book 3
Trying Hard, Book 4
Falling Hard, Book 5

FIREHOUSE FOURTEEN

Once Burned, Book 1
Playing With Fire, Book 2
Breaking Protocol, Book 3
Into The Flames, Book 4
Second Alarm, Book 5
Feel The Burn, Book 6

STAND-ALONE TITLES

Emeralds and Gold: A Treasury of Irish Short Stories
(anthology)
Finding Dr. Right, Silhouette Special Edition
Time To Heal
Dangerous Passion

Dear Reader:

To read more about Manon Rheaume—the first (and only) woman who played for the NHL (yes, a woman has really played for the NHL—and she just happened to be a goalie for the Tampa Bay Lightning in 1992!!), please check out some of the following links:

www.manonrheaumefoundation.org/

www.sportsnet.ca/hockey/nhl/manon-rheaume-realizes-nhl-debut-not-just-another-game/

www.si.com/nhl/2016/06/27/manon-rheaume-where-are-they-now

thehockeynews.com/news/article/there-is-a-hall-of-fame-case-being-made-for-manon-rheaume

If you're interested in learning more about the NWHL, please visit their website at: www.nwhl.zone/

Happy Reading!

LBK

#FightLikeAGirl
#PlayLikeAGirl

Lisa B. Kamps

chapter
ONE

Silence surrounded her. Empty and almost eerie. It shouldn't be this quiet, not with fifteen thousand people on the other side of those thick concrete walls painted red, white and blue.

Shannon Wiley pushed away from the table, empty now of fliers and brochures touting the rest of the year's schedule for the Chesapeake Blades. It would have been nice if the colorful brochures had disappeared because fans had taken them, but that wasn't the case. Charles Dawson, the team's PR Director, had boxed them up ten minutes ago then disappeared with Taylor LeBlanc, the team's captain—along with everyone else.

Shannon snorted, the indelicate sound echoing around the empty concourse. She was making it sound like something dramatic had happened when nothing could be further from the truth. Her teammates had simply gone home—or back inside to finish watching the last ten minutes of the game between the Banners and Vegas.

Which is what she should be doing—heading home. A glance outside the large window was more than enough to show her that the weather wasn't getting any better. The flurries that had been forecast had taken on a life of their own, turning into thick, fat flakes that coated the sidewalk and the street.

A trickle of worry crept along her neck when she thought of Sammie Reigler, one of the Blades' defensive players. Sammie hated driving in this shit. Shannon should have offered to take her home—

No, scratch that. Shannon was pretty sure that Sammie's ex-husband, Jon, was taking care of that. Shannon seriously doubted that Jon would be Sammie's ex for much longer, not if the sparks that had been leaping between them the last couple of months meant anything.

Good for Sammie. She deserved to be happy, and it was obvious that there was still a lot of love between Jon and her. Maybe Shannon should start a pool, get everyone to bet on how long before the couple officially reunited.

Because yeah, that was definitely going to happen. Shannon had no doubts about that. Which was perfect, because Sammie definitely deserved to be happy.

Everyone did.

"Abso-fucking-lutely," Shannon murmured under her breath then grabbed her gear bag and tossed it over her shoulder. She glanced around, looking for her stick, then rolled her eyes at her forgetfulness. Her stick wasn't here because she had given it to the young girl who had come up to the table and asked for her autograph.

Right after telling Shannon that she wanted to be a goalie, just like her.

Shannon blinked against the odd film of moisture burning her eyes then shook her head. Anyone watching her would think she was definitely losing it, the way she was standing there with a ghost of a smile teasing her lips as she swiped at her eyes.

Fuck them if they did. Wouldn't be the first time people thought she was weird, and it certainly wouldn't be the last.

And she didn't care anymore now than she did when she was growing up.

She gave herself a mental shake then headed along the concourse toward the main doors. The concession stands were already closed, their staff paying no attention to her as they cleaned off counters and swept floors, probably anxious to get home. Shannon didn't blame them, not when she felt the same. People drove like idiots in weather like this.

She rounded the last curve of the concourse then veered left, heading for the exit, when someone called her name. She hesitated, wondering if maybe she was imagining things, then heard it again.

"Shannon! Hey, Wiley. Wait up."

No, that voice definitely wasn't her imagination. Deep, rich, warm. She didn't have to turn around to know who it was, not when that same voice had caused an embarrassing blush to creep into her face fifteen minutes ago.

Kind of like it was doing right now.

She froze, torn between turning around and acting bored—or running for the door like the hounds of hell were after her. And shit, could she be any lamer than that? So what if Caleb Johnson was a star winger for the Banners? So what if he was six-feet four-inches of pure masculine deliciousness? He was just a hockey player.

Just like her.

Just like her teammates.

Except none of her teammates had ever made her skin prickle and dance with awareness as they raked her with their gazes.

"Get a grip, Wiley." She muttered the words under her breath then winced as they echoed around her. Shit, they came out louder than she had planned. Had he heard her?

She took a deep breath then turned, her sigh of relief almost as loud as her muttered words when she saw that he was still several feet away—definitely not within hearing distance. The staccato rhythm of each crutch against the shiny tile floor was another point in her favor, the sound helping to mask whatever idiocy decided to fall from her mouth.

Shannon adjusted the grip on her gear bag, swinging it from her right shoulder to her left, then watched him with as nonchalant an expression as she could manage. It was harder to manage than she thought it would be, considering all she wanted to do was rake his body with her eyes, from the thick black hair hanging over his forehead all the way down to the soft cast covering his left ankle—and everywhere in between.

No, not with her eyes—with her hands. With her mouth. With—

She swallowed back a groan of frustration and looked away, cursing the blush heating her face. What the hell was wrong with her? She didn't act this way over guys. Ever. So why now? Why with him?

She had no idea but she needed to get over. *Now*.

Caleb came to a stop less than two feet away, his weight braced on the crutches as he leaned toward her. No, he wasn't leaning—that was just her imagination.

Or maybe wishful thinking.

She pushed a few strands of hair from her face and tried to act nonchalant like sexy, gorgeous men came up to her all the time instead of running away the first time she opened her mouth. "Hey. What's up?"

"You heading out?"

Shannon almost rolled her eyes and said, *Duh*. Almost. She stopped herself at the last second, practically biting her tongue to keep the word from spilling from her mouth. "Yeah, pretty much."

Did he hear the sarcasm in her voice? She hoped not. If he did, he did a good job of hiding it.

"Are you heading home or going out?"

Shannon frowned. What kind of question was that? Of course, she was going home. Where else would she be going in this kind of weather? "Just home."

"Feel like grabbing a quick bite?"

And dammit, there went her face, heating up again at all the different images popping into her squirrel brain at his last word. Or maybe it wasn't the word—maybe it was the way he was watching her, those sparkling green eyes entirely too intense as they focused on her.

And holy shit, was he actually *flirting* with her? No. No way.

But what if he was?

Taylor LeBlanc's words came back to her in a flash of startling clarity: *Do not go there. Caleb is a nice guy but he's the biggest player ever. The.* Biggest. *So just don't go there.*

Is that what he was doing? Setting up nothing more than a quick play, looking to add Shannon's name to his list of conquests?

She narrowed her eyes at him, doing her best to ignore the way her heart skipped and danced in her chest at the sight of that dimple peeking out from his right cheek. "I'm not sleeping with you, Johnson, so just forget it."

If the words surprised him, he didn't show it. He actually leaned a little closer, his grin widening, causing that damn dimple to deepen in his cheek. "Fair enough. But the offer still stands: feel like grabbing a bite to eat?"

Shannon was speechless. Not just from his smile or his offer, but because he was still standing there instead of slinking away with his tail between his legs. That's what usually happened when she struck down an offer—which was fine by her, because the last thing she wanted was to be with a guy who was intimidated by her.

But Caleb didn't turn to leave, didn't act like he was intimated by her at all. He just stood there, watching her with those deep green eyes. Waiting. Like he really wanted nothing more than to grab a bite to eat. With her.

No fucking way.

She glanced over her shoulder, at the snow that seemed to be getting heavier, then turned back to Caleb. If she were smart, she'd tell him she couldn't. If she were smart, she'd tell him she needed to head home before her trusty car decided not to be so trusty in this shitty weather. "Aren't you supposed to hang out after the game for a meeting or something?"

"Yeah, but it won't take long."

Shannon chewed on her lip, torn by indecision. She should say no, she really should.

Caleb leaned forward and nudged her with his elbow, like she was just one of the guys he was trying to talk into doing something. "It won't be long, really. I'll even treat."

"Um—" She stepped back, trying to ignore the flare of heat caressing the skin where he'd touched her. "Yeah, sure. Why not?"

"Great. How about I meet you in the garage in—" He glanced at the watch on his wrist, an expensive timepiece that probably cost more than what she made in one season with the Blades—which really wasn't saying much. "Fifteen, twenty minutes?"

"Why the garage?"

"Isn't that where you parked?"

"Would I really be heading outside in this shit if I was?"

Confusion flashed across his face. Had she been too sarcastic? Probably—because everything that came out of her mouth ended up sounding that way. Perfect. Just perfect. Now he'd change his mind, suddenly remember something else he had to do.

"Why aren't you parked in the garage?"

"Because I was told we couldn't park there." She adjusted her grip on the bag, waiting for him to rescind his offer. "The garage is for season ticket holders and players and staff."

"They seriously told you guys not to park there?"

"Yeah, seriously." Shannon stepped back, wondering why he hadn't changed his mind yet, then decided to take pity on him and give him an out. "I should probably get going—"

"You're still going to meet me, right?"

"Um—" Okay, she hadn't expected that. At all. She started to open her mouth, to ask him why, then snapped it shut when he moved closer.

"We're heading to The Maypole. Do you know where it is?"

"Not a clue."

"It's not far from here." Caleb gave her directions, his gaze barely leaving hers as people started streaming into the concourse. He glanced around, wincing as a few people called out to him, then turned back to her. "So I'll meet you there?"

"Um, yeah. Sure."

"Great. Give me about thirty minutes." He winked—yes, he actually *winked* at her!—then started hobbling away on his crutches, weaving through the crowd like a fish swimming upstream.

Shannon waited until he disappeared from sight, then let the crowd push her toward the exit and outside. She shouldn't go, she really shouldn't. This was some kind of set-up. Or maybe some kind of weird hazing or something. She'd get to the bar—if it even existed—then sit there and wait. And wait some more. Meanwhile, Mr. Entirely-Too-Sexy-For-His-Own-Good would be having a laugh about the whole thing.

If she were smart, she'd just go home.

But what the hell. She was hungry, and bar food beat a frozen dinner any day. She'd go to the bar—if it existed—grab a bite to eat by herself, then head home. And if it turned out the bar was nothing more than a ruse, no big deal. She'd find somewhere else to eat then go home.

And call herself every name in the book for being so stupid and naïve.

chapter TWO

It wasn't a ruse. At least as far as the place existing. Whether or not Caleb showed up remained to be seen.

Shannon stepped inside the bar, brushing snow from her hair and jacket as she looked around. Rich, dark wood. Lots of open space. Tables and booths were arranged in seating areas instead of lined up like little soldiers, creating an atmosphere of intimacy. One section near the back was roped off, marked with a sign that said *Reserved*. Large screen televisions were placed around the walls and over the huge bar, each one showing a different channel. Large vases of flowers were scattered here and there, freshening the warm air with subtle fragrance.

Not exactly what she had been expecting from a sports bar.

Or maybe that was part of the joke.

Yeah, that had to be it, because the waitstaff consisted mostly of men and every single one of them could be labeled "man-candy". No way could this be a hangout for Caleb and his buddies.

A sports bar? Shannon had her doubts—a lot of them, even if the walls *were* decorated with sports memorabilia. She looked closer, surprised to see a lot of Banners items: pictures, jerseys, sticks. Some recent, some dating back more than a decade. There were even old pictures of the team holding the Stanley Cup, wide smiles on faces of long-ago players she didn't recognize.

She moved toward one, trying to read the inscription on the small metal plate attached at the bottom. A waiter—or maybe he was the host—approached her with a stack of menus, a smile on his rugged, lined face.

"A table for one?"

"Um—" Shannon hesitated then shook her head. "No, I'll just sit at the bar, thanks."

"No problem. Whenever you're ready to order, just let Bradley know. He'll take care of you."

"Yeah, sure." Shannon nodded, trying not to stare at the man as he walked toward a few of the occupied tables. He looked familiar, but Shannon had no idea why. Maybe he just reminded her of someone—

She shrugged the thought away then moved to the bar, pulling out a leather-covered stool with the toe of her boot. She climbed up then settled back with a sigh, removing her jacket as her gaze wandered around some more.

The place wasn't crowded—not surprising, considering the weather. And this was more upscale than your usual neighborhood bar, which made her think the few patrons probably drove instead of walked.

It also wasn't located in a residential neighborhood, centered as it was a few blocks away from the arena. They probably drew their crowds from the businesses nearby.

And she was spending entirely too much time analyzing things, especially since the bartender was standing in front of her with an expectant grin on his face, waiting for her order.

"I'll just have an iced tea."

"Not a problem. Did you want to grab something to eat?"

Shannon nodded, accepting the menu he slid across the smooth bar. She glanced down at it, only half-listening as he told her about the specials for the afternoon. A few minutes later, the bartender was back, placing a large glass of iced tea in front of her. He set a dainty plate holding a few lemon wedges next to the glass then looked over at her.

"Were you ready to order?"

She almost said yes—she knew exactly what she wanted, could already feel her taste buds watering at the thought of spicy crab soup and a juicy burger. Something made her hesitate. Caleb had said thirty minutes, and those thirty minutes weren't up yet. Close, but not quite. And even though she was almost positive he wasn't going to show—that this was still some kind of set-up—something made her want to give him the benefit of the doubt.

Which was probably beyond stupid on her part.

"Not yet, thanks. I'm supposed to be meeting someone here. I think."

"No problem. Just holler when you're ready." The bartender looked at something behind Shannon, then darted a glance at her and grinned. "If you're waiting for the guys, they'll probably be along any minute now."

"The guys?"

The bartender's gaze slid down for a brief second before moving up to meet her eyes. "You play hockey, right? I figure you must be waiting for some of the Banners."

Shannon glanced down, suddenly remembering she still had on her jersey. Duh. Then the man's last words finally sunk in and her head shot up in surprise.

"The Banners? They seriously come here?"

"Just about after every game, yeah." He nodded toward the reserved section in the back. "That's why we have that area blocked off. We may not need it this afternoon because of the weather but better safe than sorry, right?"

"Um, yeah. Right." Shannon took a long swallow of the tea and spun around on the stool, looking around again. So Caleb really hadn't been joking about coming here? Why was she having such a hard time believing that?

Because guys generally weren't serious when it came to things like that, not with her. At least, not once she started talking. Usually, when that happened, they learned very quickly how deceiving appearances could be. She wasn't stupid, she knew what she looked like, knew that when men first saw her, they automatically thought stripper or something—until she opened her mouth. That's when they realized she wasn't quite what they were expecting, and that it would take more effort than simply buying her dinner to get anywhere. A *lot* more.

Which suited her just fine. She hated playing games—unless it was hockey, of course. Better to have things right out front from the very beginning. Less chance of misunderstandings that way.

That also meant that things generally didn't go much past the very beginning, at least not for her. Yes, that had its drawbacks—but not enough to outweigh the positive.

Which still didn't explain *why* Caleb had invited her here this afternoon. She didn't know him, at all. Had never even met him before he stopped by their signing table a little more than an hour ago. She couldn't wrap her squirrel brain around it, especially on top of Taylor's serious warning to stay away because he was a player. Was this supposed to be some kind of joke, where she ended up as the punchline?

That and a dozen other scenarios were still running through her mind when the front door opened, letting in a rush of chilled air along with a mix of masculine voices. Shannon's gaze darted to the front of the bar and she paused, the glass of tea halfway to her mouth, as a group of suited men walked inside.

She recognized the faces right away: Shane Masters, left wing; Logan Simms, defense; Jacob Riley, center. And yes, there was Caleb, star winger for the Banners, making his way inside on crutches, that damn dimple peeking from his cheek as he laughed at something. He turned away from his teammates, his gaze sliding across the cavernous room until his eyes met hers. And oh damn, she was in so much trouble because his grin grew even wider. She gulped down a big swallow of tea, suddenly wishing she had ordered a beer instead—especially when Caleb moved away from his teammates and headed toward her.

"Hey. You made it."

"Yup. So I did." Shannon placed the half-empty

glass on the bar then wiped her damp hand against the leg of her jeans.

"Good. I wasn't sure if you were going to actually show up." He climbed onto the stool next to her, wedging the crutches against the bar beside him, then turned toward her. Their knees brushed and Shannon quickly moved her leg, cursing the heat filling her face.

"I almost didn't. I figured you were pranking me or something."

Caleb cocked his head to the side, that grin dimming just a bit—just enough that the dimple disappeared from his cheek. "Then why'd you show up?"

"Because I'm hungry."

Caleb laughed, the sound rich and warm. "Fair enough." He leaned across the bar, calling out to order a beer then looking over at her glass before asking for a refill for her. He shifted on the stool, bracing his arm along the polished bar and leaning toward her. "So, what do you think of The Maypole?"

Shannon moved away, just far enough so her leg didn't brush his. Again. "It's, uh, different. Not what I was expecting."

"That's what a lot of people say. I can't believe you've never heard of this place."

"Sorry, but I haven't."

"It's kind of a legend around here. At least with the team, it is."

"How come?"

"Because—" He stopped to accept the mug of beer from the bartender then took a long swallow. His gaze darted around, another grin teasing the corners of his mouth as he waved to someone behind her. "Do you know who Randy Michaels is?"

Shannon frowned, her mind racing as she struggled to remember why that name sounded familiar. "Maybe? I think. I mean, the name's familiar but I can't remember why—"

"Good thing my ego isn't very fragile."

Shannon jumped at the voice behind her. She spun around, her eyes widening in surprise at the man standing there—the same man who had greeted her when she first walked in.

"Randy used to play for the Banners. He owns The Maypole."

"That was a lifetime ago, Johnson. And I don't own it, my wife does." The older man reached for Shannon's hand, took it in a firm grip. "Randy Michaels."

"Shannon Wiley."

Caleb leaned in close beside her and placed his hand on Shannon's shoulder, the move almost possessive. "Shannon's the goalie for the Chesapeake Blades."

"Yeah?" Randy's hazel eyes darted from Shannon to Caleb and back again. "The jersey kind of gave it away. How's the new league doing?"

"It's, um, it's doing. Kind of a slow start so far." Talk about *understatement*. Slow? More than slow— although better than anyone had thought, at least at first. The rumor going around at the beginning of the season was that the league wouldn't last past the first four games. Yet here they were, with game number seven behind them, and they were still playing. That had to mean something, right?

Not that Shannon was about to tell either of the two men flanking her that. They'd probably think she was being melodramatic or overreacting or exaggerating or something. And why wouldn't they, considering they were both pros—current and retired? It wasn't like they had ever had to worry about not having a place to go play if their league didn't work out.

Not when their league had been around for more than one hundred years.

Randy Michaels was still talking, unaware of the doubts floating through her mind. "I'm sure it'll pick up soon enough. I'll have to try to make it to one of the games. Maybe get some Blades' gear to hang on the walls. If you ever feel like donating a signed jersey, let me know."

His offer caught her by surprise and she glanced down at her jersey, fingering the hem as she tried to figure out if the offer was nothing more than empty words. "Yeah, sure. Maybe when I buy a replacement one for this or something."

"Well, just let me know." The older man stepped back and briefly nodded his head. "I'm going to go make the rounds. You kids have fun."

Shannon watched him walk away before finally turning around on the stool. She jumped back in surprise when she saw Caleb watching her, his eyes a little too intense, their expression unreadable.

"When you buy a replacement? What's that mean?"

"Just that. We have to buy our gear."

"All of it?"

"Yup."

"No shit." He leaned back and reached for his beer, watching her over the rim of the mug as he took a long swallow. Shannon realized she was staring at the strong muscles working in his throat with each swallow and forced herself to look away.

"So when you gave that kid your stick earlier—that was really your stick? You have to buy another one?"

"Yeah. I mean, I have more than one but—yeah, I have to replace it."

"That sucks. I had no idea you guys had to pay for your own gear."

"Pretty much." Shannon reached for her glass, hesitated then propped her elbow on the bar and rested her chin in her hand. She leveled a direct look at Caleb, silently counting the seconds until he looked away.

Except he didn't. He met her direct gaze with one of his own, almost like he was silently daring her to look away first. A few long seconds went by before she finally offered him a quick smile and leaned back. "Okay, Johnson, no more games. Why did you invite me out?"

"Who says I'm playing games?"

"Me. And you didn't answer the question: why did you invite me here?"

"Why not?"

Shannon laughed, amused at his non-answer. She shook her head then drained her iced tea, placed the glass on the bar with a loud *thunk*. Then she leaned forward, not missing the way his eyes widened ever so briefly or the way they dropped to her mouth, just for a split second; not missing the way the corners of his mouth lifted in a small grin when his gaze darted back to hers.

"I already told you: I'm not sleeping with you. So if you think—"

"You shouldn't listen to everything Tay-Tay says."

"Yeah? Why not? Are you saying she's completely wrong?"

He shrugged, that grin still teasing the corners of his mouth. "Am I saint? No. But I don't know many people who are."

"That's not an answer."

"Are you always so suspicious?"

"Not *suspicious*. I prefer to think of it as being realistic."

"So the only reason anyone would ask you out is because they want something from you, is that it?"

Shannon studied him through narrowed eyes, waiting for him to look away. Waiting for him to slip and say or do something that would prove her doubts—and Taylor's warning—correct. But he didn't shift on the stool, didn't fidget, didn't look away. If anything, he looked *too* serious—like he was honestly curious and eager to prove her wrong.

"Let's just say that in my experience, men generally tend to run the other way as soon as I open my mouth."

"Yeah? And why is that?"

"Because I intimidate the hell out of them, that's why."

"Is that a fact?"

Shannon nodded, unable to hide her grin. If this was nothing more than a game, he was pretty good at it. And God help her, she was having fun—so far. "Fact."

"Well, I'm not running, am I?"

"Not yet."

"Not planning on it, either." He took another sip of beer, his green eyes glittering with amusement. "That's not to say I'd fight too hard if you decided to jump me. If you wanted to, I mean."

Shit. Was she so transparent that he could see every single thought on her face? No, impossible—

even if she had been thinking that exact same thing. She forced her tongue away from the roof of her mouth and gave him an exaggerated eye roll, praying her face wasn't as red as it felt. "In your dreams, Johnson."

He shrugged, as if it didn't matter one way or the other. "Just throwing it out there. Besides, how do you know I don't have the same problem?"

"What problem is that?"

"Intimidating women. Or realizing they only want one thing from me."

Shannon snorted her disbelief—loudly—then held her left leg out toward him. "Oh please. Here, pull the other one while you're at it."

"You don't believe me?"

"No, not really."

He watched her for a few seconds then tilted his head back and laughed, the warm sound wrapping around her. He wiped his eyes then leaned toward her, nudging her with his elbow.

Just like she was one of the guys.

"I like you, Wiley." He drained his beer then nudged her again. "But there's no ulterior motive. I just thought you might want to grab a bite with the team, that's all. You know, build up some camaraderie before our big exhibition game."

Disappointment swept through her—which only managed to piss her off. Why the hell should she be disappointed? She didn't *want* any complications with the man sitting so close to her—even if she had been thinking about it. She forced a smile to her face, refusing to let him see the disappointment. "Okay, I get it now. You're waging psychological warfare. Or trying to butter me up so we take it easy on you."

He cocked his head to the side, his dark brows raised in question. "Is that what I'm doing?"

"Yeah, pretty sure." Wasn't he? Shannon couldn't tell, not really—and she wasn't sure how she felt about that.

He laughed again then nodded his head toward the back. "Come on, I'll introduce you to the guys."

"I don't think—" But Caleb was already sliding off the stool and reaching for his crutches. He braced his weight against them then gave her an expectant look, like he couldn't understand why she was still sitting there. She hesitated for a brief second then finally stood, wondering if she had completely misread things. Yes, she must have, because Caleb simply led her to the reserved section then quickly introduced her—

As *Wiley*, the Blades' goalie.

Like she was just one of the guys.

And for the first time in her life, she wasn't sure she was happy about that.

chapter THREE

"How's the ankle?"

"Better."

"You sure about that?"

Caleb glanced down at the offending appendage, hidden by the black leather of his skate. Yeah, it was better—but it still fucking hurt if he twisted the wrong way. Damn if he'd admit it though—not that he had to, because everyone already knew, including the coach.

He glanced toward the bench, where Coach Donovan was talking with some of the other staff. The older man paused then looked over, their gazes meeting for a few long seconds. Caleb broke the eye contact first, turning back to Shane Masters with a grin.

"Yeah, sure enough."

"Think you'll be playing tomorrow night?"

Caleb shrugged, unwilling to answer for fear he'd jinx it. Whether or not he'd play tomorrow night was still up in the air. Did he want to? Hell yeah. He'd been off the ice for too long as it was. Would he? It wasn't his call.

Which was why he needed to show no weakness right now. To anyone. If he did, he'd continue to be a fucking scratch, and that was the last thing he wanted.

He tossed another grin in Shane's direction then took off down the ice, his gait nice and slow. Easy. Stretching his legs, feeling the burn in muscles he hadn't used in weeks, not like this. Ignoring the twinge in his left ankle, pretending it was nothing more than a kink that would be fine as soon as he worked it out.

And it would. Right after practice, he'd work on the additional strengthening exercises designed to get him back where he needed to be. Then he'd go home, elevate it, ignore the throbbing in the joint while he iced it down.

Good as new.

The sharp shrill of a whistle split the chilled air, signaling an end to this portion of practice. Special teams were up next—just not for him. Caleb glanced at the other end of the ice, his back teeth clenching in frustration. He needed to be down there practicing, instead of up here working out the kinks like some fucking rookie who was just starting to build his endurance.

And fuck, he hated this. Hated feeling helpless, hated feeling out of the loop, apart from everyone else. The break had been a fluke, a stupid fucking accident back during the preseason, an accident he couldn't blame on anyone but himself because he'd been showboating. Nothing more than stupid dumb luck. At least the break had been a clean one, healing quickly—for the most part.

Now all he had to do was convince the trainers and Coach Donovan that he was ready to go back in. *Show no weakness.*

Not a problem. Not when he put his mind to it.

Not when they needed him on the ice, now more than ever. The team was struggling with their goalies—both of them. Their primary goalie, Luke Connelly, had lost his fucking mojo a few weeks ago. It was like he had a huge jinx on his back that he couldn't shake, no matter what he did. And Dan Lory, their current back-up, wasn't much better. The Banners had won the last few games because of solid defense and a lightning offense, not because of their goaltending. It was anyone's guess how long they could keep that up, not without the solid goaltending.

There had been a rumor that the upper office was talking about sending Lory back down to the Bombers. The only problem with that was there wasn't really anyone else to call up. There had been more rumors about a trade that might be in the works but Caleb didn't believe those, either. No way in hell would the Banners bring Corbin Gauthier back, not if half of what Caleb had heard was true.

He still didn't know the whole story. Nobody did, not that he knew of. At least, if they did, they weren't talking. All Caleb knew was that something had happened a decade ago, something that had left bad blood between Ian Donovan and the goalie. And considering Donovan was now the Banners' head coach…

Yeah. No way would that trade happen. They'd have to make-do with Connelly and Lory until something else came up. Luke only had maybe another year or two left to play. The man was somewhere in his early thirties now, and every year he'd been playing was starting to show. Was that what his problem was? His body giving out, telling him he didn't have much longer to play?

And fuck, wouldn't that just suck? Caleb couldn't imagine life without hockey. Hell, he couldn't even remember life *before* hockey. Which was why being on the sidelines with this fucking ankle had nearly pushed him to the brink of insanity. He wasn't used to being on the sidelines.

For anything.

Which was why he needed a distraction. Something else to focus on instead of the lingering fear that he'd be a scratch for at least one more game. Something to take his mind off the irrational fear that even though the break had been relatively clean and minor, his game might never be the same as it was before.

He skated back and forth, easing into it, finding the rhythm that had come so naturally to his body as he was growing up. Yeah, he definitely needed a distraction—from the twinge in his ankle, from the fear that kept nagging at him, from the doubts that tried to eat away at his confidence.

The corners of his mouth twitched in a lopsided grin as the perfect distraction popped into his mind: a pair of large brown eyes fringed in long, dark lashes. Thick blonde hair that begged a man to plunge his hands into their silky strands. A full, pouty mouth, perfect for—

He nearly tripped, caught himself at the last minute. Yeah, that mouth was perfect—until it opened up and words tumbled from it. Christ, that woman was nothing more than one big contradiction after another.

A body designed for every male fantasy and an attitude designed to slice a man off at the knees.

Or maybe a little higher.

Caleb mentally winced at the thought, damn near reached down to adjust his cup against the phantom pain. Shannon Wiley was nothing like he had imagined. Not even close.

And maybe she was just the distraction he needed. Yeah, asking her to join the guys at the Maypole last week had been nothing more than pure impulse. And yeah, he had definitely entertained the idea of smooth talking her straight into his bed. Then Tay-Tay had to open her big mouth and warn the other woman off.

Except that hadn't stopped Shannon from showing up. It also hadn't stopped her from putting him in his place by declaring straight out that she wasn't going to sleep with him.

Almost like she was throwing out a challenge.

He'd thought about smooth talking her, changing her mind. It wouldn't be hard—he could tell she was attracted to him. But he hadn't, which surprised him. He always rose to a challenge—in more ways than one—but something told him that if he had tried, that would have been it. Yeah, he might have succeeded, but it would have been nothing more than a conquest, one he would have taken no joy in.

And that surprised him, too—the fact that he wanted more than just another easy conquest. He'd taken a gamble and backed off, deciding to treat her like she was one of the guys—when she was anything but.

Then he'd completely fucked up and failed to do any follow-through. Hadn't asked for her number, hadn't made plans to see her again. He'd simply let her leave with nothing more than a casual *see you around.*

Maybe it was time to rectify that.

Caleb slid to a stop as the whistle blew again. He bent over, bracing the stick against his legs and breathing in stale, frigid air, pulling it deep into his lungs and holding it.

The sound of steps shuffling along the ice pierced his thoughts. From the corner of his eye, he saw a pair of legs encased in blue track pants come closer. He took another deep breath and straightened, watched as Coach Donovan approached him. The man's dark eyes showed no emotion, gave nothing away as they studied him for seconds that stretched into one agonizing minute then another.

Coach Donovan rubbed the back of his hand across his mouth then exhaled, his breath escaping in a small puff. "How's the ankle?"

"Fine."

"Fine, huh?" His eyes darted to Caleb's left foot then shot back up. "Is that why you're still favoring it?"

"I'm not—"

"Bullshit."

Caleb's heart slammed into his chest as dread swept through him. He ground his back teeth together, felt the muscle twitch in his jaw. "It's fine, Coach. I'm ready."

Donovan just stared at him, his gaze giving nothing away. Then he shook his head, the motion brief and final. "Not yet. Another few days—"

"I'm ready now, Coach."

A flash of emotion sparked in man's eyes. "You really want to risk fucking it up permanently? Because that's what'll happen if you go out there before you're ready. I know you, Johnson. You go out there now, you'll push it. You'll showboat and fuck it up again—worse this time. Is that what you want?"

Caleb opened his mouth to argue, to tell Donovan he was wrong, that he wouldn't screw it up, that he wouldn't push it. Something in the coach's eyes stopped him and he snapped his mouth closed and slowly shook his head.

Donovan nodded, rubbed his hand across his mouth again and glanced around before meeting Caleb's gaze once more. "I want you back on the ice as much as you want to be there, Johnson. But I want you there at one hundred percent. Let's give it a few more days. If Doc gives you the go-ahead on Friday, I'll start you on Saturday."

Caleb wanted to argue. Hell, he wanted to do more than argue—he wanted to kick and scream and slam his stick against the boards like a two-year-old losing his shit. But he didn't do any of that, not when he knew it wouldn't help. Saturday. That was four days away. Four days wouldn't make that much difference, not in the long run.

Four days.

Who the fuck was he kidding? Four days would kill him.

He watched Coach Donovan shuffle away, knowing there was nothing he could do to change the man's mind.

Four days.

He had to find something to take his mind off the extended wait. Now, before he went totally insane.

And he knew the perfect distraction. What the hell. It wasn't like he had anything to lose.

Not that he would. He never lost, not once he put his mind to something.

chapter
FOUR

Breathe.

Shannon closed her eyes and repeated the word. *Breathe.*

In. Out. Slow and steady. Finding her center. Mentally preparing herself.

Just like she did before every game.

Only this wasn't a game. This wasn't even practice. Practice was over, had been for the last ten minutes. She stood at the edge of the ice, sweat running in little rivers down the side of her face and trickling between breasts that were bound and smashed by layers of gear. She growled, the sound low and muted, and pressed the heel of one hand against her chest to stop the annoying trickle. Then she opened her eyes and stared at Charles Dawson, the team's PR Director.

"You're worrying too much, Chuckie. Relax. I got this."

He pinched the bridge of his nose and muttered

something under his breath, the words barely audible in the chilled air of the rink. Then he blew out a quick breath and looked up at Shannon, his eyes filled with warning.

"Do not mess this up. Please."

Shannon started to roll her eyes then caught herself at the last second, figuring Chuckie would only worry more if he saw it. She reached out instead and tapped him on the shoulder—maybe a little harder than she had planned because he briefly staggered then narrowed his eyes at her.

"This is a bad idea." He shook his head and looked around, like he was seeking divine intervention. "I'll cancel the interview. Or maybe I can get Dani to do it instead."

Anger and disappointment rolled in Shannon's gut. Was she really that bad? Did Chuckie really think she'd make a mess of things? Yeah, he really did. Why else would he be searching around with that look of desperation on his face?

Maybe she wasn't the most articulate player on the team. She knew that, knew that sometimes her mouth got carried away before her brain totally engaged. Okay, maybe it was more than just *sometimes*. But she was trying, she really was. Last week at the autograph session was a perfect example: she hadn't slipped up and cussed at all. Well, not really, not in front of the fans. That was what counted, right?

Shouldn't Chuckie give her the tiniest bit of credit for that, at least? She curled her gloved hand around the stick and swallowed back the disappointment, hiding it behind a forced smile.

"Dani can't do it, she's busy." Not really, but since she was in the locker room already, Chuckie didn't know that. "And you can't reschedule because that would look bad. You don't want to look bad, do you?"

"Shannon—"

"Come on, Chuckie. A little faith wouldn't exactly be misplaced, you know."

He exhaled again, the sound conveying every single doubt he had—as if seeing it in his eyes wasn't enough. "You're positive you won't screw this up?"

Shannon nodded. "Abso-fucking-lutely."

Chuckie narrowed his eyes and leaned forward, one long finger pointing at her. "That. That right there is what I'm talking about."

"What?"

"You don't even realize it, do you?"

Shannon shifted her weight from one foot to the other and looked around, wondering what she was missing. "Realize what?"

"Shannon, you need to stop and think before you speak. One little slip-up like that will be enough to undo everything we've accomplished so far."

She almost opened her mouth to ask exactly what they'd accomplished, then changed her mind at the last second. Chuckie had been facing an uphill battle from the start. Hell, they all had, considering that the league was brand new and nobody knew what to expect of a not-quite-semi-pro women's hockey league in its inaugural year. They still didn't, not really. But Chuckie was doing his best, and so was the Blades' owner, James Murphy.

Which meant Shannon had to do her best too, and not just when she was in the net.

She tossed another wink in Chuckie's direction then headed off the ice before he could change his mind, taking a deep breath to calm her nerves. Maybe *nerves* was the wrong word—she wasn't nervous, not exactly. Anxious, maybe. Or maybe *cautious* was a better word. This was a big deal for her and in some way, she understood why Chuckie was worried. That one television interview Taylor had done at the start of the season had seriously backfired—on everyone. That still had to be weighing on Chuckie's mind.

But this wasn't a television interview—thank God, because Shannon didn't think she could handle that, not yet. This was just a sit-down interview with TR Meyers, the woman who had done that abso-fucking-lutely wonderful piece on Sammie a few weeks ago. Shannon could handle that.

She hoped.

She shrugged out of her gear, piling pads and helmet and stick off to the side. She tugged her hair from the ponytail then ran her fingers over her damp scalp, sighing in relief. Hopefully TR wouldn't want to take any pictures, at least not before Shannon had a chance to shower because yeah, yuck.

One last deep breath, then she made her way over to the metal bleachers where TR was sitting. Shannon hesitated when she saw Gordon "Mac" MacGregor standing there talking to the reporter, afraid of interrupting. Mac was a friend of Sammie's soon-to-be non-ex, a former military something-or-other. Shannon had no idea that the man knew the reporter, was surprised to even see him here. Or maybe not, considering Jon was here with Sammie's daughter, Clare.

Which would make her Jon's daughter, too. Duh.

She waited for a few minutes, shifting her weight from one skate to the other as the chilled air of the rink started to seep through her sweat-soaked shirt and hair.

If the two of them kept talking for much longer, she'd have to go back and grab her sweatshirt. She had no idea what they were discussing but they both looked intense. At least, Mac did—which meant nothing because his scarred face always looked intense.

Shannon finally cleared her throat, the loud sound echoing around her. TR and Mac both looked over at her. Moisture filled TR's pale eyes and she reached up to brush at them. Mac fixed Shannon with a penetrating stare made more intense from the reflection of the overhead lights. Then he blinked, all intensity disappearing as his ravaged face broke into a smile that transformed his features into something only marginally softer.

"I didn't mean to interrupt—"

"You're good." His voice was gruff, whether from impatience or as a result of his injuries, Shannon wasn't sure. He nodded in her direction, just the briefest of acknowledgments, then turned back to TR. "Just don't be stupid."

Shannon watched him walk away then turned back to the other woman. "Everything okay? We need to reschedule this or something?"

"No, of course not." The woman cleared her throat then shifted on the bench. She pushed her dark hair from her face then patted the bench next to her. "Have a seat."

Shannon dropped onto the bench, shifted once or twice to get comfortable, not sure how she should sit, or if it even made any difference. She finally gave up and made herself comfortable: feet and legs spread apart, slightly bent over with her elbows braced on her knees. "So…everything's good?"

"Yeah, fine."

"You sure?" She looked over her shoulder, watching Mac as he leaned closer to Jon, the two men in deep conversation. "Need me to go kick his ass or something?"

A short burst of laughter escaped the other woman. "No, it's all good. He was just, um, helping me with something."

Shannon turned back to TR, one eyebrow raised in surprise. "By telling you not to be stupid?"

Another burst of laughter, this one a little sadder somehow. "Long story." TR reached into the bag by her feet and pulled out her phone. Her fingers flew across the screen for a few seconds then she placed the phone on the bench between them. Shannon glanced down at it then nearly froze.

"You're, uh, you're recording this?"

"Yeah." TR looked up from the notepad resting on her knee. "I always record interviews. You don't mind, do you?"

"Uh——" Shannon looked away from the phone and tried to swallow back her anxiety. The thought that every single word coming out of her mouth would be recorded and stored somewhere in a virtual cloud for all eternity kind of terrified her but it wasn't like she could back out now, not after her talk with Chuckie. "Uh, no. No, it's fine."

"You don't have to look so nervous. It's just another way to take notes so I can refer back later. Just relax and—"

"So. Question." Shannon raised her hand, just like one of Sammie's kindergarten students would. She realized what she was doing and quickly dropped her arm. "If I, uh, slip and say something I shouldn't—are you going to print it and make me look like a total ass?

Because I really don't want to look like an ass. Chuckie would have a fucking fit and—yeah, like that. Please don't print that."

TR watched her for a long minute, all humor gone from her eyes. She was serious now. Intent. Seeing too much. Shannon squirmed on the bench but refused to look away, no matter how much she wanted to.

TR reached between them and clicked the recording app, stopping it. Then she leaned back, a small smile on her full lips. "My job isn't to make you—or anyone else, for that matter—look bad. I want to showcase the team. The players. *You*. I want the readers to get to know everyone, to let them see the heart and soul of each of you. To get them excited and interested. Painting any of you in a bad light would have the opposite effect, now wouldn't it?"

"Yeah but—"

"You're thinking of the television interview with Taylor LeBlanc." It was a statement, not a question. But Shannon answered anyway.

"Pretty much, yeah. That was a fu—" She stopped, looked away and cleared her throat. "That was a disaster."

"It wasn't the best piece around, no. It's also not my style."

"Okay." Did Shannon believe her? Maybe, maybe not. All she had to go on was the other article TR had done, the one featuring Sammie—which had been pretty damn good.

She blew out a deep breath then slowly nodded. "Okay, cool. So—how does this work? You ask me some questions, I answer. You clean it up and print it?"

"Yes and no. I like to dig a little deeper, learn about the real person. Try to capture their personality and make it shine. Think more human interest than exposé."

Human interest? Shannon almost laughed. Holy shit, what had she gotten herself into? Yeah, she was human—duh. But interesting? Not hardly, not in her opinion.

"Are you still up for it?"

"Yeah, sure. Shoot."

TR laughed, the sound light, then settled more comfortably on the bench. She crossed one long denim-clad leg over the other, her booted foot gently swinging. "How long have you been playing hockey?"

Shannon sighed in relief. That question was an easy one. If they were all like this, she'd ace the entire interview. "Since I was six."

TR nodded, her pen poised against the pad—unmoving. Shannon frowned, wondering why the woman wasn't writing anything down.

"Um, that would mean I've been playing for seventeen years." She stared at the unmoving pen, her breath held as she waited for it to move. Still nothing. She glanced at the other woman then reached out and tapped the tip of her finger against the blank notepad. "Are you going to write that down?"

A ghost of a smile hovered around the other woman's mouth as she shook her head. "Not yet."

"Why not?"

"Because I'm waiting for more."

"More what? You asked. I answered. What more do you want?"

TR's smile grew a little wider. "You're pretty literal, aren't you?"

"What? No, I don't think so—"

"People usually elaborate a bit more when they

answer."

"Elaborate how? That one was pretty straightforward, right?"

Another smile—but at least this time she was writing something. Shannon leaned forward, trying to read the woman's notes, but the handwriting was nothing more than an illegible chicken scratch.

Damn.

"Why hockey?"

"Um, because."

"You just woke up one morning and decided you wanted to play hockey?"

"Well, no. Not really. I mean, my older brother played. And all of his friends. And there really weren't any other girls in our neighborhood. At least, not ones I really wanted to hang out with because they were too busy playing with dolls or dress-up or whatever and that so wasn't me because I've never been into that girly shit so I—" Shannon stopped, frowning at the pen racing across the page. What the hell was she writing?

TR looked up. "Go on."

"Oh. Um, well—that's pretty much it. My brother played."

"Does he still play?"

"Steve? Nah. He gave it up before high school. Besides, he hated that I was better than he was." Shannon tried to hide her smirk but couldn't. She still loved teasing her brother about it, because he was so easy to tease.

"Any other siblings?"

"Nope, just us."

"And was that an issue?"

"What? Not having any other brothers or sisters? No, I don't think so. I mean, we were both a pretty big handful growing up, so I don't think—"

TR's laughter interrupted her. "I meant, was it an issue that you were better than your brother?"

"Oh. Not really. I mean, maybe. When we were growing up. But Steve's heart wasn't really into it, you know? He liked playing, but it wasn't *who* he was. If that makes sense."

TR scribbled something else then looked up, understanding clear in her eyes. "Makes perfect sense. What about now?"

"Um, what about it?"

"Is playing now an issue for your brother? Or for any other man in your life?"

"There is no man—" Shannon's mouth snapped closed, heat filling her face. Had that sounded as pathetic as she thought it did? She cleared her throat and dropped her gaze. "I, uh, I don't date much." And yeah, okay, *that* sounded pretty pathetic.

"Because of hockey?"

"No, that's not it. I mean, not really. I just—I don't have time. Practice. Games. Work. Not much time left for anything personal." That was a safe answer, wasn't it? And it sure sounded a hell of a lot better than admitting that men tended to shy away from her because she was intimidating. Yeah, that was one thing she'd never admit, especially not to the woman sitting next to her.

TR scribbled a few more notes then looked up, her gaze drifting to something behind Shannon. A small smile curled her mouth and she nodded in the direction of her gaze. "I think someone's waiting for you."

"What? Who?" Shannon turned around, expecting to see Taylor or Dani or one of her other teammates standing there. Her stomach did a slow roll just as her heart slammed into her chest. Caleb Johnson was standing a few feet away, watching her with a heart-stopping grin. Heat filled her face and she quickly looked away, her mind racing. What the hell was he doing here? And why did he have to look so damn delicious?

Shannon glanced behind her once more. Yeah, definitely delicious. He looked just as good in a pair of worn jeans and a Banners' sweatshirt as he did in a tailored suit—which was so unfair, considering she looked like death warmed over in her hockey shorts, socks, and sweat-soaked t-shirt.

She ran one hand through the tangled mess of her hair and quickly turned away again. The small grin on TR's face surprised her, made her realize she must look like she was primping or something just as stupid. She dropped her hand into her lap and forced a smile on her face.

"Next question?"

TR shook her head and closed the notepad. "We can pick up again on Thursday after practice."

"But—I thought this was a one-time thing. Don't you have to, you know, finish the story or something?"

"Didn't Chuckie tell you? There's no set deadline. I'm working on a series of articles featuring all of you, so no rush. Besides, it looks like your date is here."

"Date?" Shannon's voice rose an octave and she cleared her throat, cursing the fiery blush racing across her cheeks. "Caleb so isn't my date. Not even close. So please, don't even put that in there anywhere, okay? Because that would be—yeah, just don't."

"Shannon, don't worry. I have no intention of writing anything that would embarrass you or the team." TR shoved the pad and phone into her bag then tossed it over her shoulder and stood. "We can pick this up on Thursday, okay?"

Shannon nodded, watched as the woman gave her a quick smile and walked away. Then she took a deep breath and spun around, frowning as Caleb approached her. "What the hell are you doing here?"

His steps faltered, but only for a second. "Just came by to say hi."

"Seriously?" She didn't bother to keep the surprise from her voice. "Why am I not believing that?"

"No idea." He dropped to the bench beside her—too close beside her. Shannon slid away, frowning.

"Seriously. What are you doing here?"

"I told you, just wanted to stop by and say hi."

"Uh-huh, sure."

"Fine. Don't believe me."

"I don't."

Caleb's chuckle sent a shiver dancing along her spine. She frowned, praying he didn't see the way her flesh pebbled—or if he did, that he'd think it was because she was cold. "Feel like grabbing something to eat?"

"You can't be serious."

"Why can't I?"

Shannon glanced at her watch then held her wrist out for him to see. "Because it's after ten o'clock, that's why."

"You don't eat after practice? Because I'm usually starving afterward."

She did, and she was. But that was beside the point. "What do you really want?"

"I told you—just stopped by to say hi and see if you wanted to grab a bite."

Shannon snorted, the sound filled with disbelief. "Uh-huh, sure you did."

Impatience flashed across his face, there and gone so quickly, she almost thought she imagined it. "You're not very trusting, are you?"

"Not really, no."

"Fine. The truth is, I wanted to see you again."

"Why?"

Caleb's intense gaze met hers, pulling her in, making her skin feel hot and prickly. He leaned forward, the faint smell of soap and aftershave wrapping around her. His voice was low and warm, just above a whisper when he spoke. "Why not?"

She jerked her gaze from his and slid back a few more inches. Dangerous. So fucking dangerous. And she didn't trust him, no way in hell. He was after something, she knew it.

Taylor's words came back to her once more. *Stay away. He's a player.*

Maybe. No, more like *probably*. But that didn't stop Shannon from wondering what his mouth would feel like against hers, or what it would be like to have Caleb's body stretched out on top of hers, hard and—

"I'm not sleeping with you." She blurted the words out before she could stop herself, then cringed at the desperation even she could hear in them. And damn if he didn't chuckle and lean in closer.

"You keep saying that."

"Because I mean it."

He shrugged, like he didn't care one way or the other, then patted her on the leg and stood up. "I'll wait while you clean up."

"But—" She didn't bother to finish because he was already walking away, like it was a foregone conclusion that she'd go with him.

Shannon sat there for a few minutes, fighting the temptation to chase after him and tell him she wasn't going. Then she sat there for another minute, annoyed with herself because she *wasn't* chasing after him to tell him she wasn't going with him.

Because she wanted to go. Wanted to see what the hell he was up to.

Wanted to pretend, for just a little bit, that he was actually interested. In her.

"You're a fucking idiot." She muttered the words under her breath then snorted and pushed to her feet. Yeah, she really was.

Because she was going to go with him.

But no way in hell was she going to sleep with him.

chapter FIVE

Shannon leaned across the table, snagged a fry from Caleb's plate, then tossed it into her mouth. She laughed at the frown on his face, at the way his mouth gaped open ever so slightly before he snapped it closed.

Like he wasn't used to sharing. Or like he wasn't used to anyone else taking something from him. Too bad for him because she didn't care.

She reached across and grabbed one more fry, just because she could, then leaned back against the vinyl seat of the corner booth. "Okay, Johnson, out with it."

"Out with what?"

"With whatever game you're playing."

His gaze darted to hers then dropped to his plate, which he was pulling a little closer to him—probably to stop her from stealing another fry. "Who says I'm playing a game?"

"Please." She filled the word with as much sarcasm as she could muster and dragged it out into three long syllables. "Like I believe you were in the area and just decided to stop by."

"I was."

"Uh-huh. Sure you were." She rolled her eyes then leaned forward and propped her elbows on the edge of the table. "What do you really want?"

Caleb looked up, the expression in his green eyes unreadable. That didn't stop the flash of awareness from rippling through her. Damn if she'd look away, though. If she did, he might realize the effect he had on her, and that was the last thing she wanted. Let him think she wasn't interested. Something told her Caleb didn't get that very often—the new experience would do him some good.

"I told you: I just wanted to say hi. See if you wanted to grab a bite to eat."

"And you expect me to believe that why?"

"I said hi, didn't I?" The corner of his mouth kicked up into a grin. "And look: we're eating. Imagine that. Must mean I was right and got what I wanted."

"Something tells me that happens a lot."

"What?"

"You getting what you want."

He shrugged, the motion—and the expression on his face—devoid of any guilt. "Yeah? So?"

"Wow. Cocky much?"

Caleb leaned closer, his grin widening. "It's not being cocky when it's true."

The sharp bark of laughter escaped her before she had a chance to swallow it back. Caleb's smile dimmed and just the briefest hint of confusion glinted in his eyes—but only for a second, only until he blinked it away.

"You find that amusing?"

"No. I find *you* amusing. But something tells me that wasn't the impression you were going for."

"Why do you think I'm going for any impression?"

Shannon shrugged then reached for the glass of iced tea, draining it with a few long swallows. She wiped her mouth off with the napkin, balled it up, and tossed it onto her empty plate. "No idea. Call it intuition. And I'm ninety-nine percent positive you have an ulterior motive for stopping by and asking me to grab a bite to eat."

Caleb frowned but refused to look away. In fact, he actually leaned closer—close enough that she had the sudden urge to back into the corner of the booth. How ridiculous was that? There was a table full of empty dishes and glassware between them. What was he going to do? Tip the table over and push it out of his way to get to her?

Yeah, right.

"Why do you have such a hard time believing that I don't have an ulterior motive? Why can't you just accept the fact that I really wanted to see you and grab a bite to eat?"

"Because—" Shannon snapped her mouth closed and looked away, afraid he'd be able to see the truth in her eyes. Because guys like him always ever wanted just one thing. Because guys in general always seemed to want that same thing from *her*. Because she'd been burned too many times and didn't trust anyone, not when it came to the opposite sex. She'd learned long ago that guys weren't interested in her, they were interested in what they thought they could get from her. And once they actually got to know her—if they even stuck around that long—they usually took off in the opposite direction, running as fast as their poor legs could carry them.

"It's because of Taylor running her mouth, right?"

Oh, yeah—that, too. Caleb was a player. She couldn't forget that.

"Maybe. Maybe not."

"Then what is it?"

"Because you don't know me. You don't know anything about me—"

"Which is what I'm trying to fix—"

"—but I'm supposed to believe that, all of a sudden, you're so interested—"

"Yeah, that's how it generally works."

"Oh, bullshit."

"Why do you say that?"

"I'm not an idiot, Johnson. I know what guys usually think when they first see me. But as soon as they get the tiniest glimpse of who I really am, off they go, running scared."

"You don't see me running, do you?"

"No. And that's why I'm pretty sure you're after something. Maybe you're trying to prove something. Guys like you are used to the sure thing, which is why I can't figure out what the hell you want."

"Christ. Double standard much?" He tossed the crumbled napkin beside his plate then sat back, slowly shaking his head. His frustration was clear, from the way his mouth pursed to the muscle jumping along his jaw. "*Guys like me*? What the hell is that even supposed to mean?"

"Don't play stupid. You're a pretty boy, with those gorgeous eyes and that stupid ass dimple." And why the hell was she still talking? She needed to shut up, to stop while she was ahead. Caleb was passing the frustration zone and slowly skating into impatience.

But her mouth had other ideas—as usual—and the words kept falling out. "Don't tell me you're not used to women throwing themselves at you. Big name superstar. Good looks. A multi-million-dollar contract."

"That's not—"

"Don't even say that's not true. I've been around sports long enough to know better. Which means you must see me as some kind of challenge, right?"

"Yeah, you're a challenge, alright. A challenge to my patience. What the hell, Wiley? How the hell did we go from grabbing a bite to eat to—to—whatever the hell this even is?"

His use of her last name acted like a bucket of cold water thrown over her, dousing the flames of her pent-up anger and frustration. What the hell was she doing, taking things out on him? Going off on him like that when he'd done absolutely nothing wrong? Did he have ulterior motives? Maybe. Probably. But if he did, so what? He hadn't acted on them, hadn't done anything except invite her out for a bite to eat.

The heat of mortification filled her face and she looked away, more embarrassed than she'd been in a long time. What the hell was wrong with her? She glanced around, caught the attention of the waitress, and signaled for their check before turning back to face Caleb.

At least, face in his direction. She was too embarrassed to actually look at him, too worried about what she might see on his face. "Sorry, I was out of line."

"Yeah, sure."

She heard the curt abruptness in his voice, opened her mouth to apologize again. To blame her over-the-top rant on lack of sleep and stress and whatever other excuse she could come up with. No, she wasn't going to make excuses, not when none existed. Yes, she was tired—but that didn't excuse her rant. Nothing did.

The waitress placed the check on the edge of the table, not even bothering to glance at Shannon. Not that Shannon could blame her for giving Caleb a thorough once-over. Or, in the woman's case, an eight-times-over, considering she'd been watching Caleb from the moment they had taken their seats.

Whatever. Shannon bit her tongue, not bothering to use the poor waitress as an example of everything she'd just said. She simply rolled her eyes and reached for the check—

At the exact same time as Caleb.

Their hands collided, their fingers twisting together as they both fought to gain possession of the paper slip. And kept fighting, until the paper started to tear. Shannon curled her fingers tighter, squeezing Caleb's until he finally let go.

"Christ. You don't give up, do you?"

"Nope." She tried to bite back her smile, then ended up looking away because her attempt wasn't very successful. "You paid the other day. I can pick this one up."

"It's not a contest, you know. I have no problem paying. In fact, that's how it usually works. I asked you out, I should pay."

"Whatever." She dug into her jacket pocket for the wallet attached to her keys and unsnapped the back compartment, pulling out a few folded bills. She glanced at the total then peeled off enough to cover the bill.

"At least let me get the tip."

"I can cover it." And she could—the diner wasn't exactly five-star dining, thank God. If it had been, she would have been forced to use her credit card, and that would have been taking a chance since the damn thing was close to its limit.

"I didn't say you couldn't." Caleb tossed a single twenty on the table, the motion casually careless, like leaving an eighty percent tip was no big deal. For him, it probably wasn't.

Shannon bit her tongue instead of arguing. The argument wouldn't be worth it—and the urge to argue didn't make sense. If she were here with her teammates, everyone would simply toss a few bills down until everything was covered. There wasn't this urge she was feeling now to one-up the man sitting across from her, draining the last of his coffee.

Maybe it wasn't that she wanted to one-up him. Maybe she just wanted to prove…something. The problem was, she had no idea what that *something* might be.

No, she mentally corrected. The problem was that she felt the urge to prove anything at all.

She slid across the bench, dragging her jacket behind her. "Thanks for the food, Johnson."

"What's the hurry?"

"You know the saying: places to go, things to do. Like sleep." She shrugged into her jacket then reached behind her, pulling her ponytail free. "I have to work in the morning."

Caleb had been sliding out from behind the table but, at her last words, paused. A frown creased his face, the expression full of confusion. "Work? Oh, you mean practice."

"No, I mean *work*. As in, go in and punch a clock

and actually work until it's time to punch out."

"I don't get it. Why are you working?"

"We all have to work, Johnson. That's how the bills get paid."

"I get that part." He finally stood up, his body too close to her. Shannon took a hasty step back to put distance between them. Did he notice? If he did, he didn't say anything about it, just kept talking about work. "What I don't get is *why*. You get paid by the Blades, right?"

Shannon's snort was immediate, loud and decidedly unladylike. "You're kidding, right?"

"Are you saying you don't get paid?"

"Oh, we get paid alright." Shannon pushed through the door, felt the cold night air wrap around her. She huddled deeper into the jacket and headed toward her car, Caleb keeping pace with her each step of the way.

"Then why are you working a second job if you're getting paid?"

Shannon rolled her eyes as she unlocked the car. "Because what we get paid amounts to chump change. Literally. It works out to be, *maybe*, a couple hundred a game. *Maybe*. And that's not everyone. Some of them aren't even making that. So yeah, pretty much everyone has another job."

"You're pulling my leg."

Shannon leaned her backside against the driver's door and looked up at Caleb. He was standing close—close enough that she could feel the tempting heat of his body, felt herself sway toward him. She stopped herself at the last second, thankful for the dark shadows hiding her blush, thankful that he didn't seem to notice what she'd done. At least, she didn't think he noticed. He was still watching her, those deep green eyes focused on her with laser intensity.

"You're being serious, aren't you?"

Serious? What was he talking about? Oh, that's right—they'd been talking about how little everyone on the team was paid.

Shannon yanked her gaze from his and nodded. "As a heart attack. And as much as I'd love to stand here and discuss the gross unfairness of it with you, I really do need to get home."

Caleb nodded and took a step back. He stopped, another frown creasing his face, then cocked his head to the side and watched her for a long minute. Like he was considering something.

And yeah, there was a scary thought she didn't need. What could the man in front of her be thinking to put that expression in his face? Like he wasn't sure what to do, and just the mere thought of whatever he was thinking was enough to worry him.

Shannon had no idea what that could be and she didn't want to find out. So she did what she always did, and let her mouth run free.

"Are you constipated or something?"

And yes, that definitely did the trick. Caleb's face cleared and he took another step back, like he couldn't get away from her fast enough. Then he stopped and oh shit, she was in so much trouble because one corner of his mouth curled into a devilish grin.

"You really don't have a filter at all, do you?"

"I do. I just don't use it very often."

He nodded then did something completely unexpected: he stepped closer. Shannon curled her hands and jammed them behind her back, afraid she'd do something really stupid, like reach up and trace the fullness of his lower lip.

"What are you doing tomorrow night?"

"Uh—" She snapped her mouth closed, frowning as she tried to think of something, anything, that she had to do. Her mind was disgustingly blank.

"You should come to the game with me."

"Uh—what?"

"Come to the game with me. We can watch from the owner's suite."

"The game? You mean, the Banners? Aren't you, uh, aren't you going to be playing?"

A shadow flashed across his eyes but only for a second before it was replaced with a carefree sparkle. "Not yet. I'll be cleared to play on Saturday. So how about it? Feel like going with me?"

"Um…" Shannon hesitated, her mind still trying to deal with the unexpected disappointment. He was asking her to go to the game, that was it. Not a date, not like she'd been afraid of.

Not like she'd been hoping.

He simply wanted her to go to the game, that was it. Two hockey players, hanging out and chilling. Nothing more.

"Um, yeah, sure. Okay."

"Perfect."

And then he did the one thing she hadn't been expecting: he reached out and cupped her chin with one large hand then leaned down and kissed her.

He. Kissed. Her.

Just the briefest touching of lips against lips. Warm. Soft. Almost tender. Certainly nothing that anyone would write down in their diary, if they had one.

Which did nothing to explain the heat flaring

inside her, the warmth that spread from where his mouth touched hers all the way down to her toes. Her heart slammed against her ribs, her breath lodged in her throat. At least she didn't do anything completely stupid, like jump into his arms and jam her tongue down his throat.

Yeah, right. Only because Caleb was already pulling away, a small grin on his mouth as he looked down at her.

"I'll call you tomorrow with the details."

Shannon managed to nod. At least, she thought she did. Not that it mattered because Caleb was already walking away. She watched him get into his expensive SUV, saw him wave as he pulled out of the parking lot.

Only then was she able to move. She jerked open the door and dropped into the driver's seat, cursing herself for not warming the car up.

Cursing herself for letting one tiny little kiss fry her brain. It was just a kiss. Not even a real kiss. It was barely even a peck.

And it meant nothing. Absolutely nothing.

Yeah, sure it didn't. That's why her heart was still fluttering and why heat still raced over her, warming her enough that she didn't even need to turn up the heat.

One little kiss, my ass.

Yeah, she was definitely in trouble.

With a capital T.

chapter SIX

"You're being unreasonable."

"And you're being an ass."

Caleb clenched his jaw against the retort, knowing that Taylor was expecting it. He needed to catch her off-guard, not play into her expectations. That was the only way he was going to get what he wanted.

He'd have it already if he hadn't been so fucking preoccupied last night. How the hell could he have forgotten to get Shannon's number from her? Especially after telling her he'd call her today. If he hadn't been so focused on that full mouth of hers, on the way she had tasted after that damn kiss that was embarrassingly brief—

He still wasn't sure why he kissed her. It hadn't been planned. At least, not like that. The first kiss should have been one that knocked her off her feet. One that emptied her mind of everything except him and the next kiss. And the next one after that, until she was trembling in his arms, ready to follow wherever he led.

Yeah, his fucking mistake. But she'd been leaning against the car, her head tilted back as she looked at him, full of attitude and sass. He didn't stop to think, just leaned down and pressed his lips against hers, just to see what she would do.

Which was nothing. No clinging to him, no swift intake of shocked breath, no flash of desire. Shannon just stood there, staring up at him, her face scrunched up in confusion.

Not exactly the reaction he'd been hoping for.

Fine. No problem. He could rectify that starting tonight.

If he could manage to get her damn phone number from Taylor.

He leaned against the boards and crossed his arms in front of him, a small grin on his face. "Come on, Tay-Tay. It's just a number. What's it going to hurt?"

She slid to a stop next to him, spraying snow against his legs. She raised her stick and he almost flinched, worried that she was going to slash him across the chest with it. Instead of hitting him, she simply used the blade to point at him.

"No. I don't know what the hell you're up to, but no. I'm not going to help you set-up my friend that way."

"Set her up? What the hell do you mean by that?"

"Just what I said. I know you, Caleb. I know how you operate. So you can just wipe that Look-At-Me-I'm-So-Charming grin off that stupid face. It's not happening."

Caleb's mouth flattened but only for a second. He schooled his face into something a little less charming, a little more offended. "I can't believe you'd even think that—"

"Oh, please. Don't bother, Johnson. It's not working."

"Tay-Tay—"

She cut him off with another slice of her stick, this one even closer to his face. He jerked back and almost lost his balance, caught himself before his feet shot out from under him. Wouldn't that be just perfect, to land on his ass in front of Taylor and have her laugh at him? Or worse, have her go back and tell everyone about it.

"Shannon isn't one of your playthings, Caleb. Let it go."

"I never said she was a plaything."

"Really? I'm supposed to believe that you actually like her?"

"Yeah. I do." It wasn't a lie, which surprised him as much as it obviously surprised Taylor. He *did* like Shannon—when he wasn't trying to keep from rolling his eyes at whatever came out of her mouth, like when she asked if he was constipated. Or maybe that was why he liked her: she didn't have a filter. At all. She didn't simper and coo around him, didn't fall all over herself trying to impress him.

She was a challenge. And Caleb liked nothing better than a challenge.

So of course he liked her. It made perfect sense when he thought of it that way.

Taylor jammed the blade of her stick against the ice and stared at him, her gaze too direct, too intense. He almost looked away, caught himself at the last second. Looking away would be bad. Looking away would make him seem guilty—and he wasn't. Not at all. It was just that his idea of *liking* was completely different than Taylor's…in this instance.

Caleb grinned, hoping it would throw Taylor off-balance, then shrugged. "Fine. Don't give me her number and I won't take her to the game tonight. Then she'll be sitting home, waiting and thinking exactly what you don't want her to think and then *you* can explain why I stood her up."

"You're seriously taking her out tonight?"

"Well, I *was*. But since I have no real way of calling—"

"Don't try to put that on me. If you were that worried about it, you would have gotten her number." Taylor tilted her head to the side, frowning. "Unless you already asked her and she wouldn't give it to you."

"I didn't—"

"Oh, man. I would have loved to see her put you in your place."

"She didn't—"

"Yeah, right." She started skating past him, heading toward the players' bench. Caleb hurried after her, shuffling his feet along the ice so he wouldn't slip and fall. Was she really going to leave and not give him Shannon's number? No way. No fucking way.

"Taylor, just give me her number."

"Not happening."

What the hell? She was serious. She really wasn't going to give it to him.

Something like panic swept over him. No, that couldn't be right, he never panicked. Maybe it was just disbelief that this wasn't working the way he wanted. That had to be it.

A dozen different persuasive arguments raced through his mind. He dismissed all of them. Taylor was immune to his charms and he couldn't think of anything else to do.

Well shit. This wasn't going the way he planned at all.

Unless—

"Then can you call her for me? That way I can at least talk to her and make arrangements for tonight." His voice carried just a hint of desperation, just enough to sound convincing. He ignored the fact that he wasn't acting and chalked it up to simple surprise that things weren't going the way he wanted.

Taylor spun around, the surprise on her face matching his own—not that he'd admit it to her. Hell, he couldn't even admit it to himself.

"You're really serious, aren't you?"

He jammed his hands into the back pockets of his jeans and nodded. "Yeah, I am."

She studied him for a long minute through narrowed eyes, like she was trying to gauge his sincerity. Or like she was trying to figure him out. Yeah. Good luck with that. *Nobody* figured him out. Ever.

Taylor finally blew out a quick breath, her gaze darting to the stick in her hand before shooting back to him. "Fine. I'll call her for you. Just give me five minutes to change. But if I find out you're playing her—"

"I'm not."

She muttered something under her breath, too low for him to hear, then spun around and headed back to the locker room. Caleb released his own sigh then made his way off the ice and over to the metal bleachers. He sat down, stretched his ankle, then looked around.

The place was a fucking dump. Several of the overhead lights were burned out, and the insulation covering the steel ceiling beams was worn in more than a few spots. The warped and scratched metal bleachers had seen better days. So had the rubber mats surrounding the scarred and chipped boards around the ice. At least the glass looked relatively new.

Maybe, if *new* meant replaced sometime in the last three years.

Christ, how could anyone even play here? It reminded him of one of the rinks he played at when he was growing up, before he'd started climbing his way up on the road to the pros. It wasn't just how the place looked—it was the smell, too. That odd combination of stale water and sweat, of damp gear shoved into a bag and left to ripen for too long. Of faded dreams and hopes and—

What the fuck was his problem? He dropped his head, reached up and pinched the bridge of his nose hard enough to make his eyes water. Why would those thoughts even pop into his mind? He had no idea. All he knew was that he didn't have to worry about shit like that now. He'd made it to where he wanted to be: on top. Not in some shit league, pretending to play at a game most people didn't understand. Only the best made it to where he was now.

And the best didn't play in shit holes like this.

Taylor's voice pulled him back to the present. He shifted on the bench, watched as she moved toward him, the phone held to her ear. She came to a stop a few feet away, frowning as she watched him and listened to whoever was on the other end of the phone.

Fuck. Had she called Shannon already? Of course she had. Taylor probably didn't want to take the chance of him seeing the number.

Right. Like he wouldn't have it for himself by the

end of the night anyway.

"Are you sure? Because I can tell him to get lost, no problem."

Caleb started voicing his objections but Taylor simply waved him away as she listened to whatever Shannon was saying. She nodded once, made a soft humming sound, then frowned and shot him a dirty look. "And you don't think this is a bad idea?"

"Taylor—"

She waved him off once more and moved back a step. "If you want to, fine. Just don't forget what I told you. Yeah, I know, but still…yeah, okay."

Taylor blew out a quick sigh, lowered the phone, and looked over at him. "What time should she meet you there?"

"I was going to pick her up—"

Taylor's laugh was sharp and abrupt. "Nice try. What time?"

"I was going to take her to dinner first."

Taylor held up one finger, silencing him as she listened to whatever was being said before moving the phone away from her mouth. "Dinner isn't happening because she doesn't get off work until five."

"Then how about five-thirty?"

Taylor rolled her eyes. "That's not going to work. She has to go home and change and stuff."

"Then—"

"Six? Yeah, I'll tell him. Just remember what I said." Taylor disconnected the call then jammed the phone into the pocket of her warm-up pants. "She said she'd meet you in front of the will-call window at six sharp."

Caleb pulled a deep breath in through his nose and willed his jaw to unclench. "Is there a reason you wouldn't let me talk to her?"

"Why would I do that?"

"Hm, let me think. Maybe so I could make the arrangements myself?"

"No need to. They're made. Just meet her outside at the will-call window at six. Simple as that."

"It's not as simple as that."

"Sure it is. Nothing could be simpler." Taylor's smile flat-lined and she stepped forward to level a single finger at him. "And I'm telling you right now, Caleb. Don't you dare play her. If I find out—"

"I'm not playing her."

"Excuse me if I don't believe that. You know, on second thought, go ahead and try it. Shannon will eat you up and spit you out if you try. She'll shred you. And when she's done, if there's anything left, I'll have a go at you myself."

Caleb's grin felt cold on his face. "Am I supposed to be worried?"

"If you're smart, yeah."

Anger washed over him—at Taylor's words, at her obvious low expectations of him, at his own reaction. He had no intention of *playing* Shannon. Did he want to have fun? Absolutely. Was he looking for a commitment? Not in this lifetime. And there was nothing wrong with that, not if he was upfront about it—and he was always upfront. Taylor making assumptions otherwise only pissed him off.

And it wasn't like it was any of her business anyway.

"Maybe you should let Shannon decide, don't you think? She's a big girl. Something tells me she wouldn't appreciate you running interference. Or whatever this is that you think you're doing."

Taylor laughed, the sound mocking his words. "Just remember what I said."

"Yeah, I'll do that." Did she catch the sarcasm in his voice? No, probably not. She was already walking away, heading for the door leading to the plush offices upstairs.

Leaving him standing there, trying to figure out why her words of caution—her *threats*—irritated him so much.

chapter SEVEN

"You okay? You look uncomfortable."

Shannon shrugged and forced a smile to her face, barely nodding in response to Caleb's question. Uncomfortable? Why should she be uncomfortable? This was nothing more than a hockey game, right?

Yeah. Sure.

She'd never been so uncomfortable in her life. It was like she a was in a giant fishbowl, on display for everyone to see. Or like she was some exotic specimen on display behind a glass wall at a weird zoo. People were *staring*. At him. At her. At *them*.

And she hated it.

She knew Caleb would be following dress code and be in a suit, so she wore black slacks and a nice sweater instead of jeans. Not because she wanted to look nice for *him*—she didn't, even if it had taken forever to decide on what outfit to wear. She had taken time with her hair instead of pulling it back in her usual ponytail. She'd even tossed on a little make-up…just in case.

But in case of what?

Not even in her wildest imaginings had she thought they'd be sitting in the owner's box. The freaking *owner*. On display. For everyone to see. It didn't help that James Murphy—the Blades' owner—was here, too. He'd looked surprised to see her, had even squinted at her for a few seconds like he couldn't believe it was her. Then he smiled and laughed and leaned over to the owner of the Banners and said something. The reaction was enough to make her paranoid for the first ten minutes of the game.

With good reason, too, because five minutes ago, the arena's announcer introduced her as a special guest in his bellowing voice and she looked up just in time to see her face plastered on the giant screen hanging above center ice. And yeah, that stupefied expression on her face hadn't helped. At all.

Neither did the small spattering of polite applause that left her even more mortified than seeing her stupid face up on that stupid screen.

Uncomfortable? Nah. What the hell did she have to be uncomfortable about?

So she kept her bright smile firmly plastered in place as Caleb studied her. "Nope. All good."

"You sure? Because you don't look it."

"I'm fine." She reached for her iced tea—served in a real glass without a straw—and took a quick sip. Anything more and she might dribble it all down the front of her sweater. "I just wish you would have told me we'd be in the owner's box."

"I did."

"I don't remember you saying the owner's box."

And she didn't—which meant nothing. Her brain had been a little scrambled last night because of that stupid kiss.

"I thought you heard me. Sorry." Caleb crossed his right ankle over his left knee and fixed the seam of his dress pants, the movement casual and almost absent-minded. And he had that devilish grin on his face, the one that made his dimple deepen and made him look totally unapologetic and entirely too charming.

Was he sorry? Maybe. Maybe not. It still would have been nice to have a little reminder, just in case—so she could have prepared herself. She said as much to Caleb, then had to refrain from hitting him when he chuckled.

"I can't believe sitting here makes you nervous. It's no different than when you're playing, when people are watching your every move."

"Trust me, this is a hell of a lot different." Shannon raised the glass to her mouth then lowered it without taking a sip. How many people were here tonight? Fifteen thousand? Twenty? She had no idea how many seats the arena held, only knew that it was a hell of a lot more than the eight hundred—barely—seats at the rink where the Blades played.

And unlike the rink where they played, damn near every seat was filled.

Caleb shifted in the leather seat, his green eyes suddenly focused on her with an intensity that made her want to squirm. "How is this any different?"

She turned away from him, pointedly ignoring his direct gaze as she looked around. "For one thing, there's more people. For another, I'm not paying attention to the piddling crowd when I'm playing. I'm in my zone, focused on the game, watching the puck and the plays. Always ready, you know?"

Caleb chuckled again, the sound low and warm and way too close to her ear. Shannon turned her head then nearly jumped when she saw how close Caleb's face was to hers. When had he shifted so close? And why the hell did her heart do that stupid little skip when she saw the way his gaze dropped to her mouth?

She jerked back, putting a few inches of space between them as she focused on the game. It should have been easy to do—she had a great view of the ice and the Banners were on fire tonight, having already scored twice. But instead of watching the game, she was thinking of last night and that stupid kiss, wondering again why he'd done it.

Wondering if he was going to kiss her again.

Shannon gave herself a mental shake and muttered incoherent words under her breath. What the hell was wrong with her? She was acting like a silly fourteen-year-old girl fawning over her first crush instead of a twenty-three-year-old woman who knew better than to get involved with a player. And that's exactly what Caleb was: a player. Smooth, suave, charming. Dangerous. And definitely up to something. The question was: what? And *why*?

She was fairly certain she knew the answer to the first question. It was the second question that confused the living hell out of her. Why was he bothering? What was he trying to prove?

Why *her*? And what was she going to do about it?

Too many questions, and she was entirely too short on answers. She shifted, ready to turn around and tell him again that she wasn't going to sleep with him— more to convince herself than anything else—when a player from Tampa snagged the puck and headed down the ice on a breakaway. Caleb jumped to his feet at the same time Shannon did, their shouts blending with the other twenty thousand screams of dismay.

Shannon's gaze darted to Luke Connelly, the Banners' goalie, noticed the way he scrambled back to the center of the net and nearly lost his balance. He hadn't been paying attention! What the hell?

She groaned and elbowed Caleb in the side. "He's out of position, there's no way he's going to stop it."

"He'll stop it."

"He's off-balance, he wasn't watching—"

"He'll stop it." Caleb's voice was sharp, edgy, the tone contradicting the words. Shannon glanced over, saw the way his jaw clenched, the way his dark brows lowered in a slash over his eyes. She turned back to the ice, holding her breath as the player moved closer to the net and pulled back on his stick. Connelly shifted to the right, anticipating the shot—

And missed it when the player readjusted and shot high and to the left. The puck sliced through the air and hit the back of the net before dropping to the ice. The red light above the net flashed as thousands of people groaned their anger and disappointment.

"Fuck." Caleb dropped back to his seat, his own anger clear in the set of his broad shoulders. "How the fuck did he let that in?"

"He wasn't ready. He was out of position. He wasn't paying attention. He—" Shannon's mouth snapped shut at the look Caleb leveled at her. It wasn't a bad look, not really. More like impatient and disbelieving.

"You could see all that?"

"You couldn't?"

"I was talking to you, not watching. I didn't think you were watching, either."

"I didn't need to be watching. I could tell as soon as I saw him what was going to happen."

"How?"

"What do you mean, *how*? It was obvious, even with a glance."

"Yeah, but how could *you* tell?"

Anger and disbelief unfurled in her chest. She opened her mouth, snapped it shut, then narrowed her eyes and leveled a cold stare at Caleb. "Seriously?"

Confusion flashed across his face. "What?"

"I cannot fucking believe you just asked me that question. I'm a fucking goalie, remember? I *play* hockey. I know the fucking game—"

"I know that."

"Are you sure about that? Because if you did, you wouldn't have just insulted me."

"You think—?" Caleb shook his head and started laughing, the deep sound unleashing a sharp bite of anger inside her. She thought about slugging him, thought about just standing up and storming off. He must have sensed her intent because he draped one strong arm around her shoulders, holding her in place. "That's not how I meant it."

"Sure as hell sounded like it to me."

"It wasn't. Honest. I was just wondering what you saw, what you were looking at. How you could tell at such a quick glance."

Did she believe him? She honestly wasn't sure. But she didn't want to draw attention to them, so she gave him the benefit of the doubt—and it had nothing to do with the way his arm was still draped around her, or with the way he was leaning in close and watching her.

"I'm a goalie, remember?" It was the same answer she had given him seconds before, only without the stinging bite. Laughter danced in his eyes and he leaned closer, his arm tightening around her.

"Yeah, I remember."

And holy shit, was he going to kiss her again? Right here, in front of everyone? No. No, no. No. Absolutely not. He couldn't.

Could he?

No, he wasn't. His hold around her was already loosening as he looked away. She expected him to move his arm, to stop holding her as he glanced around, but he didn't.

Shannon wasn't sure what to make of that, didn't know if she should move away from him or dislodge his arm herself. The fact that she wasn't sure what to do was almost as disconcerting as the weight of his arm around her shoulders. Since when was she so indecisive? And why was she getting so flustered?

Caleb's arm tightened around her, like he was trying to get her attention. He pointed at the giant screen suspended above center ice. "Hey, look. It's the Kiss Cam."

"What?" Shannon looked up then rolled her eyes. "Ugh. I hate that stupid thing."

"Hate it? Why?"

"Because I do. It's stupid. It puts people on the spot."

"Nah. It's all just fun."

Shannon watched as the camera panned in one unsuspecting couple. The guy was watching his phone, completely ignoring the embarrassed woman next to him. The woman nudged the guy, then slid down in her seat and covered her face with her hands as the crowd booed.

Shannon looked over at Caleb with a smug smile. "See? I rest my case. It's stupid and embarrassing and puts people on the spot."

The crowd broke out in a loud cheer, applauding and whistling and shouting encouragement. Shannon ignored the sudden grin on Caleb's face and rolled her eyes. "Let me guess: some couple is really hamming it up."

Caleb's grin widened, laughter dancing in his eyes as he looked at the screen then back at her. "Not yet, no."

"Then what—"

"Look." He motioned with his head, his eyes never leaving hers as the crowd cheered even louder. Shannon turned, her gaze darting to the giant screen—

And froze when she saw her shocked face staring back at her from center ice. Only it wasn't just her face—it was her and Caleb, their faces framed by a flashing pink heart.

A flush heated her cheeks and she looked away from the screen, shaking her head as she tried to say *no*. This wasn't funny, she didn't want people to think they were together.

And she didn't want him to kiss her again, not like this. Not for show for some stupid camera.

But Caleb leaned closer, laughter and something else flashing in his eyes. She saw his lips move but she couldn't make out his words, not over the sound of the wildly cheering crowd. She wanted to tell him no, tried to move away, but it was too late.

His lips met hers. Soft and warm. Tempting. Inviting. His tongue swept across the seam of her lips, dipped inside her mouth and tangled with hers. Slow.

Deep. Thorough.

This was nothing like last night's brief meeting of the lips. Not even close. This was…this was too tempting. Too dangerous.

She told herself it was for the camera, that was it. It meant nothing. She couldn't let it mean anything.

For the camera. The crowd. Nothing more.

But she didn't care. Couldn't make herself care. Not yet. Not right this second.

Because Caleb was kissing her.

chapter EIGHT

"He kissed you!"

It wasn't a question. It wasn't even really a statement. It was more like an accusation, leveled with the same fast accuracy of each of Taylor's practice shots tonight.

Shannon had deflected most of Taylor's shots but she wasn't going to be as lucky with this one, not when the other woman was standing right in front of her, shock and dismay and frustration clear on her face. It didn't help that several of Shannon's other teammates flanked Taylor, similar expressions on their own faces.

"It wasn't a real kiss!" And dammit, even she didn't buy that. How could she expect her teammates to when just the memory of the kiss was enough to heat her face? She ignored her flaming cheeks and forced even more conviction to her voice. "Seriously. You're all overreacting. I told you, it was just for the stupid Kiss Cam."

"Kiss Cam my ass." Taylor slid closer, moving to within inches of Shannon. "He had his tongue down your throat!"

"Oh for fuck's sake, he did not." Not really. If his tongue had been down her throat, she would have choked. His tongue had simply been in her mouth. Hot. Wet. Tempting.

Too damn tempting.

"Don't tell me it wasn't! It's all over social media, Shannon. Any moron can look at the video and tell where his tongue was."

"And again, you're overreacting." Shannon pushed away from the net, wanting to do nothing more than fly across the ice and hit the locker room so she could change and leave. She wasn't even going to take a shower until she got home. She should already be walking out the door—practice had ended a good ten minutes ago. But she was penned in, unable to push her way past Taylor and Sammie and Dani. She was bigger than Sammie, she could probably just push her out of the way and make a dash for it—

Dani stepped in front of her, stopping her from doing just that. Shannon narrowed her eyes, ready to give her friend a warning when Taylor popped her on the shoulder to get her attention.

"And you're underreacting. I told you, Caleb's a player. He'll drop you as soon as he gets what he wants."

"Yeah? And? What makes you think I'm not playing him? What makes you think I'm not going to drop him as soon as I get what *I* want?" Shannon mentally cringed as soon as the words left her mouth and it took all her effort not to snort in disbelief. Yeah, right. Like she was capable of doing something like that.

The identical expressions of her teammates were nothing more than a reflection of her own thoughts. They didn't believe it any more than she did. And why would they? That wasn't her. She wasn't like that. She'd never been like that.

Maybe she should be. Maybe it was time to change and go after what she wanted for once. That's what she did on the ice, why should her personal life be any different?

Because she didn't have a personal life, that was why. But what if—

"Are you crazy? Did you get hit in the head or something and not tell anyone?" Dani's even voice—steady and controlled—cut through the surprised silence. Shannon narrowed her gaze and stared at the other woman.

"What's that supposed to mean?"

"Just what I said. That's not you. You wouldn't know how to play a guy if your life depended on it."

"How would you know?"

"Because I know."

"Yeah? Is that what you think? Because you don't know. For all you know—"

"Ohmygod would you two please knock it off! You're giving me a headache." Sammie wedged herself between them with a playful smile. "Besides, I have news."

"You're pregnant."

Sammie spun around, her light brown eyes wide with shock as she faced Shannon. "What? No! Why do you always think that whenever someone has news?"

"I don't know. Just sounds good, I guess."

"Well stop. Okay? It's silly."

"Fine. Whatever." Shannon draped her arm along the top bar of the net and stared at the smaller woman. "So what's this news?"

Sammie took a deep breath, her gaze resting on each woman for a long second. A slow smile lit her face and laughter danced in her eyes a second before she bounced up and down in excitement. "Jon and I are getting married!"

Silence greeted her announcement, dimming Sammie's smile. She blinked, glanced around, blinked again. "Well? Aren't you guys excited?"

"How exactly is that news? You guys are already married."

"No. We're divorced. Remember?"

"So you're getting remarried."

"Well…yeah. I guess."

Dani slid closer to Sammie and pulled her in for a quick hug. "Ignore Shannon. She doesn't have a romantic bone in her body."

"Hey! I do so!" Her half-hearted objection was largely ignored as the other two women congratulated Sammie. Shannon released a heavy sigh then skated closer to the small group, pulling Sammie in for a big hug. "Congratulations, Reigs. As long as he makes you happy."

"He does."

"Good. Because I'd hate to have to kick his ass for you."

Sammie hugged her back with a laugh. "I don't think you need to worry about that."

"So you guys have worked everything out, then? No more issues? Discussed how he screwed up last time?" Taylor's questions were sharp and direct, fired one after another. Sammie pulled away, ran a hand through the damp curls of her short hair, and nodded.

"Yes, yes, and yes. I mean, we're still working on what happened and I asked him to get counseling." Sadness filled Sammie's dark eyes, there and gone in a heartbeat. "You know, for everything he went through over there."

"And he agreed?" Taylor's voice held just the slightest edge, tinged with a little disbelief.

"Yeah, he did. Not right away but he agreed."

"And you're absolutely sure about this?"

Shannon looked over at Taylor, frowning. Why was she being so short? First with that bit over that stupid kiss, and now with Sammie's news. That wasn't like Taylor. Shannon opened her mouth, ready to ask what was going on, then snapped it shut. She could ask later, when Sammie wasn't gushing about her ex-husband. Or rather, her future husband.

"I'm positive. I love him. He loves me. That never stopped, you know?"

"Are you sure—"

Shannon nudged Taylor in the side, hard enough to make the other woman grunt. "You heard her. She's sure. Now drop it."

"I just want—"

"So when's the date?" Shannon moved in front of Taylor, speaking right over her before she ended up saying something stupid. "Let me guess: a June wedding, right? With lots of lace and flowers and—hey, can you wear white again? I mean, considering you guys have already been married and have a kid and all."

"Three weeks."

"What?"

"We're getting married in three weeks."

Silence, stunned and heavy, hung in the air at

Sammie's announcement. Shannon exchanged a disbelieving glance with Taylor and Dani then turned back to Sammie. "Three weeks? Are you fucking crazy? You can't plan a wedding in three fucking weeks!"

"What about the rest of the season? You can't just quit in the middle of it!"

"And the exhibition game. Please tell me you aren't going to miss that." Taylor's voice was a little strangled, the words coming out in a croak. "After everything Chuckie did—"

"Guys, stop! Holy crappola, you're supposed to be excited for me, not freaking out!" A playful smile filled Sammie's face as she rolled her eyes. "We're not doing a big wedding. We already had that. And no, I'm not wearing white. I don't think, I haven't given it much thought yet. And I'm not quitting. And I'm not missing the exhibition game, so relax. We're just going to have a small ceremony, that's all."

Dani edged closer and tilted her head to the side. "Like, how small?"

"Not so small that you guys won't be there."

"Whew. Okay, good." Shannon reached out with her stick and tapped Sammie on the leg. "Because I was going to have to go off on you if we weren't invited."

"Of course, you're invited! You guys are like my family." Sammie's voice wobbled on the last word, a second before she hurtled toward them, her arms open wide for a group hug. Shannon stiffened for a brief second then rolled her eyes and joined in the hug. No, it wasn't her thing, never had been, but Sammie's excitement was contagious and she couldn't let her friend down.

Or maybe she was just starting to soften a bit.

She shook off the horror of that last thought and

stepped back, not really paying attention to the chorus of voices echoing around her. Taylor skated away first, followed by Dani. Shannon hesitated, ready to follow, but Sammie's stare stopped her.

"What?"

"You shouldn't pay attention to Taylor. She's just being a grump. I think she's worried about ticket sales. And the exhibition game. And Chuckie."

"Yeah, no kidding. And I'm not. Um, what about Chuckie?"

"I'm not sure but I think he's feeling added pressure because sales haven't picked up."

"But they will. Right? I mean, it's still early. And it has to mean something that he got the whole exhibition game set up. That's, like, a huge deal. Bigger than huge. It's abso-fucking-lutely amazing.

"Yeah, I guess." Sammie nodded then shifted her weight from one skate to the other and twirled the stick in her hand. "We don't have a shot at winning at all, do we?"

"Of course we do. Why would you say that?"

"Why? Um, because we're going to be playing against the Banners, that's why. Those guys are the real deal."

"Newsflash, Reigs: so are we. They just get paid a hell of a lot more."

"They also play more and practice more and have a lot more experience than we do."

"Doesn't mean we can't kick their asses."

Sammie laughed, the sound a little forced, a little hollow in the chilled air. "I guess. So…do you like him?"

"Who?"

"Don't play stupid. You know who."

Shannon shrugged and started skating away. Not to get away from Sammie and her questions—that wouldn't work, not when Sammie was right beside her. She was skating just to move. She thought better when she was moving, when the ice was under her feet, when she was *part* of the ice. Who cared if it didn't make sense? It worked for her. It had always worked for her.

Only the ice wasn't giving her answers, not to this question. She didn't know how to answer. Did she like Caleb? Yeah. But was there something more to it than that? How could there be when she still didn't know what he was up to? When she had no idea what it was he wanted?

"Well? Do you?"

"I don't know, Reigs. Maybe." Shannon pushed through the door, waiting for Sammie to follow before slamming it shut. "But I don't think I trust him."

"Why not?"

"Because I don't know what kind of game he's playing."

"Why do you think he's playing a game?"

"Oh please. Really? This is me we're talking about. My mouth opens and God only knows what's going to pop out. Guys like him don't want someone like me."

"I think you're selling yourself short."

Shannon grunted but didn't say anything as they entered the locker room and started removing their gear. Was she selling herself short? Maybe...but what else was she supposed to do when experience had taught her otherwise? And why was she suddenly so worried about it now, when it had never bothered her before?

Because she liked Caleb, that was why.

Which meant she was already in over her head.

She tossed everything into her bag—because they weren't the only ones who used this locker room so they couldn't leave anything behind—then pulled a heavy sweatshirt over her head and slid her shoes on. She needed to get over this…this *thing* she had for Caleb before she did something really stupid. Like sleep with him.

Or worse.

"You should bring him to the wedding."

"What?"

Sammie tossed her gear bag over her shoulder with a shrug. "You heard me. Bring him to the wedding."

"No. Not happening."

"Why not?"

"Because…because it's not, that's why. We're not dating. Not even close. And bringing him to your wedding would be like a date."

"But you like him. And judging from that kiss, he must like you."

"I told you, it was just for the stupid camera. It didn't mean anything."

"Uh-huh. That's why you're blushing."

"You're seeing things." Shannon turned away and hurried toward the door in a vain attempt to hide her flaming face. Sammie's laughter followed her, letting her know she hadn't succeeded in hiding anything.

chapter NINE

Sweat ran down his face, stinging his eyes behind the shield. Caleb ignored the burn, kept his focus on the puck as the forward from Anaheim raced toward the net. The score was tied three-to-three with two minutes left in the game. If Anaheim scored, they'd end up winning. Caleb knew a lot could happen in two minutes. Hell, he'd played in games where the final score had been decided in a tenth of a second. But he couldn't shake the feeling that nothing like that would happen tonight.

If Anaheim scored, they won, as simple as that. Caleb knew it in his gut.

Which meant they couldn't score.

He didn't have to look behind him to know that Connelly was struggling in the net. He'd been struggling all fucking night, sliding out of position, losing sight of the puck. It was a fucking miracle the Banners weren't down by five.

Anaheim couldn't score. No fucking way could that happen.

Caleb skated backward, his legs burning, his ankle throbbing. He ignored the pain, gritted his teeth against the mouthguard, and moved to the right. Watching, waiting…

Now.

He pushed forward, a burst of speed propelling him in front of the net a second before the puck went flying. He leaned forward, skates digging into the ice as he reached with his stick and shot the puck away. Shane Masters caught the pass, spun around and headed up the ice.

Caleb sucked in a deep breath and pushed after him, catching up as thousands of fans jumped to their feet. Shouts and curses mingled with the boos as Anaheim's chance of scoring disappeared. It was their puck now, and Caleb would make damn sure it went in.

He shouted at Shane and tapped the blade of his stick against the ice, waiting for the pass he knew was coming. A second later, the puck connected with his blade, nice and easy, like it knew it belonged there. With him.

Caleb bit back a smile as he darted to the left and spun around Anaheim's D. Jaxon Miller was several feet away, already in position, wide open. All Caleb had to do was pass the puck to him—

Except Anaheim's goalie was ready for that move, Caleb could see it in the way the man was already leaning to the side, his glove hand ready. Fuck that shit. Caleb hesitated, pulled back like he was going to pass, watched as the goalie followed-through on changing positions.

There. Now.

Caleb pulled the puck toward him, leaned low and drove toward the net. The goalie realized his mistake and struggled to get back into position but it was too late. Caleb shot the puck through the air, his legs sliding out from under him as he watched the hunk of galvanized rubber sail toward to the net—

And hit the back with a satisfying whoosh that Caleb could hear over the echoing jeers of the crowd.

He bit back another smile as his teammates crowded around him, clapping him on the back. Jaxon leaned in close, something flashing in his eyes before he could blink it away.

"Nice shot. You should have passed it, though."

"No fucking way. He was ready for you."

"I would have gotten it in."

"I told you, no way." Caleb tapped him on the helmet and skated toward the bench, grabbing a towel to wipe his face as he took a seat. He looked up, watched the replay on the giant screen, and nodded when he saw the puck careen into the net in slow motion.

Ninety seconds later, the Banners made their way back to the locker room, cheering and celebrating their win. Coach Donovan pulled him to the side, leaning in close to be heard over the noise. Was that irritation in the coach's eyes? No, he was just seeing things, that was all.

"You're up for interviews, Johnson. Keep it simple. And humble. For fuck's sake, stay humble."

Caleb frowned, wondering what the hell the other man meant by that. He shook it off with a shrug then made his way to the outer locker room where interviews were conducted. A few reporters were already talking to Connelly, which gave him enough time to get his helmet and jersey and pads off. He ran one hand through his wet hair and dropped to the bench, a wide smile on his face as several reporters crowded around him.

"Johnson, how's it feel to be back in the game after being out for so long? Ankle giving you any issues? Are you at one hundred percent?"

Caleb glanced down at his ankle then looked back at the reporter with a bright smile he knew would look great on the cameras. "Well, it feels like it to me. We've got the coaching staff, the trainers—you know they're not going to let me back in before I'm ready. And you saw that last goal. Yeah, I'd say I'm a hundred percent."

"About that last goal—" Another reporter shoved a microphone at Caleb. "Why didn't you pass it to Miller? He was wide open, he would've made the shot."

Caleb swallowed his frustration, keeping his smile in place. "Yeah, he was wide open. But I was watching Anaheim's goalie, he was waiting for it. I had to make a quick judgment call. I saw the opportunity and I went for it. Any one of the other guys would have done the same thing."

"There were rumors earlier this season about some discontent in the locker room. That some of the guys weren't happy with what's been called your showboating. Any comment on that?"

Caleb tossed his head back and laughed, the sound low and deep and completely void of the frustration growing in his chest. He shook his head, ran a hand through his hair again, and kept on smiling. "Just rumors, I'm afraid. You guys know how it goes. And there's no showboating. We're a team, each of us giving two hundred percent every time we're on the ice."

He turned away from the reporter, using subtle body language to shut him down before he could ask any more questions. Another microphone appeared in front of him, the hand's owner speaking above the other voices to be heard.

"Speaking of rumors—any truth to the one about you being involved with the goalie of the Chesapeake Blades? With Shannon Wiley?"

Caleb had been wondering if someone was going to ask him about that, but he hadn't expected to hear the question here, in the locker room after a game. It didn't matter because he was prepared. He looked up at the reporter, knew that the cameras—both video and still—were focused on his crooked smile, on the dimple appearing in his cheek, on the teasing sparkle in his eyes. "Now you know a gentleman doesn't kiss and tell."

It was the perfect answer, drawing a chuckle from the surrounding crowd. The words admitted nothing while his expression hinted at something completely different. Would Shannon see or hear it? It didn't matter if she did or not, because he knew someone would definitely be telling her, one way or the other. It was just enough to force a reaction out of her—and he was pretty damn confident it would be the exact reaction he wanted. Sure, she'd be pissed at first. But after…yeah, he was looking forward to *after*, because he had no doubt she was interested. She just needed a little nudge, that was all. And if that didn't nudge her, he didn't know what else would.

"Speaking of the Blades, what are your thoughts about the exhibition game coming up in a few weeks?"

"We're looking forward to it. It's a great way to raise some money for charity, and it'll give us a chance to play a nice, relaxed game."

"So you're not worried about any real competition?"

Caleb choked back his laughter, turning it into a small cough. He covered his mouth with the back of one hand and quickly smothered his smile. The back of his neck itched with a faint tingle of warning and he reminded himself he needed to be careful with how he answered. Insulting Shannon and her team certainly wouldn't win him any points.

"I don't think any of us are looking at it as a competition. Like I said, we're doing this for charity. It'll be fun."

"So you don't think the ladies have a chance of winning?"

Christ, couldn't the guy move on to another question already? How many times did Caleb have to answer? His smile dimmed but he was careful to keep the edge from his voice when he spoke.

"Again, we're not playing to win. It's just a fun way to raise money, that's all." Caleb turned his attention to another reporter, eager for a change in topic, but the first guy wasn't quite ready to concede.

"The game might be a fundraiser but, if you had to bet, who would your money be on?"

Caleb turned back, his smile just a little forced, an irritated edge clear in his voice. "Well, if I was forced to bet, you know my money would be on the Banners. That's the only thing that makes sense, right? We're the professionals, after all—"

"So you're saying the Blades aren't a professional team?"

"No. Of course not. It's just—"

"Or is it because it's a women's team?"

"That's not what I said. All I meant was that—"

"So you don't think they have a chance at all, do you?"

"If we were really playing? I'd have to say no, I don't. The Blades are too new, too inexperienced. You can't even compare them to us—"

Coach Donovan appeared out of nowhere, placing his body between Caleb and the reporters. "Okay gentleman, that's all for now. We've got our postgame meeting then a flight to catch."

One by one, the reporters grabbed their gear and made their way out of the locker room. Caleb breathed a sigh of relief then bent down to undo his skates, pausing when he noticed that Coach Donovan hadn't moved. He looked up and felt another tingle of warning dance along his skin at the stormy expression on the coach's face.

"For fuck's sake, Johnson. What part of *humble* don't you understand? Do you have any idea what kind of shit storm you just caused?"

"I didn't—"

"Yeah, you did. Christ. Tomorrow's going to be a real treat."

"But—"

"I don't want to hear it. Just get your ass in the shower. And start thinking long and hard about how you can spin this when you get called on it tomorrow."

Caleb stared at the coach's retreating back, wondering why the hell the man was so convinced there was going to be a shit storm. Could Caleb have said things differently? Yeah, of course. But nothing he said had been *bad*. Not even close.

Which did nothing to explain why that tingle of warning was getting worse with each passing second.

chapter TEN

Shannon hurried along the hall, the heels of her dress flats clicking against the polished tile as Chuckie practically dragged her behind him. She pulled on her arm, finally tugging it from his desperate hold. "Tell me again why this is so important, it couldn't wait?"

"I told you: damage control."

"But why do you need *me* here? I'm not the one who ran his mouth off during the interview!"

Chuckie spun around to face her, his eyes flashing with impatience. "No, but you're the one who had his tongue jammed down your throat for all the world to see."

"You have got to be fucking kidding me. I told you, it was just a show for that stupid kiss cam." Did he notice her blush? How could he not, with the way he was studying her? And yeah, sure enough, he rolled his eyes in disbelief.

"Why don't I believe that? And for the last time,

watch your mouth. You absolutely cannot let anything slip like that during the press conference." His vivid blue eyes raked her from the top of her head to the tips of her shoes and back again. "Don't you have any lipstick or something you can put on?"

Shannon's mouth dropped open, his words momentarily robbing her of speech. She tried to say something but the only thing that came out was a strangled gurgle. Or maybe it was a growl, she wasn't sure. It didn't matter because Chuckie wasn't paying attention.

"Forget the lipstick, that would just make you look even more like sex-on-a-stick. The look you've got going now is more wholesome. Almost innocent." He almost choked on the last word then grabbed her wrist and started tugging her again. "Wholesome is good. That's the image we need—"

"Whoa. Hold up. What the hell?" Shannon dug her heels against the floor and yanked her arm free. "Lipstick? Could you get any more sexist? Taylor needs to kick your ass. And *sex-on-a-stick*? Did you seriously just fucking say that? About *me*?"

His small chuckle surprised her, but not nearly as much as the blush spreading along his jaw and cheeks. He glanced down at the floor then finally looked up and met her gaze with a sheepish expression. "Yeah, sorry. It's just, that was the first thing I thought of the very first time I saw you—until you opened your mouth and I realized you had the lethal bite of a striking cobra."

"Seriously? *Sex-on-a-stick*?" Shannon didn't know whether to laugh—or haul off and slug him. Both. Neither. She settled on clearing her throat and giving him a stern look of warning. "Keep it up and I really will have Taylor beat you up for me."

Was it her imagination, or was that a gleam of excitement that flashed in his eyes? Shannon shook her head, knowing there was no way in hell she was even going to ask. Not that Chuckie would even give her a chance because he wrapped his hand around her wrist once more and tugged her along the hallway.

"I still don't understand why I have to be here. Or why it's even a big deal. Half of what Caleb said was taken out of context."

"Yeah, but the other half wasn't."

"So? I still don't understand why there has to be this big press conference about it. It's not like—"

"Because it went viral—and not in a good way. Because it's a slow news day in the sports world. Because coming right after that kiss made things even worse."

"And I told you, that was just for show and—"

"And you need to actually look at it. Trust me, it didn't look like it was for show. And there isn't a single person out there who would believe it if you told them, so don't. It'll just make things look worse."

"I still don't—"

Chuckie silenced her with a single glance then led her into a small room. Shannon stumbled to a halt, her eyes widening at the small crowd gathered there. James Murphy, the owner of the Blades; Paul Branton, the owner of the Banners. A lithe woman she had never seen before with dark blonde hair and high cheekbones stood in the far corner, talking to Ian Donovan, the Banners' head coach. Even Diane Reynolds, her own head coach, was here.

And sitting on one of the leather sofas all by himself was Caleb, immaculately attired in an expensive suit. Shannon glanced down at her own outfit: dress slacks, black flats, and a fitted blue blouse. She thought she had looked crisp and professional—until seeing Caleb.

He glanced over at her then slowly straightened, obviously ready to say something. Shannon narrowed her eyes at him and spoke before he could get the chance. "You are such a fucking jerk."

Caleb straightened even more and pinned her in place with a glare. "Excuse me?"

"You heard me. And people talk about *my* mouth? At least I never—"

"Shannon, enough." Chuckie pulled her further into the room and shut the door behind them. Then he led her over to the sofa and motioned for her to have a seat next to Caleb. One look at the expression on his face was enough to keep her from arguing so she simply took a seat—and made a point of sliding away from Caleb, just to irritate both men.

She was rethinking her decision a few seconds later when the eyes of everyone in the room zeroed in on her. No, not just *her*—*them*. Her *and* Caleb. She shot a questioning glance in his direction then turned back to Chuckie, wrongly assuming he was the safest one in the room.

"Are you two dating?" His abrupt question split the heavy silence. Shannon straightened with a frown and shook her head.

"No."

"Yes."

Her mouth dropped open in shock. She twisted toward Caleb, surprised to see him casually sprawled out on the sofa, his arm draped across the back near her shoulders. That crooked smile teased one corner of his mouth as he watched her.

Shannon leaned toward him. "No. We are *not* dating."

Caleb's grin grew a little wider. "How many times have we gone out to grab a bite to eat?"

"That doesn't mean—"

"And how many times have we kissed?"

"We did *not*—" Her objection was cut off by the sound of light-hearted music underscored by thunderous applause and cheers. Shannon tilted her head to the side then swallowed a groan when she saw the replay of the kiss cam splashed across a large screen hanging on the far wall. The lithe blonde hit a button on the remote she was holding, replaying it one more time before turning it off and facing them.

"If it was just the kiss, we could play this off as a joke—even if the expression on each of your faces says otherwise." The woman hit another button and a replay of Caleb's interview flashed across the screen.

Well, if I was forced to bet, you know my money would be on the Banners. That's the only thing that makes sense, right? We're the professionals, after all.

You're saying the Blades aren't a professional team?

No. Of course not. It's just—

Or is it because it's a women's team?

That's not what I said. All I meant was that—

You don't think they have a chance at all, do you?

If we were really playing? I'd have to say no, I don't. The Blades are too new, too inexperienced. You can't even compare them to us.

Caleb groaned, the sound barely audible. Shannon looked over at him, felt a tiny twinge of sympathy—but not enough to stay quiet. "Just had to run your mouth, didn't you?"

She whispered the words so only he could hear. His head shot up and he stared at her, something unreadable in his green gaze. It looked like he wanted to say something but he never got the chance. The screen went blank and the woman turned toward them again.

"Unfortunately, both the kiss and the interview went viral, which means we need to respond."

Shannon raised her hand then leaned forward, her eyes never leaving the other woman's. "Who the hell are you?"

The woman floundered for a second, her gaze shooting to the Banners' owner then darting to their head coach. Shannon didn't miss the small blush fanning across high cheekbones and for a split-second, she could almost *feel* the other woman's embarrassment.

"This is Lori Evans. She's a digital media specialist for the Baltimore Banners. She's also the one who worked with me in setting up the exhibition game." Chuckie broke the silence before it became more than an awkward pause. Shannon nodded then leaned back, stiffening when she felt Caleb's arm brush against her shoulders. She almost moved but one of his hands squeezed her shoulder in subtle warning. She looked over at him, saw that same warning flash in his green eyes and in the small shake of his head.

What the hell was that all about?

Shannon mentally rolled her eyes then turned back and tried to listen to the rest of the conversation. And listen was all she got to do because it quickly became obvious neither she nor Caleb was going to be allowed to talk.

At least, not yet. Not until they were herded out in

front of the reporters to recite the story they'd been given.

They were colleagues, yes. Yes, they were also friends. They'd gone out a few times but they weren't ready to comment on the status of any relationship, choosing to keep it private.

As for Caleb's unfortunate words during the post-game interview in Anaheim, they'd been taken out of context. Yes, they were both looking forward to the game. Yes, it was nothing more than a friendly game for charity, but that didn't mean there wasn't some lighthearted competition going on at the same time.

And yes, either team could win. The Blades were just as good as the Banners and could boast a winning record for the season so far. They'd have to wait and see how it played out.

Shannon glanced over at Caleb during that last bit and nearly choked on her laughter. No, he wasn't happy about that last part, not at all. And she wasn't the only one who picked up on his expression, either, because Coach Donovan leaned down and said something to him, the words too quiet for Shannon to hear. Whatever the man said must have carried some weight, though, because the color drained from Caleb's face before he gave the coach a curt nod.

And then they were being ushered out of the room and down the hall, around a corner and into another room. Shannon stumbled in surprise at the unexpected crowd, felt the heated weight of Caleb's hand in the middle of her back as he steadied her.

"Just smile and pretend you're in the zone."

Shannon nodded at his whispered words of encouragement, her gaze scanning the reporters with their cameras and microphones and tablets. Her eyes rested on a familiar face and she released a quick sigh of relief when TR's gaze caught hers.

The other woman hurried over, ignoring the glares of the other reporters in the room—mostly men. She rested her hand on Shannon's arm, gently nudging her away from Caleb and the others.

"Bet you didn't think you'd be facing something like this, huh?"

"No. It feels like a firing squad."

TR laughed then leaned in closer. "You can handle it. Just look over at me if you get nervous or stumped. Now go give them hell."

Shannon barely had time to nod before she was whisked away to the large table in the front of the room. The logos for both teams had been placed on the wall behind the table, creating a colorful backdrop that would make an impressive picture. Shannon could already hear cameras clicking as she took a seat in the center, next to Caleb. And it wasn't just the two of them: Chuckie and Lori flanked them, along with each owner and each coach.

Shannon swallowed nervous laughter and tried to ignore all the cameras. She felt something press against her leg and glanced down to see Caleb's hand give her thigh a reassuring pat. She almost brushed it away but Chuckie nudged her in the side and shook his head, just the tiniest bit. Then it didn't matter because Caleb's hand was gone and the questions started flying.

Were they dating?
How long had they been seeing each other?
What was the story behind the kiss?

The answers to those were short and sweet, using the responses they had both been coached on. Shannon glanced around, saw the clear doubt on some of the faces looking back at her, but she didn't care. They could doubt all they want but there wasn't much more to say since the questions had already been answered.

Mostly.

Then came the questions about the game. How had it been set up? Were they expecting a large turnout? How had the logistics been handled and how had it been approved in the middle of the season?

Shannon relaxed just a little as those were answered by the owners and the two PR people flanking them. She didn't even worry when Caleb was questioned on his poor choice of words—he sat beside her, cool and relaxed, a hint of a smile on his face as he calmly explained each comment away.

The questions were finally dying down and she breathed a sigh of relief. It was almost over. She'd done it. A few more minutes then she'd be able to go back home, change, and get to work without missing any more time. Just a few more minutes…

Another reporter stood up, jumping to his feet like he was afraid the party would end before he got a chance to get there. "Ms. Wiley, a question."

Shannon stiffened as a trickle of unease danced along her spine. She leaned forward, her brows raised in question. "Yes?"

"Don't you think it's unrealistic for women to even think of competing with men on a professional level? And what makes you think any man would even tolerate something like that?"

Shannon felt Chuckie stiffen next to her, felt his elbow nudge against her side in silent warning. Even Caleb seemed to stiffen, whether in outrage or for some other reason, she didn't know. What she did know was that he was getting ready to answer and if he did—

No, she couldn't let him. Whatever he was about to say wouldn't be good, she knew that as sure as she knew the reporter was just waiting for a juicy soundbite. The question had been directed at *her* and she was the one who needed to answer.

She kicked Caleb's foot under the table and leaned forward, ready to let the first thing that sprang to mind drop from her mouth. Her gaze darted around the room, coming to rest on TR for a quick second. The woman smiled and nodded, giving her a thumbs-up in encouragement.

Shannon smiled back, the tension leaving her as she faced the reporter. She could do this. She knew she could.

"It's not unrealistic at all. And if you've ever seen us play, you'd know that. As for any man being expected to *tolerate* it..." Shannon couldn't quite the stop eyeroll when she forced the word past her lips. "I don't think a real man would have any issues about it. And to be honest, that's why not many men can meet my high standards. So far, Caleb's measuring...*up*...just fine."

chapter ELEVEN

"So I'm measuring up just fine, huh?"

Shannon ducked her head so a thick hank of hair hid her face—but not before he saw the bright flush spread across her cheeks. Caleb tossed back his head and laughed, then choked it back when she elbowed him in the side.

"It's not funny. And it sounded a whole lot better in my head."

"It didn't sound that bad."

"I'm sure it didn't, not to you." She shook her head then reached up and brushed the hair from her face with a sigh. "I don't think Chuckie is ever going to forgive me. Or let me in front of a camera again."

"I think you're worrying over nothing. It really wasn't that bad. And that little pause you added, right before you said *up*—" Caleb laughed again, sidestepping so he'd be out of reach of her elbow.

"Yeah, go ahead and laugh. Everyone else did. It

was embarrassing."

At first, he thought she was just being overly-dramatic, in a funny sort of way. But he caught a glimpse of worry in her eyes and saw the way her shoulders hunched around her ears. The movement was as brief as that expression on her face but not brief enough. Was she really worried about it?

Yeah, she really was.

There was something about that small glimpse of vulnerability that stopped him in his tracks—literally. He grabbed her hand and moved off to the side of the sidewalk, tugging her with him. The fact that she came willingly told him how upset she really was. Caleb ignored the tug of emotion he felt at her expression, telling himself he was imagining things. Did he feel sympathy for her? Yeah, of course he did. He wasn't that heartless or uncaring. But that's all it was: sympathy. And it had nothing to do with the way he kept her hand cradled in his, or with the sudden urge he had to pull her into his arms and tell her everything would be okay.

Or the urge to kiss her until she forgot everything about this afternoon.

He ignored both urges and dropped her hand then leaned against the wall. The coldness of the bricks seeped through his jacket and shirt and into his skin, a contradiction to the heated blood flowing through his veins. This was a bad idea, he should have never asked her out tonight. Not because there was anything wrong with going out for pizza but because he wanted one hell of a lot more than pizza.

He wanted *her*.

Only he couldn't have her, not the way he wanted. Shannon wasn't a one-night stand, even if he had been considering just that not too long ago. But the more he was around her…

He liked her, dammit. Which meant his former plans had to be scratched. Which meant he had to put all thoughts of her long legs wrapped around him and sturdy curves pressed against him completely out of his mind.

Yeah, sure. Easier said than done.

Shannon shifted in front of him, curling her arms in front of her and huddling deeper in her coat to fight off the chill of the night air. "Is there a reason we're stopped in the middle of the sidewalk?"

Was there a reason? Caleb gave himself a mental shake. A reason. Yes, there had been a reason. He wanted to reassure her, to tell her there was no reason for her to be embarrassed. He just needed to stop looking at her mouth and thinking—

He cleared his throat and finally met her gaze. "It wasn't that bad."

"You said that already."

"And I'm repeating it because it's the truth. The guy was an ass. You pretty much put him in his place."

"Yeah. Uh-huh. And made you sound like some sex god in the process."

Caleb choked back his laughter and wondered if she had any idea how close her words were to his own thoughts. Not about the sex god part—although yeah, that certainly wouldn't hurt his reputation—but the sex part.

Definitely the sex part.

Only no, she didn't have a clue. Not about what he was thinking. Not about what she did to him. Not even about how she looked, standing there in her worn denim jeans that hugged every inch of those long legs, her head tilted back and her mouth slightly parted as she watched him with wide brown eyes.

"I hope you know this is all your fault."

He frowned, wondering if he had missed something while his mind was somewhere it shouldn't be. "What's my fault?"

"Everything. But especially this afternoon. If you hadn't run your mouth during that interview last night, none of this would have happened."

"It was taken out of context."

Shannon's brows shot up in disbelief. "Out of context? Oh, please. You were smooth about it but you're not going to stand there and tell me you didn't mean every single word you said. You really don't think we can beat you."

"Could you? Maybe. But it's not a fair game. We've been playing a hell of a lot longer. We've got more experience—"

"I've been playing for seventeen years. How about you?"

"I—" Caleb frowned when he realized he'd only been playing two years longer. He shook his head, brushing her question away. "That doesn't matter. We've been together longer as a team. We have more game experience, more practice time, more ice time. It only makes sense to think we'd win against a brand-new team. We have the advantage."

"Yeah, okay. If you say so. It's still your fault. You should have just kept quiet. If you hadn't let that guy goad you, we wouldn't have had that awful press conference today and I wouldn't have embarrassed myself."

"You didn't embarrass yourself."

"Yeah, I did." She uncrossed her arms and poked

him in the chest with her finger. "But you were the one responsible for the other night. You and that stupid kiss—"

"Stupid?"

"Yeah. Stupid. You just had to show off—"

Caleb didn't stop to think, just reached out and pulled her closer and claimed her mouth with his own. It was stupid. A bad idea. A *really* bad idea.

But he didn't care, not when her mouth opened beneath his with a soft gasp. Not when her hands rested on his shoulders as she stepped even closer, fitting her body against his. Hard and soft and warm.

Caleb cupped the back of her head with one hand and deepened the kiss, swallowing her soft moan. Or maybe the noise had come from him, the sound born from both desire and surprise. It didn't matter, not when she pressed against him and kissed him back.

And this…this was so much better than he'd imagined. A hundred times better than that open-mouthed kiss he'd given her the other night in front of eighteen thousand screaming fans. A million times better than that lame ass closed-mouth peck in the parking lot of the diner.

This…this was hot and wet. This was what he wanted, what he'd hadn't been able to stop thinking about. Carnal desire and need and excitement all rolled into one powerful punch strong enough to bring him to his knees. And when her hips pressed against the length of his erection…yeah, fuck. His knees damn near buckled right then and there.

He broke the kiss with a silent growl, his breath leaving in a strangled gasp when she looked up at him with eyes glazed with desire. Then she blinked, her tongue darting out and sweeping across the swell of her bottom lip, and he damn near groaned again.

"I thought we were getting pizza."

Pizza? How could she think about pizza right now?

Caleb cleared his throat and tried to step back, damn near knocked himself out when his head smacked against the brick wall.

"Pizza. Yeah. Sure." He rubbed the back of his head, watching the playful smile that curled the edges of her mouth. "We, uh, we could get it to go. I don't live too far from here—"

"I told you, I'm not sleeping with you."

"Who said anything about sleeping?" And shit. Damn. *Fuck*. He hadn't meant to say that out loud, hadn't meant to give her a reason to haul off and slug him or verbally slay him.

To his surprise, she didn't do either of those things. And she didn't give him a withering look or storm off, either. She just stood there, her head tilted to the side as she watched him.

And watched him some more.

A slow smile spread across her face and danced in her eyes, one that filled him with both excitement and terror. Maybe he had counted himself lucky too soon, maybe now was when she would haul off and throttle him.

Except she didn't. Instead, she reached down and grabbed his hand, tugging until he had no choice but to follow her.

"I actually think getting take-out is a great idea."

chapter TWELVE

"You don't like losing, do you?"

Caleb raised one brow and pinned her with a disbelieving expression that silently asked if she was crazy. "Does anyone like losing?"

Shannon shrugged, a smile teasing her mouth. "Probably not, no. But *some* people handle it better than others."

She shifted on the sofa, stretching her long legs and crossing them at the ankles before placing her feet back on the coffee table—right next to his. Caleb stared at their feet, both covered in matching white socks. His were large, almost clumsy looking next to her smaller ones. He'd never been into feet, had never even paid that much attention before tonight—until seeing Shannon's resting so comfortably next to his. He wondered if her toes were crooked like his from being jammed into skates for most of his life, or if any of them had been broken like his. Were her toenails painted at all? Maybe a delicate color, like a pale pink. No, Shannon wouldn't pick something pale. If her nails were painted, they'd be something bright and colorful and—

What the hell was he doing, sitting here thinking about whether or not the woman next to him painted her toenails? He needed his fucking head examined. Not just for that, but for this whole night.

Because this was *not* what he had planned. Not even close.

Not that seduction had been on the schedule, not really, but there had always been a tiny hope in the back of his mind. Especially after that kiss. Yeah, definitely after that kiss.

He sure as hell hadn't planned on bringing her back to his place and playing video games. But that's exactly what they'd been doing for the last hour: eating pizza and playing video games.

And she was kicking his ass while doing it, too.

She uncrossed her ankles and nudged his foot with her own. "Come on, one more. I'll even let you win this time."

Caleb tossed the controller onto the table and shook his head. "I think I'll pass."

"Aw, look. You're pouting."

"No, I'm not."

"Yeah, you are. Admit it."

"I'm not pouting."

She playfully elbowed him in the side. "You are. It's kind of cute, in a weird, immature way."

Caleb turned his head to the side, his gaze dropping to her mouth before darting back to her laughing eyes. "Did you just call me cute?"

Shannon rolled her eyes and looked away, but not

before he noticed the flare of interest in their depths. "Oh please, don't go getting all excited. I also called you immature."

"But cute. You definitely said cute."

"I didn't mean it. Lord knows, your ego doesn't need more feeding. Just forget I said anything."

"That's not feeding my ego. No more than it would be feeding your ego if I said I thought you were cute."

Shannon snorted, the sound just a little too loud to be called delicate. Caleb watched the color bloom on her cheeks, noticed how she looked away and fidgeted just the tiniest bit. No, she wasn't fidgeting—she was easing away from him but trying to be subtle about it. And she didn't ask him to repeat the compliment or even try to fish for more, like most other women he knew. In fact, she looked uncomfortable, like she wished he hadn't said anything at all.

Caleb lowered his legs from the table and shifted sideways on the leather sofa so he was facing her. He draped his arm along the back, let his hand drift down to her shoulder. She stiffened but didn't move away. She also wouldn't look at him.

"You don't like compliments, do you?" It was a statement, even if he did phrase it as a question. She lowered her gaze to the twisting hands in her lap and shrugged before forcing a laugh.

"Don't be an idiot. Everyone likes compliments."

"Then why are you blushing and trying to scoot away from me?"

"I'm not."

"Liar." He didn't say anything else, just sat there and waited for her reaction. She held herself still for a long minute as the silence stretched around them, broken only by the low music coming from the paused video game. Caleb sighed and leaned over for the remote, hitting the button that would turn the entire entertainment center off. Now the room was completely silent, the stillness heavy and absolute.

He mentally cursed himself for turning the thing off. At least before, there had been that annoying background music instead of this uncomfortable silence. He shifted positions again, his hand once more brushing against her shoulder. Shannon stiffened and for a second, he expected her to jump to her feet and storm out. Instead, she turned and faced him, her eyes narrowed as she watched him.

"What game are you playing, Caleb?" There was nothing light or playful in the clipped words, or in her expression. This was a different side of Shannon, one he'd never seen before. Quiet. Serious. Untrusting.

Wary.

He dropped his hand and moved away, his gaze never leaving hers. "Why are you so convinced I'm playing a game?"

"Because I'm not your type. And don't lie and say I am because we both know it's not true."

"You keep saying that. So tell me: what's my *type*?"

Shannon rolled her eyes then looked around the large living room, like she was searching for an answer. She finally sighed and waved one hand, the motion taking in the leather furniture and glass and chrome accents, the large wall of windows and sliding door that led to the balcony, the twinkling lights reflected on the harbor just beyond.

"Not me, that's for sure. I mean, look at this place. We're not in the same league. Hell, we're not even in the same fucking zip code."

Frustration bloomed in his chest, some of it slipping into his voice when he spoke. "Why the hell do you keep saying that?"

"Because it's true. I mean, look at you. You're…you. And me—I live in a studio above my brother's garage. I'm the one with the lethal strike of a cobra. Even Chuckie said so."

Caleb started to laugh and choked it back at the last second, nearly strangling with the effort. "A striking cobra, huh?"

"It's not funny!"

"It's a little funny—*oomph*." He grabbed his side where Shannon had elbowed him then moved back just a little, out of range.

"It's not. And that's exactly what I'm talking about."

"Okay, you lost me. Hell, this whole conversation has lost me. What are even talking about?"

She waved her hand between them. "This. You. Me. And…and whatever it is you're doing. I'm not your type. Not even close."

"How do you know what my type even is?"

"I don't know but I'm pretty sure it's not someone who's just one of the guys—which is what I am."

"What the hell ever gave you that idea? Trust me, you are definitely *not* just one of the guys."

"Really?" Disbelief was clearly etched on her face. "How many dates do you bring home for pizza and video games?"

"I—well, none. But that doesn't mean—"

"I rest my case." She placed her hands on the edge of the sofa, started levering herself up. Caleb grabbed her, the motion throwing her off balance. She toppled back to the sofa and landed in his lap. He released her, just long enough to give her a chance to move if she wanted.

She didn't move.

Caleb breathed a quick sigh of relief then wrapped one arm behind her, his touch light, his grip loose. "Why do you have such a hard time believing that maybe I just like you? That maybe I'm comfortable enough with you to bring you back here and let you kick my ass in video games?"

Shannon snorted. "*Let* me? Oh, please. We both know I kicked your ass because I'm better than you."

"Yeah, you keep telling yourself that. Now stop avoiding my question."

"I'm not."

"Yeah, you are. Now, why are you so convinced I'm playing games? Why can't you believe that maybe I actually like you and want to spend time with you?"

"Why?" Shannon shifted, not enough to move off his lap, but enough to put just a little distance between them. "Because most men tuck their tails between their legs and run off because I intimidate them."

"I'm not most men."

"No, you're not. You're a player."

Caleb bit back another sigh then reached up and ran his free hand through the long strands of her hair. Soft, satiny-smooth. Entirely too tempting. He tucked the hair behind her ear and reluctantly dropped his hand before capturing her gaze with his own. "You need to stop listening to Taylor."

"Are you saying you're not?"

"Am I a saint? No. Never said I was. But that doesn't mean I'm playing you."

"We haven't even been out on a date."

"Wrong. We've been out on four."

"Four?" Her brows shot up, then quickly narrowed. "Where the hell did you come up with that number?"

He counted off on his fingers. "The Maypole. The diner. The hockey game. Tonight."

"None of those count."

"The hell they don't."

"They don't. They're not even real dates."

"You're so full of it! They certainly are real dates."

"I say they're not, so they don't count."

Caleb chuckled—not at her words, but at the small pout that played around her mouth and the hint of laughter that danced in her eyes. He reached up, swiped her lower lip with the pad of his thumb, felt her lean a little closer to him. "Then what counts as a real date?"

She propped one hand on his shoulder and placed the other in the center of his chest. She shifted on his lap and he swallowed a groan at the feel of her tight ass wiggling against the hard length of his erection. How could she feel that and not think he was interested?

He almost asked her but she started talking, silencing him.

"A real date is when you get dressed up and go out. You know: dinner. The movies. Something like that."

"We can do that." The words came out in a ragged whisper, hoarse and almost desperate. He cleared his throat and repeated them.

"We could, yeah." Shannon leaned even closer, so close he could feel the weight of her breasts brush against his chest. So close he could feel the heat of her breath against his mouth. He swallowed back a groan and tilted his head up, wanting to capture her mouth with his own, wanting to taste her. She pulled back just the tiniest bit, a smile teasing her lips.

"Or we could go to a wedding together. That would count, too."

"Wedding?" The word was strangled, filled with feigned horror. "What wedding?"

"Sammie Reigler, one of my teammates. She's getting married in two weeks, and I need a date."

"Weddings are—" He cleared his throat, searching for the right words. A wedding? Holy shit, that was the last place he wanted to take a date. Weddings made women get crazy-stupid ideas. Weddings gave him hives. "I'm allergic to weddings."

Shannon leaned back then shifted so she was straddling his lap. He groaned, swallowing back both frustration and laughter when he noticed the teasing expression in her eyes. "Then take some Benadryl."

"Real funny. Haha. I can't make it. I'm sure we have a game that day."

"You don't, I already checked."

"How about we go to Vegas instead? Or maybe a quick trip to the Bahamas? That would count as a date, right?"

"Nope. It has to be the wedding."

She wiggled against him again, eliciting another groan from him. He grabbed her hips and held her in place, rocked his own hips against her then nearly swore. Stupid. So fucking stupid. The only thing that move accomplished was making him more frustrated. At least he wasn't the only one—he saw the way her lids fluttered, noticed the way her chest rose and fell on a quick breath as she pulled her lower lip between her teeth.

He leaned up, caught her lower lip with his mouth and sucked, ever so lightly. "And, uh, what happens if I take you to this wedding?"

"Well..." She rocked against him once more, nice and slow, her fingers curling in the thin cotton of his shirt. "It's at a hotel and we'd probably be drinking. Which means we'd have to get a room."

"*One* room? Or two?"

"Just, um, just one."

"Doesn't that mean we'd have to sleep together?"

"Who said anything about sleeping?" She tossed his earlier words back at him and rocked against him again. Once, twice. He sucked in a deep breath and tightened his hands around her hips, holding her still.

"That's blackmail."

"No." She leaned forward, brushed her mouth against his then pulled away before he could kiss her. And damn if she wasn't smiling. "It's actually bribery. So—is it a date?"

He pulled her closer, half-expecting her to stiffen or push against him, then leaned up and captured her mouth. The kiss was hot, needy, filled with promise and frustration. He broke the kiss with a small groan, knowing instinctively not to push things, not to push *her*. Not now. Not tonight. He was only slightly appeased to see that her breathing was as harsh as his own; slightly mollified to see her dark eyes smoldering with the same desire burning in his.

"It's a date."

chapter THIRTEEN

Shannon crouched low, bounced twice on her skates then swung her stick from side to side, tapping each post before rolling her head. Deep breath in, hold it. Release, nice and slow. One more time for good measure before getting into final position just before the puck dropped.

Action exploded at center ice as Taylor fought for the puck, finally hitting the winger from New York with her shoulder as she dug with her stick. The puck broke free from the melee and slid across the ice, hitting the blade of Rachel's stick. She turned and skated up the ice, passing the puck behind her to Taylor. Back and forth, moving into the offensive zone, setting things up for an early shot.

Shannon straightened, allowing herself to relax for a fraction of a second as the action unfolded at the other end. She held her breath, watching as Taylor made a final pass to Rachel then skated around the back of the net. It was a classic set-up. All Rachel had to do was shoot. If she scored, fan-fucking-tastic. If not, Taylor would be there for the rebound—

And fuck, fuck, fuck. How the *fuck* had Rachel missed? She totally whiffed the shot! Now the puck was heading back this way, being propelled through center ice by one of New York's D-men. Shannon dropped to a crouch, her gaze focused on nothing but the puck. From her periphery, she saw one of the Blades—it had to be Sammie, nobody else was quite as small as she was—dash across the ice to intercept. Bodies collided with a dull thud but not before the puck shot free, straight toward another player from New York.

Shit, fuck. Breathe. Focus.

Closer…closer. Shannon watched the other player's stick, watched as the woman shifted her weight from one leg to the other. Just a small sign, a little tell…Shannon didn't move, just kept watching as the player moved closer and pulled back on her stick—

Now!

Shannon followed the motion of the stick with her eyes, watched as the woman followed-through on the shot. The puck sailed straight toward her, low and fast. She reached out with her glove hand and snagged it before it crossed the line, started to throw it to the side for Sammie. But Sammie wasn't close enough and there were two players from the other team waiting on it, skating in fast to knock it free and shoot it in on a rebound. Shannon pulled her glove hand into her chest, cradling the puck and waiting for the whistle.

The shrill blast echoed in the chilled air, followed by a short burst of subdued groans from the home crowd. A split-second later, Shannon felt the slash of a stick across her lower back, sharp and stinging. She straightened, dropping the puck to the ice and jumping to her feet, ready to swing at the woman standing a foot away. But then Sammie was there, and Dani and Maddison, coming between her and the player from New York. And then the ref was there, separating all of them before anything else could happen.

Yeah, because God forbid if they actually started fighting.

Shannon reached down for the puck, tossed it to the ref then stared at him, waiting for him to call a penalty. He simply looked at her then skated away.

"What the hell? No penalty? Come on! How could you miss that?"

The ref turned back, frowning, then shook his head.

"What? Are you fucking blind? She slashed—"

Taylor skated closer, practically shoving her hand in Shannon's face to quiet her. "Don't. You'll draw a penalty."

"Me? What about her? Did you not fucking see that?"

"Yeah, I did. Let me handle it." Taylor nodded once then skated off toward the ref, her face a mask of fury as she started talking to him. Shannon couldn't hear what was being said but she could tell Taylor was losing her cool. Her face was turning a dangerous shade of red and she was motioning wildly with one hand. The ref shook his head again, his mouth thinning into a hard line.

And then Sammie was there, pulling Taylor away, saying something to her in a low voice as she tugged. The ref skated away, getting into position for the next puck drop.

Son of a bitch. He wasn't going to call it! Shannon bit down on her mouthpiece and got back into position, anger coursing through her veins.

Brush it off. Focus. Get back into the zone.

Her eyes darted to the board, noticed the time left on the clock. Twenty seconds. They could do this. Twenty seconds and the game would be over, and the Blades could put another point in the win column. No problem.

Just breathe. Focus.

The puck dropped again only this time, New York won the draw. Fuck! Shannon crouched lower, barely blinking as her eyes followed the puck. Close. Closer. She waited for the shot, watched as the puck was passed right in front of her. She moved toward it, realized her mistake and scrambled back. And shit, here it came, she wasn't in position—

Shannon leaned backward, arching her back and stretching to the right, the muscles of her thighs and abdomen pulling…pulling. She threw her right arm to the side, reaching across the net with her stick, knowing it was too late, knowing New York had just tied the fucking game.

Stretching more, her breath held, her thighs and abs burning, everything moving in slow motion as she reached…reached—

The puck hit her stick and bounced out, away from the net and straight toward Rachel. Holy fucking shit, no fucking way! The other woman looked as stunned as Shannon felt.

"Go! Go!" Shannon shouted at her over the background noise, breathed a sigh of relief when Rachel spun around and skated away from the net.

Three seconds. Two. One—

The horn blared, signaling the end of the game. Shannon collapsed onto her knees and bent over from the waist, her helmet touching the ice as she sucked frigid air into her lungs.

Holy shit. Holy fucking shit.

Hands reached for her, pulling her to her feet then gathering her in for a group hug. She heard excited voices and mingled words of congratulations and disbelief as she was pulled toward the bench. Coach Reynolds tapped her on the helmet with her ever-present clipboard as Shannon made her way back to the locker room with everyone else.

"Holy crappola, you are the Limbo Queen!" Sammie pulled her into a big hug, bouncing up and down and nearly clipping her in the chin with the top of her head. Shannon laughed, finally extricating herself so she could start getting out of her gear.

"I don't know about all that." She pulled her jersey off and tossed it to the side, then removed her chest and arm pads. She twisted, trying to see her lower back, then gave up and turned toward Dani. "Is there a mark there?"

Dani leaned over, frowning as she traced a line on Shannon's back. "Yeah, you've got a nice welt going. It's not bleeding, though."

"Well, that's something, I guess. I can't believe that dumb fuck didn't call a penalty on that." She dropped to the bench and removed the rest of her pads, then started unlacing her skates. "Taylor, did he say anything to you when you went over to talk to him?"

"Yeah." Taylor's mouth thinned out and an angry blush stained her cheekbones. "He told me not to tell him how to do his job."

"Are you serious?" Shannon yanked her sock off

and tossed it to the side. "What an ass."

"Don't worry, she got him back." Sammie dropped to the bench next to Shannon, a grin on her face. "Taylor told him that if he was actually good enough to do his job, he would be playing for us instead of wearing stripes."

Laughter echoed around the dingy locker room. Taylor's blush deepened and she shrugged. "Sorry, but he pissed me off. The ass."

Conversation dwindled to a low roar, then faded to nothing as Coach Reynolds came in to congratulate them and discuss what they needed to work on. Then it was time to hit the showers and head out to the bus for the long ride home. Shannon tossed her gear bag into the outside compartment then climbed onboard, wincing just a little when she took her normal seat in the back. Taylor and Sammie and Dani all frowned at her.

"Are you okay?"

"Yeah, just a little stiff. I stretched muscles I didn't even know I had."

"I still can't believe you made that save!"

"Yeah, neither can I. It was pure dumb luck, that was all."

Taylor shook her head, contradicting Shannon. "No, that was pure skill."

"No, it was luck. If I hadn't been out of position, I wouldn't have had to stretch like that. My mistake."

"You're being too hard on yourself. Trust me, it was a beautiful save. Keep playing like that, and we're going to give the Banners a game they aren't expecting."

Dani spun around in her seat, leaning over the back to stare at Taylor. "You're delusional if you think we can beat them. We don't have an ice cube's chance in hell."

"Why not? We're good. There's no reason we *can't* beat them."

Sammie raised her hand then quickly dropped it. "Um, hang on. Isn't this supposed to just be a charity game? You know, for fun?"

"Yeah, but that doesn't mean we can't win."

"Taylor, you're delusional. Just like Dani said."

"What is with you guys? Why so negative? Why so convinced we're going to lose?"

"Um, let's see. They're bigger. They're faster. They're more experienced—" Shannon started to say more but her phone began vibrating. She pulled it from the front pocket of her slacks and glanced down at the screen, then bit back a smile when she saw the text notification from Caleb. It was just a simple text, there was absolutely no reason for her heart to be dancing in her chest the way it was. That didn't stop her from smiling when she swiped the screen and brought the text up.

Awesome save. I'm impressed.

He watched the game? But how? The Banners were on the road this weekend, playing in Florida then in Nashville. The only way he could have watched the game was if he had been streaming it on his phone through a social media app, because it sure as hell wasn't playing on any of the networks.

Her fingers flew across the screen, typing out a reply.

Thanks. It was nothing but luck.

I think skill might have had something to do with it. Did you hurt anything?

No.

Too bad. I was going to offer to kiss everything to make it better :)

Shannon bit back a grin and wondered if her face was as red as it felt. Probably. Yes, she knew it was silly. Not silly—stupid. They hadn't done anything except kiss…which sounded so juvenile, it was almost embarrassing. But it had almost become a game now, one filled with teasing suspense, all leading up to Sammie's wedding next week.

And God help her, but she was enjoying herself. Yes, she was going to sleep with him—although she really hoped there wasn't much actual sleeping involved. Was it a smart move? Maybe. Maybe not. But she didn't care. She liked Caleb. She enjoyed hanging out with him, enjoyed their bantering and teasing. She didn't *think* he was playing her, but if he was…so what? Maybe she was simply playing him, too. They were both having fun, not looking for a relationship. Her heart wasn't involved, not even close. As long as she kept that in mind, she'd be fine.

No response, huh?

She looked back at her phone, realized she'd been sitting there for several minutes without saying anything. She bit back a smile and typed back.

I'll hold you to that next weekend.

There was a slight pause before her phone vibrated again. She opened the message and almost laughed out loud at the gif of a bottle of champagne being popped and exploding everywhere that flashed across her screen. Yeah, that could definitely be taken in more than one way.

Gotta run, time to get ready for game. I'll text later.

Shannon replied with a quick *ok* then tucked the phone back into her pocket…and looked up to see three sets of eyes staring at her. "What?"

"Who was that?"

"Why do you have that shit-eating grin on your face?"

"Yeah. And holy crappola, why are you blushing like that? I've never seen you blush like that before."

"I am not blushing."

Sammie reached over and placed the back of her hand against Shannon's forehead. "Yup, you're definitely blushing. And your face is hot. I'd almost think you had a fever but I'm a mom and know better. Okay, out with it. Was that Caleb?"

"He just—"

"Are you seriously still hanging out with him?" Taylor's voice was flat, a little impatient. "Shannon, did you not listen to anything I told you?"

"Yeah, I did. I'm ignoring it."

"You need your head examined."

"We're just hanging out. Having fun. There's nothing else going on."

"Wait. Aren't you still bringing him to the wedding? Or did something change? Because I thought you said—" Sammie's mouth snapped shut under Shannon's glare. She dropped back into her seat with a little bounce, a bright smile on her face. "So yeah, anyway—"

"You're bringing Caleb as your date?"

Shannon thought about denying it, but why? It wasn't like Sammie hadn't already told them. And it wasn't like they wouldn't find out anyway, especially since they were all sitting together at the small reception.

"Yes, I'm bringing him." She pointed a finger at Taylor, stopping the other woman before she could say anything. "And I don't want to hear another word about it. Besides, I thought you liked him. You said he was a nice guy."

"Yeah, I did. I do. He is. But not to date. I just don't want to see you get hurt."

"I'm not going to get hurt."

Taylor opened her mouth, hesitated, then closed it. She looked around then finally shook her head. "I just hope you know what you're doing. I mean, you do realize you're now sleeping with the enemy, right?"

A short burst of laughter escaped Shannon. "We're not sleeping together—"

"Yet."

"—and he's not the enemy. Why would you even say something like that?"

"Because he plays for the Banners. And we're going to be playing *them*. That makes him the enemy."

"You're crazy, you know that, right? Abso-fucking-lutely crazy."

"No, I'm desperate. We can beat them. I know we can."

"Shannon's right—you're crazy." Dani leaned further over the seat, then leaned up and swiped the bright red hair from her face. "You're beyond crazy— you're obsessing. And I'm starting to worry about you."

"I'm not obsessing. Don't you guys realize how much is at stake with this?"

"Taylor, it's a charity exhibition game. There's nothing at stake!"

"Yeah, there is. Think about it. Do you have any idea how much publicity we would get if we go out there and kick their asses? People would finally notice us. Ticket sales would go up. The team would make more money. And if the team makes more money, *we* make more money. People would start to take us seriously."

Silence followed Taylor's passionate speech, a silence filled with thought and consideration. Dani finally broke it with a small sigh. "More money would be nice. I'm getting tired of working extra nights just to pay my rent."

"Yeah. And it would be nice if we didn't have to keep buying our own gear. I broke two sticks last week at practice." Shannon held up two fingers. "*Two*. That adds up real quick."

"See? I told you, there's a lot more to this than just a charity exhibition game. We need to really wow everyone. And we can do that if we beat the Banners."

Sammie sighed, the sound filled with quiet desperation. "I still don't see how we're going to do that."

"It's not impossible. We just need to come up with a game plan."

"Fine. You're the Captain. How do we come up with a game plan?"

"We need a team meeting. And not one at the rink. There's always some team or another playing or practicing there when we're not."

"So why not just have it after practice? There's nobody there that late."

"No, we need somewhere else. Someplace big enough for everyone so we're not standing on top of each other."

"Then ask your parents. Their place is huge."

Taylor frowned, her head tilted to the side as she considered it. "No, I don't want to do it there. I don't want Uncle JP hearing about it and trust me, as soon as the twins overhear any little thing, they'll be running off to spread the news to everyone."

Sammie raised her hand, kept holding it up until Shannon reached over and forcefully lowered it. "You need to stop doing that."

"Sorry, force of habit." Sammie leaned in closer and lowered her voice. "We could have it at the warehouse."

"What warehouse?"

"Jon and his buddies just leased a new space for everything and the place is huge. I'm sure they wouldn't mind if we used it for a meeting."

"Don't they have, I don't know, top secret shit and everything hidden there?"

"No, of course not. It's just stuff for the security business. And all that would be locked up anyway."

"You don't think they'd mind?"

Sammie shrugged. "It doesn't hurt to ask."

"Okay then, now we're getting somewhere." Taylor held her hand out, palm down, then looked at each of them, waiting. Shannon rolled her eyes, watching as Dani placed her hand on top of Taylor's, followed by Sammie's.

Taylor turned to her, an expectant look on her face. "You know you want to. We can do this. I know we can."

Shannon laughed and rolled her eyes. "You're all crazy but fine, I'm in." She placed her hand on top of Sammie's. "Here's to fighting like a girl."

Chapter
FOURTEEN

Caleb frowned at the phone, surprised to see a blank screen staring back at him. It wasn't completely blank, of course—the icons for the dozens of different apps were still there, along with the phone icon and the message icon. It was that last one that had him frowning: it was empty. Zero messages. None. Nada. Zilch.

He opened the app and checked his last incoming message from a few hours ago. More than a few, actually—it was right before the game, when he had been texting Shannon.

I'll hold you to that next weekend.

A flare of heat tightened his groin at the underlying meaning in that message. At least, he hoped there was an underlying meaning to it. And how big of an idiot was he, to send his lame ass response? That popping champagne bottle followed by a stupid, casual text.

Gotta run, time to get ready for game. I'll text later.

Nothing since then. Fuck.

"Something wrong with your phone?"

Caleb glanced over at Logan Simms, relief pushing away his worry. That had to be it: something was wrong with his phone. *That* was why he wasn't seeing any messages from Shannon.

"Yeah, must be. Can you send me a quick text?"

Logan pulled the phone from his pocket, his fingers flying over the screen. A few seconds later, Caleb's phone beeped and he looked down at the notification signaling the incoming message, frowned when it popped up on his screen.

Asshole

"Nice. Real nice."

"Whatever." Logan pocketed his phone then reached up and undid his tie, pulling it off and tossing it onto his bed. "Your phone works. Now come on, let's go. The guys are waiting."

"Yeah, okay. Coming." Caleb pushed off the bed, still staring at the phone, still wondering why he didn't see any messages from Shannon. Maybe they got jammed somewhere along the line and just hadn't come through yet.

He paused in the middle of the room and dashed a quick reply, then muttered a curse when Logan's phone beeped in response. Well shit. He didn't have any problems getting a text from Logan or sending one to him. So where were all the other texts?

Unless Shannon hadn't sent him one.

No, that couldn't be right. Of course, she'd send him at least one. Wouldn't she? The bus ride from New York to Baltimore didn't take that long, she had to be home by now. Actually, she should have been home to catch at least the last ten minutes of his game. Wouldn't she have texted him to at least congratulate him on that game-winning goal?

Yeah, of course she would have. Which meant his phone had to be acting up or something. That was the only thing that made sense.

"For shit's sake, Johnson. Are you going to be glued to that thing all fucking night?"

"Hm? Hey! What the hell?" Caleb jerked back in surprise as Logan snagged the phone from his hand. "What do you think you're doing? Give that back to me."

"Not happening." Logan jammed the phone into his pants pocket then yanked open the door. "You can have it back later. Right now, the guys are waiting. And babes. Lots of babes, all ready to do their part in congratulating us on kicking Florida's ass. Now let's go."

Caleb hesitated, no longer in the mood to head down to the lobby bar. Hell, he hadn't really been in the mood earlier, either. No way in hell he could tell Logan that, though—he'd never hear the end of it. And he couldn't exactly make a grab for his phone, not without Logan laughing his ass off after pummeling him.

Okay, fine. He'd go down for one beer, get his phone back, then come back up to the room and—

And he didn't know what. Try texting Shannon, maybe. It wasn't that late, not really, and it *was* a Saturday night so she should be awake. Unless she was out somewhere—

"Johnson! Let's go."

"Yeah, fine. I'm coming." Caleb reached behind him, making sure he had his wallet, then stepped out into the hallway. Logan pulled the door closed with a loud bang then led the way down the hall to the elevators. And shit. Just his luck, because Christian Harper and Jacob Riley and Hunter Billings were standing there, holding the elevator doors open for them.

Caleb bit back a sigh of frustration and piled into the elevator with everyone else. One beer, he told himself. One beer, and then he'd call it a night.

Hunter leaned his shoulder against the back wall of the elevator and pinned Caleb with his dark, penetrating gaze. "Why the hell do you look so grumpy? I figured you'd be downstairs already, celebrating with a hook-up."

"I'm not grumpy."

A chorus of rough laughter echoed around him. Caleb bit his tongue, refusing to take the bait. If he showed any annoyance at all, they'd pounce on him and give him shit.

"He's pissed because I took his phone away."

"Not even close, Simms."

One of Logan's dark brows shot up in clear disbelief. "Oh, that's right. You're pouting because your woman hasn't texted you. What's the matter, Johnson? Not used to being on the other end, are you?"

"What the hell are you talking about?"

Christian nudged him out of the way with a hand to the chest. "Details, Simms. Now. What woman? And if she's ignoring Loverboy over here, I need to meet her."

"You already did. It's the goalie from the Blades. What's her name? Shelly. Sharon. Something like that."

"It's *Shannon*. And she's not my *woman*." Caleb's

voice was low and tight, filled with a warning he didn't understand. He realized his mistake almost immediately, knew he should have kept his fucking mouth shut as soon as he saw the expressions on the faces of teammates. Surprise. Disbelief. Amazement.

Laughter.

He leveled a scowl at Christian, the expression feral enough that the man should have been backing away in fear. Instead, he laughed even harder, nearly bent over as he tried to catch his breath. He finally straightened and ran the back of his hand across his eyes.

"No. Fucking. Way. Are you seriously dating her?"

Caleb opened his mouth to say *yes*, then just as quickly snapped it shut. Yeah, he had used some creative spinning when he'd told Shannon they had technically been out on four dates but that's all it was—creative spin. They'd been out, yeah, but they weren't *dates*. Not even close. It was like she had told him: a date was when you got dressed up to go out to dinner and the movies or dancing or clubbing or something. What they'd done hadn't even come close.

But damn if he didn't *feel* like they were dating, especially with some of those kisses they had shared. Kisses that left him reeling and panting for more.

Panting? Christ, what was he, some kind of fucking dog?

He thought back to the other night at his place, remembered the feel of Shannon's body as she straddled his lap and rocked her hips against him.

Yeah, definitely panting like some damn dog. He'd be damned if he'd admit that to any of these guys.

"Well, are you?"

Caleb gave himself a mental shake then slowly

focused on Christian. He cleared his throat, nodded, shook his head. "We're still working out the details."

Hunter nudged him in the side. "Well hell. If you're not, let me know, because she is *smoking* hot. Like, I'd gladly get burned by her."

"Don't even think about it, asshole. She's off-limits so don't even try." He ignored the surprise on everyone's face, breathing in a sigh of relief when the elevator finally reached the lobby level. The doors opened and Caleb pushed his way out, wondering again if he should just go back to his room.

"Well shit." Hunter nudged him forward, away from the escape the elevators offered. "I thought that whole thing was just a publicity stunt for that stupid fucking game we're being forced to play."

"Yeah, seriously." Jacob moved in front of them then started walking backward, a frown on his face. "How the fuck did that thing even get approved? The last thing I want to do is play against a bunch of women. We're going to have to tone down our play so much, we might as well just go out on the ice blindfolded."

"Um, yeah. I wouldn't be so sure of that."

"What are you talking about?"

Caleb shook his head as they walked into the hotel bar. The noise level was a little higher here, music and conversation mingling to create a low din. He glanced around, noticed the crowd already gathered around the bar, the lack of open tables. And fuck, this was the last place he wanted to be right now, especially since the puck bunnies were already moving toward them.

Caleb backed up a step then stopped, his gaze landing on a set of tables in the back corner. And thank God, some of the guys were already sitting there—

Shane Masters and Jaxon Miller and Marc Sanford, guarding the empty chairs around them.

He headed straight toward the table, blatantly ignoring the come-hither looks on the faces of a few women. He didn't bother to look their way, or even acknowledge them when they called his name. The only time he paused was to grab Christian by the back of his collar and jerk him away from the two bunnies who had latched onto him.

"Hey. I was talking—"

"Talk later." He released Christian's collar then grabbed a chair and dropped it into it. Then he turned to Logan and held out his hand. "I need my phone."

"Nope. No way. Not if you're just going to sit there, pouting, while you keep checking it all night."

"I'm not checking it. There's something I need to show you guys."

Logan watched him for a few long seconds, then finally heaved a sigh and dug Caleb's phone from his pocket. "Fine. But the first time I see you checking it, I'm taking it away."

Shane Masters leaned across the table, his bruised hand wrapped around a dark glass bottle. "Check what? Why's he pouting?"

"Nothing. Not important." Caleb waved the question off, staring at the screen on his phone as he scrolled through several social media apps. What the hell? Why wasn't he finding it anywhere? That save should have gone viral by now. His little show for the kiss cam last week had gone viral in a matter of minutes, not to mention the clips from his botched interview.

So why the hell couldn't he find a replay of Shannon's save?

He shook his head in frustration then gave up and went to the Blades' social media page. Sure enough, there it was. He frowned, wondering again why the hell nobody else had picked it up, then tapped the short video. He gave it a quick share from his profile then nudged Jacob.

"Hey, Riley. Check this out. Still think we need to tone-down our play for that exhibition game?" Caleb turned the phone so everyone could see then tapped the play button. You couldn't hear anything, not with the noise in the bar, but you didn't need to—the video didn't need any narration.

"What. The. Fuck." Shane sagged against the table, nearly spilling his beer. Identical expressions of amazement filled the faces staring back at him.

"No fucking way."

"Holy shit."

"Wait. Play it again. There's no way—" Hunter leaned forward, frowning as he stared at the video. He sat back in his chair, his dark eyes wide with the same surprise Caleb had felt when he'd first seen it live.

"Hey. Do you think she does that move in bed? Because damn, can you imagine how—"

Caleb's hand shot out and clipped Shane on the shoulder before he could stop himself. The reaction was entirely hypocritical because Caleb had that same exact thought hours earlier. That didn't mean he was going to put up with listening to any of his teammates voice the same question. "You're a fucking ass. Don't talk about her that way."

"Whoa. Seriously? What the hell is your problem?"

"That's Caleb's woman, leave her alone." Logan reached for the phone, replaying the video again as half-a-dozen faces turned to study Caleb. He ignored the questioning glances, tried to hide the spurt of possessiveness shooting through him.

Caleb's woman. Why did he like the sound of that?

Logan slid the phone across the table then sat back in his chair. "Damn. She's good."

"Yeah, no shit."

"Does the rest of the team play as well as her?"

Caleb shrugged, almost embarrassed to admit he didn't know. "I'm not sure, but probably. Hell, Taylor LeBlanc is the team's captain and she's good enough to play for us."

"Isn't Sonny LeBlanc her dad?"

"Yup. And JP Larocque is her uncle."

"Well shit." Jacob's eloquent words echoed around the silent table. The silence lengthened, finally broken when Shane smothered a small belch then uttered a curse.

"Maybe we can get your woman to give Connelly a few pointers because *his* game has been sucking wind."

"You can say that again." Caleb pocketed his phone then glanced around the table. "Speaking of Connelly, where is he?"

"No idea. He dropped his shit as soon as we got here then headed out."

"He didn't say where he was going?"

"Not a word. He's still pissed he got pulled in the second."

"What the hell did he think was going to happen? He's been playing like shit lately. I'm surprised Coach even started him tonight."

"Yeah, well—I heard a rumor he might not even be with us for much longer."

Silence greeted Jaxon's announcement. He

glanced around the table, a furious blush coloring his face at being the center of attention. He slid down in the seat then offered a half-hearted shrug. "Hey, it's just a rumor. No idea if it's true or not."

"What are they going to do, send him down to the Bombers?"

"If what I heard was true, they're looking to completely cut their losses and trade him. I also heard they're looking to make a deal and bring Corbin Gauthier back."

"Gauthier? Are you fucking crazy?" Shane took a long swallow of beer then slammed the bottle on the table. "Where the fuck do you even hear these things? Gauthier's what, thirty? Thirty-two? He's at the end of his career. Why the hell would they want to bring him back now?"

"Hey, don't go tarring the messenger. I'm just repeating what I heard. And Gauthier's still pretty damn good. He's got at least a few more years left in him."

"And he's definitely been playing better than Connelly has."

Several heads nodded in agreement with Hunter's quiet statement. Caleb brushed off the rumors, chalking them up to nonsense—even if he had heard the same thing a few weeks ago. Yeah, trades happened all the time. And yeah, Connelly was playing like shit. They'd probably just send him down to the Bombers and pull one of the goalies from there. That's the only thing that made sense.

"They're not going to trade Connelly. No way. We just need to talk some sense into him, get his head back in the game—especially before this exhibition game."

"Why before the exhibition game? Wait. No

fucking way." Jacob swallowed back a bark of laughter then popped Caleb in the shoulder. "You're not actually worried about it, are you? I mean, I don't care how good you think they might be, there's no way the Blades can touch us. Not happening."

"No, probably not," Caleb agreed. "But how fucking mortifying would it be if they did?"

"Yeah. Again—not happening."

"But what if—"

"No *buts*." Jacob leaned to the side and draped a heavy arm around Caleb's shoulders. "And if you're that worried about it, I suggest you start working on your woman."

"What the hell are you talking about?"

"Just what I said. She's your woman, right? Maybe you need to think about working a little harder to wear her sweet ass out. Make her so tired the night before the game, she won't be able to think about anything else except soaking her bruised muscles."

Shane tapped him on the shoulder with a leer, one that made Caleb cringe. Christ, had he ever talked that way? Yeah, probably. And just like Shane, he hadn't really meant it, it was nothing more than just talk—which made him feel even worse. And he couldn't say a damn thing in response, not unless he wanted to be on the receiving end of a dozen jokes. So he kept quiet as Shane pushed away from the table.

"Now if you guys will excuse me, I have some women to enlighten."

Laughter greeted Shane's parting words. Several of the other guys stood up to join him, making their way over to the group of waiting bunnies. Caleb glanced around, realized it was just him and Jaxon and Hunter left.

What the fuck was wrong with him? Usually he was the first one to leave, the first one to find eager company for the night. The idea held no appeal and hadn't for a long time.

"You're not really thinking of taking Jacob's advice, are you?"

"What? Hell no. And I don't think it was really advice. I'm pretty sure he was just talking big, trying to show off."

"I wouldn't be too sure of that. He's got an ego the size of an Olympic rink." Jaxon guzzled the last of his beer then pushed away from the table. "I'm heading up."

Hunter looked up in surprise. "What? Already? I thought we were going to find a club or something."

"Nah. I'm done." He turned toward Caleb. "You going out with these guys?"

Caleb hesitated. Should he go out? It was still early, plenty of time to go find a club somewhere and have a few drinks. It was what they usually did if they got the chance.

But he didn't want to. Not tonight. Not after Jacob's careless comments. Not when there was a chance he might miss a call or text from Shannon. He'd be able to hear his phone better in the quiet of his own room—as long as Logan didn't drown everything out with his snoring.

Caleb shook his head and stood up. "No, I'm calling it a night, too."

chapter FIFTEEN

Shannon jammed her hands into the pockets of her jacket, wishing again that she was wearing one of her heavy sweatshirts underneath instead of a dressy sweater. The sweater might look nice with the black slacks and low-heeled boots, but it sucked as far as warmth went.

If she had known the warehouse was going to be so cold, she would have reconsidered her wardrobe choices—especially since several of her teammates were watching her with unveiled curiosity. *That* she had anticipated. What surprised her so far was that nobody had said anything about the way she was dressed, not even Taylor.

Although Taylor looked preoccupied, even a little worried, so maybe it wasn't a surprise she hadn't said anything. Yet.

Shannon glanced at her watch then bit back a sigh as she looked around. Almost everyone was here—

everyone except Rachel and Amanda. Not that Amanda counted, not really. She was still officially on the roster but she wasn't playing because she was still going through rehab. The latest rumor was that she was finishing up and might actually return in time to finish the season. Shannon wasn't sure how she felt about that. Part of her was sympathetic—a very small part. The rest of her? Not so much. How could she just throw everything away like that for a quick fix? It wasn't just Amanda's potential career—it was the reputation of everyone else on the team. Hell, the reputation of the league itself. There had been a major shit storm when Amanda collapsed on the ice a few months ago—even more when they discovered it was because of her drug problem. Yeah, that had been ugly. Beyond ugly.

And yeah, Shannon knew it was an *addiction*. Knew that addicts had no control and didn't know what they were doing. The logical part of her brain understood that. The emotional side of her—the one filled with passion for playing—struggled to understand the *why* behind it. Which was stupid, because *why* didn't matter when drugs and addiction were involved.

She bit back another sigh—this one filled with impatience—and pushed all thoughts of Amanda from her mind. This meeting wasn't about Amanda—it was about their upcoming exhibition game.

And Shannon was going to miss it if Taylor didn't start soon. She had a date with Caleb tonight—a real, actual *date*. They were going out for a late dinner then catching an even later movie. And after that...she wasn't sure. She knew what she *wanted* to do, she just wasn't sure if it was the *smart* thing to do.

"How much longer are we going to wait before

getting started?" Dani finally asked the question that everyone else had been thinking. A few more voices chimed in, echoing around the cavernous room before finally disappearing in the dark shadows overhead.

Taylor glanced at her watch then leaned against the back of the worn sofa. Springs creaked with the movement and she quickly sat back up, shooting a frown at Sammie. The other woman shrugged, a small smile of apology on her face.

"It's a warehouse, not an office. What did you expect?"

Shannon looked around again, taking in the concrete floors. The large sturdy cabinets secured by even larger locks. The interior doors leading to what she assumed were offices, also securely locked. Well, almost all. One door was open, light spilling from it in a harsh slash along the floor. Sammie's ex-husband—or rather, her soon-to-be-husband—was back there with one of his buddies, their voices nothing more than deep rumblings seeping into the chilliness of the large room.

Shannon hunched her shoulders around her ears to ward off the cold. She'd bet anything that they had heat in that office.

"How come they're in there where it's warm and we're stuck out here?"

"Because that room is too small for all of us." Sammie glanced over at the office then leaned closer and lowered her voice. "Besides, they're having a meeting."

Jordyn Knott stared at the open door then turned toward Sammie. "What exactly do they do again?"

"Oh, you know." Sammie laughed and waved her hand from side-to-side. "Security and, um, stuff."

"'Stuff'? What kind of 'stuff'?"

"Just, you know, um, *stuff*."

"We could tell you, then we'd have to kill you."

At least seven of her teammates jumped at the menacing words uttered in a gravelly voice. Twelve of eyes turned to stare at the men standing just outside the door. Large, foreboding, their bodies nothing more than intimidating silhouettes framed by the light coming from behind them. The only thing missing was dramatic music.

Shannon bit back her laughter, nearly choking on it. She didn't think either man would appreciate it, especially Mac. He was so damned scary, even though he was doing nothing more than simply standing there.

At least, he would be, if not for the three-year-old girl clinging to him like he was her favorite teddy bear.

Shannon quickly averted her gaze and covered her mouth, trying to hide the strangled laughter that threatened to fall from her mouth. She cleared her throat then snapped her fingers in Taylor's attention.

"Can we get started already? I need to leave in—" She glanced at her watch and frowned. "In twenty minutes."

"Where are you going?"

"It doesn't matter. Just get started already, will you?"

Taylor studied her with a frown. She opened her mouth then snapped it shut, obviously reconsidering whatever she had been about to say. Well, that was a first. Shannon had expected the third degree, had been waiting for it ever since she pulled through the automatic gate at the end of the long drive leading up to this place. Now she started to worry, wondering why Taylor wasn't questioning her.

A quiet Taylor couldn't be good. Unless she had already figured out where Shannon was going. But if that was the case, wouldn't she be giving Shannon a hard time about it?

Maybe. Probably.

Or maybe Shannon was just starting to get paranoid, probably a result of sitting in this dark cavern filled with untold secrets.

"Just a few more minutes. We're waiting on one more."

"You mean Rachel?" Dani rolled her eyes then took a sip from her fountain soda. "I don't think she's coming. She pitched a fit about it last night at practice, saying she didn't get paid for 'unscheduled meetings'."

"No, not Rachel. TR was going to try to make it."

"TR?" Shannon straightened in the lumpy seat and tamped down the spurt of guilt. She still owed TR the rest of that interview. Was the woman going to collect tonight? God, she hoped not. She didn't have time. "Why would TR be here?"

"Relax, Wiley. She's not going to hold you up. She's coming because I invited her. And because she wants to fit this into part of that whole thing she's doing."

Dani finished her soda with a loud slurp then placed the empty cup by her feet. "Doesn't that kind of defeat the whole purpose of having a strategy meeting? I mean, why bother if the Banners find out about it beforehand, you know?"

"She's not going to publish anything *now*. This is for later."

Shannon rolled her eyes then looked at her watch again. Fifteen minutes. She must have made a sound or something because Taylor looked over at her with another frown.

"Fine, we'll get started." Taylor grabbed the pad next to her and balanced it on her knee. "Let's talk strategy."

"How's this: we play our best and hope for the best."

"I'm just hoping we don't get killed." Sammie muttered the words, but they were still loud enough for everyone to hear. And loud enough to earn a frown from Taylor.

"Guys, enough. We can beat them. I *know* we can. We just have to focus on our game. Outshoot them. Outscore them."

"Taylor, this is supposed to be an exhibition game. You know, for fun. Don't you think you're going just a little overboard?" Maddison Sinclair asked the exact same question Shannon had been ready to ask. More than a few of her teammates nodded in agreement, which only seemed to upset Taylor. She tossed the pad beside her then stood up and started pacing, each clipped step echoing around them.

"Am I the only one who thinks we can do this? Because if I am, let me know now."

Shannon looked around, noticed that everyone else suddenly seemed preoccupied with staring at the floor. She rolled her eyes then spoke up. "Taylor, it's not that we don't think we can do this. We're good. We all know that."

"Then why is everyone just sitting here looking resigned to losing?"

"We're not *resigned to losing*. We're just...I don't know. Being realistic. The Banners have been playing together a lot longer than we have. They have more ice time. More practice time. They have more experience as a team." Shannon mentally cringed as the words left her mouth. Wasn't that exactly what Caleb had told her? Yes, it was. And yes, it made sense. But when the hell did she start letting other people dictate what she should believe?

She blew out a quick breath and ran her hands through her hair. "Okay, forget that. Those are nothing but lame-ass excuses. You're right. We *can* beat them. We're just going to have to focus. Play hard. Harder than we've ever played before."

Taylor stopped next to her and gave her a high-five. "Now that's more like it. So—what's our game plan?"

Silence greeted her question. Long. Heavy. Filled with doubt. Not doubt that they could do it—or at least give the Banners one hell of a run for their money—but doubt on *how* to do it.

Shannon rolled her eyes. "Goaltending."

"What? You mean yours?"

"No, not mine. I mean, yeah, mine, to a point, if you guys don't do your job. But I'm talking about *them*. Let's face it, their goaltenders are struggling right now. Connelly has some serious fucking issues. And Lory still hasn't found his zone, hasn't been played enough to really adapt to the Banners' system yet. So...we play to their weakness. They both have them."

"Like what?"

"Yeah. And how do we know which one's going to be in the net that night?"

"We don't, but it doesn't matter. Not if you know what to look for."

Sammie leaned forward, excitement dancing in her eyes. "What do we look for?"

"I need a television. And an internet hook-up."

She glanced around the cavernous room then looked at Sammie, who turned toward the two men lounging against the far wall.

"Jon?"

"We can make that happen." He pushed away from the wall and headed toward one of the locked doors, motioning for them to follow. The alarm on Shannon's watch went off with a small beep and she hesitated. It was time to leave, or else she'd be late for her date with Caleb.

Twelve of eyes stared at her. Watching. Waiting. She glanced around, her gaze finally meeting Taylor's own serious one.

And shit. Shit, fuck shit.

She thought of Caleb's deep green eyes. Of the dimple that made her heart skip a few beats. Of hot kisses that made her knees buckle.

Of the unspoken promises that filled her with anticipation for their first real date—and what might happen after.

Caleb...or her teammates?

Fuck it. She couldn't leave, not when her teammates needed her.

"Come on. Let's do this."

chapter
SIXTEEN

She stood him up.

Caleb couldn't believe it. She had really stood him up. He reached for the glass of wine that had been sitting in front of him, untouched, for the past thirty minutes. It was warm now but he didn't care, just tossed it back, swallowed it with a wince, then slammed the glass onto the table. Would the restaurant let him take the bottle to go? Probably not, even though he was paying for it.

A whole damn bottle wasted except for that one glass. And he didn't even fucking like wine.

Shannon had stood him up.

What the fuck?

He glanced at his phone, staring at the blank screen, willing it to beep or ring or vibrate. Something. But it didn't move, didn't make a single noise, no matter how long he stared at it. It had been silent for the last thirty minutes, ever since Shannon had sent him that quick text saying she was running a few minutes late.

A few minutes? It had been more than a few minutes. A hell of a lot more, considering they were supposed to meet an hour ago.

And what the fuck was he doing, sitting here by himself? The wait staff had been watching him, no doubt whispering among themselves. Probably laughing. What kind of asshole hung out at a restaurant for an hour, waiting for a date that wasn't going to show?

The pathetic kind, that's what kind.

Which didn't say much for him, since he was still sitting here. Still waiting.

Fuck.

He clenched his jaw and looked around, searching for his waiter. The man was nowhere in sight. Of course not, now that Caleb was ready to leave. Wasn't that the way it usually worked? The man had appeared at his side every five minutes, asking if he was ready to order no matter how many times Caleb had told him he was waiting for his date. He didn't miss the doubt in the man's eyes, or the pity—which only pissed him off. He'd finally told the guy that he'd wave him down when he was ready.

Caleb was ready now, so where the hell was the damn waiter?

He swore under his breath and pushed away from the table, ready to hunt the man down. Or maybe he should just throw some bills on the table—enough to cover the damn bottle of wine and an outrageous tip—and get the hell out of here.

And *fuck*. She stood him up. He still couldn't fucking believe it.

He grabbed the suit jacket from the back of the chair and shrugged into it, not bothering to straighten his collar or sleeves. Why the hell should he, when he was just going to take it off as soon as he got home?

Of all the—he bit back another curse and pushed the chair in. Carefully, even though he'd rather slam it against the table hard enough to send the fancy place settings crashing to the polished terracotta floor.

Doing that would accomplish exactly nothing. It wouldn't even make him feel better because he'd end up having to pay for it.

He still couldn't believe she'd stood him up. That never happened to him before. *Never*. And he wasn't sure how to act. The anger he felt made sense, was even welcomed. Anger was normal.

What *wasn't* normal was the disappointment coursing through him—strong enough to drown out the anger. Why the fuck was he disappointed? It didn't make sense. He had nothing to be disappointed about. Nothing at all.

That's what his brain kept telling him. The clenching of his gut was saying something completely different. Neither of which explained why he was still standing there like an ass, staring at the phone gripped in his hand.

"Hey. Sorry I'm late."

Caleb frowned at the phone, wondering why the words were coming from *behind* him. Then his brain finally clicked and he turned, surprised to see Shannon walking toward him, her hair drifting around her face with each step. He clenched his jaw, told himself not to stare, not to smile because she was finally here.

She stopped in front of him, leaned up and pressed a quick kiss against his jaw, then shrugged out of her coat and dropped into the seat with a breathy sigh.

"You said you were going to be a few *minutes* late."

She looked up at the sharpness in his voice then offered him a bright smile and a shrug. "I know, sorry. Things ran longer than I thought."

"We were supposed to meet an hour ago."

She tilted her head back to look up at him, her brows lowered in a small frown. "I know, but I was running late. I told you that."

Caleb opened his mouth, snapped it shut again. He had no idea what to say—at least, not without sounding like he was snapping at her, not without sounding angry. Maybe he didn't even have to open his mouth, maybe Shannon could tell anyway. Her own jaw clenched, just for a split second before she pushed away from the table.

"Maybe we should just do this another time. You're pissed—"

"I'm not pissed."

One sculpted brow shot up. "Really? Because your face is doing one hell of an impression of that right now."

"I'm not—" He snapped his mouth closed again and pulled his chair out, dropped into it with a heavy sigh. "I'm not pissed. I'm just..."

His voice trailed off. Just...*what?* He had no idea. And he hoped Shannon didn't press him because he wasn't sure how to answer if she did.

She rested her arms on the edge of the table and leaned forward, the motion giving him an eyeful of soft, creamy skin peeking out from the V of her sweater. Caleb blinked and forced his gaze to the center of the table, wondering why he suddenly felt like a complete ass for even looking.

"You're not used to waiting, are you?" There was humor in her voice, a hint of laughter that irritated him.

"Waiting, yes. For an hour? No. I was ready to leave, thinking you had stood me up."

She laughed again, the sound laced with disbelief and maybe even a little bit of sympathy—although he wasn't sure if it was genuine. "You've never been stood up before."

It was a statement, not a question. "No, I haven't."

"But I bet you've stood up a date once or twice before, hm?"

"I—" He snapped his mouth closed and frowned as heat filled his face. Had he? Yeah, he had. Probably more than once or twice. Usually because the date suddenly thought that *date* meant a lifetime commitment.

"Yeah, thought so. Sucks, doesn't it?"

"Are you telling me you've been stood up before?"

"Duh. Of course. I told you, men generally run the other way—usually without the guts to tell me first."

"You don't see me running, do you?"

"Nope. And I still haven't figured out why." She reached out and patted his hand, maybe a little harder than necessary. "But I'm here now, neither one of us stood the other up. So. Do you want to do this thing or not?"

His gaze shot to hers, confusion filling him at her words. But only for a second, only until reason finally asserted itself by smacking him upside the head. *Dinner.* She was talking about *dinner*.

"Yeah, fine. We can eat."

"Good, because I'm starving." She opened the menu, studying it for a minute before looking over at him. "Aren't you going to look?"

"I already have. I memorized the damn thing forty minutes ago."

Shannon laughed, the sound rich and warm. She closed the menu then nudged the empty wine glass toward him. "Sorry. Again. Now how about some of that wine?"

He pulled the bottle from the stone holder, brushed the water from the bottom, then filled her glass. He hesitated then filled his own before putting the bottle back.

Shannon pulled her glass toward her, cradling the base with her fingers. "I really am sorry. I didn't think I'd be quite this late."

Caleb nodded, glanced at his glass, looked back at her. "What were you doing, anyway? I didn't think you had anything else going on."

"I didn't. I mean, I *did*, but it ran late. It was just some team stuff."

"Team stuff? I thought you only had practice on Tuesdays and Thursdays."

"We do." She took a small sip of the wine, her nose wrinkling in a ridiculously cute way that made the last of his anger fade away. "This was a meeting, not practice."

"A meeting for what?"

She grinned, the sight slamming into him with a force he didn't understand. "On how to kick your asses at the exhibition game."

Caleb choked back what might have been laughter. Did they seriously think they really had a chance? He almost told her she was crazy—they were all crazy if they thought that—but the waiter chose that moment to finally show up. Again. Probably a good thing, because Shannon would no doubt give him hell for spouting the truth.

She ordered a salad with steak and sides, almost identical to his except she opted for the loaded baked potato instead of the hand cut fries. Caleb bit back a grin, trying to remember that last time he'd been on a date where the woman had ordered anything besides a salad and a diet soda.

"What's so funny?"

"Nothing. I guess we have the same tastes in food, huh?"

"Well, it's a steakhouse. What else would I order? Oh. Wait." She sat back in the chair, an amused smile curling the corners of her full mouth. "I hope you weren't planning on me ordering a stupid salad and calling it dinner. You weren't, were you? Because yeah, that's not going to work."

"No, that's not what I was planning on." And he wasn't, not if he had given it any thought. Shannon burned a lot of calories on the ice, just like he did. There was no reason to expect her to eat like a bird.

He leaned back in his chair and watched as she sipped her wine. The way her fingers curled around the stem of the glass, the way her lips touched the rim as she sipped. The way her tongue darted out and swept across her upper lip after she took a drink. His groin tightened, even as he cursed himself for being such a stupid damn cliché. Getting worked up over the way she licked her lips? Really? Talk about clichés. But damn if the sight didn't do something to him.

He shifted in the chair, searched his brain for something to say—anything to get his mind off Shannon's mouth and tongue and what he wanted her to do with them. "So tell me about this meeting."

"Ha. No way. Not happening."

"Why not?"

"Because I'm not spilling secrets. Taylor already accused me of sleeping with the enemy."

A bark of laughter escaped him, the sound just a little too loud, filled with just a hint of frustration. "You told her we weren't, right?"

"Not yet, anyway."

Caleb damn near dropped the glass. Holy shit. Had he heard her right? Yeah, he must have, because she refused to look at him, suddenly more interested in the intricate design etched into the handle of the silverware. But he could see the blush fanning her cheeks, turning her fair skin a delicate pink. Shannon was blushing. He couldn't believe it.

Or maybe he could, because he was pretty sure his own face was turning a little red. Not from embarrassment, but from the promise of her words.

Not yet.

Christ, he didn't know what to think, was afraid to hope...and shit. Now he didn't know what to do. Should he say something back? Tease her? Drag her out of the restaurant and straight back to his place?

That last option held the most appeal—that's what he'd been wanting to do for the last few weeks, ever since he met her. Hell, he couldn't remember ever wanting another woman like this.

He couldn't remember ever waiting this long for another woman, either. He'd never had to, not when they were eager for his company. So what the hell was it about the woman across from him? Shannon herself had joked and said it was because she was a challenge. And she was, in more ways than one. The way she didn't hold back, the way she wasn't afraid to speak her mind, the way she did her own thing. She was comfortable with who she was and didn't go out of her way to impress anyone.

That must be why her blush, why that hint of embarrassment, tugged at him. It hinted at vulnerability—something he would have never associated with Shannon. She was the least vulnerable woman he'd ever met. Hell, she was one of the least vulnerable *people* he'd ever met. Except maybe she wasn't. How many times had she made comments about the way she intimidated men? How many self-deprecating little jokes had she made? At first, he had thought it was nothing more than her own personal brand of sarcasm. But now...now, he was second-guessing himself.

All because she had blushed with embarrassment because of three little words.

Not yet, anyway.

Christ, he needed his fucking head examined.

That didn't stop him from thinking about it—her vulnerability *and* those three little words of promise—all through dinner and dessert. While they chatted about hockey and movies and the upcoming wedding in a few days. While he paid the bill and walked her out of the restaurant, her hand held in his larger one.

While he walked her to her car, parked two levels above his own in the parking garage.

Shannon unlocked the door and leaned in, jammed the key into the ignition and started the engine while he stood there, doing his best not to stare at the firmly-rounded curves of her ass. Then she was standing next to him, that same ass pressed against the back door of her car, out of his sight *and* his reach.

She rubbed her hands against her thighs, twisted

them together for a second, then jammed them into the pockets of her wool coat. "I guess we missed the movie, huh?"

Caleb grinned and reached for her arm, tugging until her hand was freed from the pocket and safely wrapped in his. "Yeah, we did."

"I'm sorry. I really didn't think I'd be that late."

"Not a big deal." He realized he was telling the truth—it *wasn't* a big deal, even though he'd been angry and disappointed while waiting for her to show up, convinced she wouldn't. "We'll just have to do the movie thing another night."

She tilted her head back, her gaze meeting his before darting away. "We, uh, we could always go back to your place and catch something on television."

Her words slammed into him, unleashing the desire that had been simmering deep inside all night. Hot, powerful. Primal. He swallowed a groan, ignored the way his cock hardened and pressed painfully against the zipper of his trousers.

Was she suggesting what he thought she was suggesting? Yeah, she was.

He cupped her chin with his free hand and captured her mouth with his own. Sweet, hot. Full of promise. He deepened the kiss, caught her small sigh as she pressed against him. Soft curves and hard flesh, a sensory contradiction that left him wanting more. *Needing* more. He groaned again when her hips rocked against his erection. When the tips of her trembling fingers trailed along his throat, his chest, lower. Each little touch hesitant. Teasing.

No, not teasing. *Promising.*

And fuck. He wanted her. Here. Now. Wanted her with a desperation that scared the living fuck out of him.

Caleb broke the kiss, his breath coming in short gasps as he rested his forehead against hers. He was an idiot. A grade-A fucking idiot who deserved to be shot for what he was about to do.

"We could." And fuck, was that harsh growl his voice? He cleared his throat, took a small step back and tried not to groan in disappointment when her hand dropped to her side. "But I have an early game skate in the morning, and you have to work."

"Oh. Yeah, sure." She stepped to the side, her head lowered. "No prob—"

He grabbed her, pulled her into his arms and kissed her again. Hard. Fast. "Neither one of us will get any sleep if you come to my place, Shannon."

"I—"

"No sleep. At. All." He put every ounce of desperation and desire he felt into his voice, filling the words with promise. Her eyes widened, understanding flaring in their depths when she realized what he meant. And damn if she didn't smile—a slow, seductive smile that damn near did him in right then and there.

"Sleep is overrated."

Fuck. She was killing him.

"Yeah, it is. But when I finally have you in my bed, I'm not letting you out of it. And I'm going to need more than a few hours." He pressed another kiss against her mouth, stepped back before it could explode into more—before *he* exploded. He reached beside her, opened the door for her. "I'll pick you up Saturday afternoon before the wedding."

She nodded, her thick hair falling in front of her face and hiding the blush coloring her cheeks. She didn't say anything else, just lowered herself into the driver's seat and fumbled with the seatbelt. He closed the door then stood back, watching as she pulled out of the parking space. Watching as her taillights disappeared around the corner as she drove away.

Fuck.

Had he just let her drive away? Yeah, he had.

What the fuck was wrong with him? He *really* needed his fucking head examined.

Chapter
SEVENTEEN

"I do."

Cheers and applause erupted around the room, growing louder when Jon pulled Sammie in for a deep kiss. Shannon whistled a few times as she clapped her hands, helpless to stop the big shit-eating grin spreading across her face. The grin faded when she turned toward Caleb and noticed him watching her, his deep green eyes focusing on her with an intensity that made her blush.

Again.

She stopped clapping and dropped her hands into her lap, wondering why he was staring at her. He'd been mostly quiet the entire day so far—all two hours, since he had picked her up. At first, she thought it might have something to do with the way she was dressed, in an actual dress and heels. No, she didn't dress up often, or do the whole hair-and-make-up thing, but she *did* know how to. It just caught people off-guard when she did.

Then she thought his unusual quietness might be because he didn't really know anyone here. The wedding was a relatively small one, with Sammie's immediate family and Jon's sister and her husband, Jon's former Army buddies and co-workers, and everyone from the Blades. Even TR was here, but Shannon couldn't figure out if she was here as part of whatever she was doing for work, or as Mac's date. They were sitting together but damn if they were acting like they were actually *together*. At least, Mac wasn't. He was sitting straight up, his back rigid, his jaw clenched and his gaze focused on something straight ahead as TR leaned across him and said something to one of Jon's other buddies.

Not that much different from Caleb. No, that wasn't exactly true. Caleb wasn't sitting like that, all stiff and rigid. He was sitting back, relaxed and comfortable, one hand resting on his knee and his other arm draped casually along the back of her chair. And he certainly wasn't looking at anything in front of him. He was looking straight at *her*, his intense expression completely unreadable.

Shannon pulled her gaze from his and stood, watching as everyone slowly made their way to the other side of the room where the tables and a small buffet had been set up. Sammie had said they were originally going to have the wedding at her parents' house but once they counted up the invitees and their plus-ones, they realized that even the small guest list was just a little too big for that. So they had it here instead, in a ballroom at one of the few hotels in Hunt Valley. There would be the buffet dinner and dessert, the cake cutting, some dancing, and then...

Shannon stumbled and almost tripped but Caleb caught her by the elbow and steadied her. He probably thought it was because of her shoes and the ridiculously high heels. Heat filled her face because the stumble had nothing to do with the heels...and everything to do with the *and then* part of the night.

She already had a room here at the hotel, had checked in as soon as they got here. They had gone up there already, dropped their overnight bags on the huge king bed that sat so conspicuously in the middle of the room. Well duh, of course it was conspicuous. It was a hotel room, not like there was really anything else in it besides the bed.

Just the remembered sight of their two small bags, sitting side-by-side on that huge bed, was enough to heat her face. And dammit, Caleb was studying her again, probably wondering what was wrong with her, wondering why she was suddenly blushing every five minutes. Not that she'd tell him. Oh hell no. No way would she ever admit to being nervous and excited about what was to come later.

Or worried that he might change his mind, just like he'd done the other night after their date.

"You okay?"

"Hm?" Shannon turned, nearly bumping noses with Caleb. "Yeah, fine."

He didn't say anything, just watched her for a long minute before pulling the chair out and holding it for her. She sat down and reached for the glass of water at her place setting, drained half of it in two long swallows. And great, now even Taylor was watching her. "What?"

"I didn't say anything." Taylor's whiskey-colored gaze darted to Caleb, her brows lowering just a fraction of an inch as she nodded in his direction. "Caleb."

"Tay-Tay."

Shannon rolled her eyes and nudged Caleb in the side. "No fighting, children."

"Who said we were fighting?"

"Yeah. We're not fighting." Taylor reached for a roll from the basket in the middle of the table and for a second, Shannon was convinced she was going to throw it at Caleb. Chuckie must have thought the same thing because he reached over and snagged the roll from Taylor's hand.

"Behave."

"I *am* behaving." Taylor took the roll back, pinched off a piece, and popped it into her mouth. "I'm not going to waste food by throwing it at him."

Dani dropped into the seat next to Shannon and snorted. "Yeah, right. Sure you weren't."

"I wasn't." Taylor slid a sideways glance at Caleb, her mouth widening in something that might be called a smile. "I'll just wait until the exhibition game to kick his ass."

"Taylor! Enough. Not tonight, okay? No hockey talk. At least, not about the exhibition game."

"Since when don't you want to talk about hockey?"

Shannon shrugged, trying to ignore the astonished looks from her teammates. Even Caleb was watching her—again. Except his mouth was curled in a devilish grin. He draped his arm around her shoulders and leaned closer, his breath warm against her cheek. "I can handle Tay-Tay, don't worry."

"I know you can." She darted a glance at Taylor then rolled her eyes. "Well, you can *try*. But I'm putting the ban in place because we're here for Sammie. No arguing about ass-kicking during the exhibition game. Especially since we're so kicking your ass."

Everyone started laughing, even Caleb. Some of the tension and worry drained from her, tension and worry she hadn't even realized she'd been feeling. Nervousness, yes. Excitement, absolutely. And okay, maybe just a little worry since she still wasn't sure what had happened the other night, why Caleb had turned down her not-so-subtle offer.

She probably shouldn't be worrying, not with the way Caleb's arm was still draped around her shoulder. Warm, comforting. His thumb traced small circles on the bare flesh of her shoulder, prickling her skin with awareness, filling her with need. Good Lord, just that little touch and she was ready to climb into his lap and beg him to take her upstairs.

She reached for her water and took another long swallow then turned to Dani. "Where'd your date go?"

"He's not my date. And he went outside to make a phone call."

"Who ditches his date at a wedding to make a phone call?"

"I told you, he's not my date. Harrison is just a friend. And he's a detective so he's always on-call, even when he's out."

Maddison leaned across the table with a teasing smile. "I call bullshit. That hottie is way more than a friend."

Dani frowned and glanced over her shoulder then turned back and shook her head. "Just friends. He lives next door to my mom. We're talking total friend-zone here. Trust me, there's nothing there."

Shannon didn't miss the disappointment in Dani's voice, or the hint of regret. Even in the candlelight from the table centerpiece, Shannon could see her blushing. Friends? Maybe, but it was obvious Dani was hoping for more.

"You should put the moves on him if you want him."

Chuckie choked on his water, grabbed his napkin and blotted his mouth before shooting a glare at Shannon. "I'm not hearing this."

"What? It's a wedding. People get all crazy romantic and do stupid shit at weddings. I'm just saying if she wants him, now would be a perfect time to put the moves on him."

Now Caleb was choking, too. Shannon turned toward him, her face heating when she realized what she had just said. "Um, I didn't mean—"

"And on that note, I think I need a drink." Chuckie pushed away from the table and stood. "Anyone else want anything from the bar?"

"I'll join you." Caleb leaned over and pressed a quick kiss to her cheek before standing. "Beer or wine?"

"Um—" She almost said *beer*. That's what she normally drank. But she had a sudden nightmare of belching later, at the worst possible moment. She didn't want that, and she certainly didn't want beer breath, either. "Wine. White, please."

She watched as the men walked away—Caleb, Chuckie, and Maddison's date. Then she turned back and saw three sets of eyes staring at her. Dani laughed and hit her in the arm.

"Way to go, Wiley. You just announced you were going to jump your date to the whole world."

"I did not!"

"Sure sounded like it to me."

Taylor leaned forward, frowning. "I thought you said you guys weren't sleeping together."

"We're not."

"But aren't you staying here tonight?"

"Yeah but—"

"Is he staying with you?"

"Yes. I mean, I guess, but—"

Dani let out a loud *whoop* and pumped her fist in the air. "I knew it! Damn girl, you go for it. I knew there was a reason you were all dressed up."

"Hey, I'm not the only one dressed up. It's a wedding. You're supposed to dress up."

"Yeah, but you're the only one wearing fuck-me heels."

Shannon opened her mouth to argue then caught Taylor's eyes and snapped her mouth closed. Her friend didn't look angry, not really, but there was no mistaking the concern in her eyes. "What?"

Taylor shook her head and looked away. "I just hope you know what you're doing."

"Taylor, would you lighten up? You've been giving Shannon shit about him for weeks now. Leave it alone already."

"Excuse me for not wanting to see her used and tossed to the side."

"That's not going to happen." The words fell from Shannon's mouth, filled with a conviction she felt all the way down to her pinched toes.

"How do you know that? I told you, he's a player—"

"Maybe he is, maybe he isn't." Or maybe he *was* but not anymore. A player wouldn't have turned her down the other night. "But you know what? So what if he is? Maybe *I* just want to have some fun. Have you ever thought of that?"

"No, but—"

"Then drop it."

"I just don't want to see you get hurt."

"And I appreciate it. I really do. But Taylor, your captaincy doesn't carry over off the ice and into our personal lives. I'm a big girl. I know what I'm doing." At least, she hoped she knew what she was doing. And if she didn't...so what? She meant what she told Taylor: maybe she just wanted to have some fun.

She locked eyes with her friend for a long minute, willing her to understand. Taylor finally nodded, a small smile teasing the corners of her mouth as she leaned forward. "As long as you give us a full, detailed report and let us know if he lives up to his reputation."

Laughter and cheers greeted Taylor's words. Shannon shook her head, unable to stop her own smile. "Oh hell no! That is so not happening!"

"What's not happening?"

Shannon jumped then spun around, surprised to see Caleb standing there. She shook her head, cursing as her face heated. How long had he been standing there with Chuckie and Maddison's date? Had he heard them talking? No, he hadn't. No way would Taylor have said that if they'd been within hearing distance. At least, Shannon didn't *think* she would.

No, she didn't. Taylor's own blush of embarrassment told her that much. And she was saved from answering when TR approached the table, dragging Mac with her.

"Hey guys." She sat down, looked over her shoulder and frowned at the big man behind her, then patted the empty seat next to her. "That was such a beautiful ceremony, wasn't it? I think I almost cried.

You don't mind if we join you, do you? I'm trying to broaden Mac's horizons. I figure making him sit with a bunch of strong women would do him good."

Shannon glanced over, watched as the big man reluctantly lowered himself into the chair next to TR. Like he was afraid the thing would topple under his weight—and like he'd rather be anywhere else but here.

Shannon bit back a grin and turned to TR. "You're, uh, you're not actually *working* or anything right now, are you?"

"No, you're safe. Although you still owe me the rest of that interview." Her gaze landed on Caleb, interest clear in her pale blue eyes. "Especially since I think I need some clarification on a few things you told me."

Shannon frowned, wondering what the other woman was talking about. Then she remembered their talk all those weeks ago, when TR had asked her about any men in her life and if they had any issues with her playing. TR just sat there and watched her, one brow raised in silent question, a smile teasing her mouth.

Shannon shook her head and looked away, suddenly feigning interest in the centerpiece. Caleb shifted beside her, pushed the wineglass in her direction, then leaned forward.

"Why do I feel like there's a whole lot of something that I'm missing?"

TR waved off his concern with a wide smile. "There's not, don't worry. Have you guys met Mac?"

A few of them had, but only because they'd seen him at the rink with Jon and again at their team meeting the other night. TR placed her hand on Mac's arm, the action both flirty and possessive somehow, and made quick introductions. The man offered everyone a curt nod then simply sat there like an immovable wall, looking like he'd rather be dodging bullets than sitting there making small talk.

Music finally filled the room, drowning out the low hum of conversation and the clanking of glasses. Jon and Sammie made their way across the room, a perfect picture of a couple in love. Jon pulled Sammie into his arms and led her around the dance floor in their first dance as husband and wife. Well, their first one the second time around.

Sammie motioned for everyone to join in, a bright smile on her face. Her daughter Clare ran across the floor and jumped toward them, giggling when Jon caught her in one arm and held her between them as a collective *aww* filled the room.

A warm hand clasped hers and tugged. Caleb leaned closer, his mouth close to her ear when he spoke. "How about a dance?"

His voice was low, filled with husky promise. Shannon met his gaze, her heartbeat tripling when she noticed the desire in those deep green eyes. She nodded, knowing speech was beyond her when he was looking at her that way.

He led her to the dance floor with the other couples, his arm warm and solid against her back. He folded his free hand around hers and brought it to his chest, right above the steady beat of his heart. His gaze never left hers, holding her captive as surely as he held her in his arms.

"I guess we get to share the bride and groom's first dance, hm?"

"Yeah. But don't they always do that? I mean, invite other couples out on the floor to join them—"

"That's not what I meant."

Shannon tilted her head to the side, ignoring the hammering of her heart as Caleb watched her. "Then what did you mean?"

The dimple deepened in his cheek when he smiled. "I mean this is our first dance, too. As a couple. Now, whenever I hear this song, I'll think about you."

"Oh. Wow. Um..." Shannon cleared her throat and looked away, wondered if her smile looked as silly as it felt. "That's, um, that's pretty sappy. And romantic."

Caleb laughed, the rich sound sending heat throughout her entire body. "Yeah, well, it's a wedding. People get all crazy romantic and do stupid shit at weddings."

chapter
EIGHTEEN

Caleb fumbled with the key card, damn near dropped it before he finally managed to insert it into the card reader. He had to do it twice before the green light blinked and he was able to open the door.

Why the fuck was he nervous? There was nothing to be nervous about. It wasn't like he hadn't done this before—lots of times before. Meet a woman, have a few drinks, take her back to his room for a few hours.

Except this wasn't going to be a few hours. And this wasn't just any woman he'd met in a bar. This was Shannon. Gorgeous, funny, quirky Shannon.

Who was just as fucking nervous as he was.

She pushed past him with a quick smile, barely looking at him when he closed the door. Her gaze darted to the bed and he could have sworn her face paled just the smallest bit. Then she turned away, her back to him as she made her way over to the thermostat.

"It's chilly in here, don't you think? I should have turned the heat on before we went downstairs."

She thought it was *chilly*? Christ, he was burning up, his entire body caught up in the fever that had been plaguing him since he'd picked her up before the wedding. How many hours ago was that? Six? Seven? Too many.

He wasn't sure how much longer he'd last if he didn't have her in his arms. Here, now. Not downstairs, sitting next to her with his arm draped around her shoulders. Not on the dance floor, with that sweet body pressed against his even though he couldn't do a damn thing about it. Hold her hand. Press a soft kiss against her mouth or cheek or just below her ear as they danced.

How many hours? He wasn't sure, only knew that every single minute had been pure torture leading up to when he could finally have her.

Here.

Now.

Except he was afraid to fucking move, afraid she'd suddenly bolt if he so much as looked at her, let alone touched her.

But he couldn't stop staring at her, at the creamy flesh of her back, bared by the emerald green dress she was wearing. The dress had a collar that wrapped around her neck, leaving her back and shoulders bare. The satiny material clung to the curves of her full breasts, nipped at her waist, then flared out past her hips before falling to just below her knees. And those shoes...holy fuck, those shoes. He'd been having fantasies about those shoes ever since he picked her up. Christ, she looked so damn sexy, it had taken all of his willpower not to keep her right here in this very room when they first checked-in. And he'd been thinking of nothing else except getting her back up here during the entire wedding and the reception that followed.

Touching her but not touching, exchanging flirty looks and heated glances, claiming nothing but the briefest of kisses. The past six or seven hours had been nothing but tortuous foreplay, leading to this very minute.

Here. Now.

He was ready to fucking explode...and he couldn't even move because he was worried about her bolting.

He dragged his gaze away from that sexy back, pulled in a deep breath, then reached for his small duffel sitting on the edge of the bed—right next to hers. Maybe if he disappeared into the bathroom, gave her a few minutes to relax, she wouldn't be quite so nervous. Wouldn't be worried that all he wanted to do was jump her.

He did, but that was beside the point.

"I'm just going to go and—"

Shannon whirled around, her eyes flared with surprise. "You're leaving?"

"What? No. Hell no. Why would you think that?"

"You said you were going."

"Yeah. To, um, the bathroom. You know. In case you needed a few minutes...in case you needed some space or something." The relief that flashed in her eyes eased some of the tension in his chest, removed any worry that he sounded like a total fucking ass stumbling over his words.

She offered him a small smile, almost shy as she closed the distance between them. Then she turned around and lifted the fancy coil of thick blonde hair from her neck. "Could you unsnap me please?"

And holy fucking shit.

Caleb muttered under his breath, the words unintelligible, sounding more like a cross between a groan and a growl. He dropped his bag to the floor then reached for the collar of her dress, his fingers shaking as they scraped along her skin. It was just a snap. He could do this. He'd done this dozens of times before, no problem.

Except he couldn't find the fucking snap or button or hook or whatever the fuck was holding the pearl-studded material together. He stepped closer, frowning, his fingers thick and clumsy as they pawed at the material.

"There are two small elastic loops that fit over the pearls. Do you see them?"

Caleb leaned closer, searching for elastic loops while he inhaled the fresh scent of her perfume. God, she smelled so good, like sunshine and coconut. And fuck, he needed to stop sniffing her before she asked him what the fuck he was doing then hauled off and slapped him.

And finally! He found the stupid elastic loops, struggled with them for a minute before freeing them. Shannon turned, watching him from beneath lowered lashes as she held the green satin in front of her. A small smile teased her mouth.

"Thank you."

He opened his mouth, ready to tell her no problem, when she moved her hand and let the front of the dress fall away. Creamy flesh filled his gaze, from the delicate flare of her collarbone down to the firm mounds of her bare breasts to the flat planes of her stomach. His gaze moved back to her breasts, his mouth completely drying as the rosy nipples tightened into sharp points.

He licked his lips, curled his fingers into his palm to keep from reaching for her. "Fuck. Shannon—"

"Is something wrong?"

He heard the doubt in her voice, saw her hand reach for the front of the dress. He shook his head and clamped his hand around her wrist, stopping her. Then he looked at her, not bothering to hide the need and desire in his eyes. "You're beautiful. So fucking beautiful."

A delicate blush swept across her skin: her face, her neck, even her breasts. And fuck, he couldn't stop himself, didn't *want* to stop. He reached out, cupped her full breasts in his hands, filling each palm with their weight. Soft, firm, so fucking smooth. He scraped his thumbnail over one nipple, watched it tighten even more. Then he dipped his head and took the hard bud into his mouth. Sucking, pulling. Teasing. He heard Shannon's breathy sigh, felt her hands dig into his shoulders for balance.

And fuck yeah. This. Christ, he'd never imagined she would be so soft, so sweet, so responsive. Her hips rocked against his, her breathy moans driving him to the edge. More. He wanted more. *Needed* more.

He reached between them and grabbed the satin material of the dress, pushed it past her hips until it fell into a puddle at her feet. Then he stepped back, drank her in with hungry eyes. Tall, lithe, a contradiction of toned muscle and soft curves in all the right places. She tossed her head to the side and the fancy coil of her hair came loose. A cascade of thick waves fell over her shoulder, the ends curling around the tightened peak of one rosy nipple.

Caleb couldn't stop looking at her, couldn't stop watching. Hunger? No, this was more than hunger. This was something earthy. Primitive. Desperate. This need to see her, to touch her. To *have* her.

He shrugged out of his jacket, let it fall to the floor as he fumbled with the tie and shirt. Shannon's gaze never left him, those beautiful eyes watching every move of his fingers as he reached down to undo his belt and button and zipper. As he kicked off his shoes and pushed trousers and boxer briefs down and off.

He was burning, her gaze licking flames over every inch of skin as she studied him. His neck, his shoulders. His chest and abdomen. Lower, following the thin line of dark hair down to the base of his thick erection, jutting proudly.

Proudly hell. His cock was fucking *begging*.

Just like him.

And damn if she didn't lick her lips as she stared at his straining cock. Like she couldn't wait to touch him. Taste him. Suck him.

Fuck. He'd fucking lose it if she did that right now.

She took a step toward him, hesitated then lifted one foot and leaned down, ready to take off her shoes. He reached for her, steadying her with one hand on her elbow as she straightened. Then he shook his head, just once.

"No."

Her eyes widened, filled with sharp desire. Then she was in his arms, bare flesh to bare flesh, breath mingling, tongues tangling. Caleb ran his hands along her shoulders, her back, down lower to cup the firm curve of her ass. He swallowed back a groan, dipped his hand inside the delicate waistband of the lacy scrap of underwear, and tugged them down her legs so she could step out of them. Soft skin, warm flesh, hard muscle. Christ, he couldn't get enough of her, didn't understand this burning hunger swallowing him whole.

He dragged his hand up her leg, his fingertips brushing the sensitive skin of her inner thighs. Higher, until his hand skimmed the soft barely-there curls covering hot flesh. Hot. Wet. He slid a finger along her clit, felt her shudder beneath his touch.

He dragged his mouth from hers, down along her neck, nipping and tasting. Then he lifted her, groaned when she wrapped those long fucking legs around his waist. It would be easy, so fucking easy, to drive his cock into her wet heat. Her pussy was right there, rubbing against him. All he had to do—

Not yet. There were other things he wanted to do, *needed* to do.

He turned around, gently lowered her to the bed and eased her legs from his waist. She sighed, her lids fluttering as she pushed up on one elbow and looked at him.

The need in her eyes sucker-punched him, leaving him breathless. Had anyone ever looked at him like that before? Like they wanted *him*, needed *him*. Not who he was or what he could give them or what he could do for them...just *him*.

He swallowed back another groan then dipped his head and caught one tight nipple in his mouth. Sucked, pulled. Teased the hard point with the tip of his tongue. Shannon reached for him, her fingers tangling in his hair as her back arched. He sucked even deeper, pulling the tight peak against the roof of his mouth before gently nipping it. The breath left her in a rush, the sound a sharp hiss of need. He released her nipple with a small groan, taking in the sight of her damp flesh reflected in the light from the single lamp on the nightstand. Then he dipped his head and kissed his way down her stomach, peppering her flesh with gentle kisses. Lower, his shoulder nudging her legs apart as he reached her pussy. He spread her damp flesh, slid a finger across her clit and watched as her hips rose toward him.

"Caleb. Please." Her voice was hoarse, throaty, the words filled with need. He dipped his head, ran his tongue across her damp flesh, bit back a groan when her fingers dug into the hard muscle of his arm.

He sat back, blindly reaching for his duffle bag somewhere on the floor. Where the fuck was it? It was right here, somewhere—there. His fingers curled over the handle and he hauled it onto the bed, quickly unzipping it just enough to dip his hand inside. He searched by feel, his eyes never leaving Shannon's flushed body. There!

His hands closed over the foil pockets stuck near the bottom, pulled them out and tossed them on the bed next to Shannon. Then he pushed the bag off the bed and stretched out between her spread legs, dipped his head and pressed his mouth against her swollen flesh.

And fuck, she tasted so sweet. So fucking hot. Like warm honey on a cold day. He drank from her, each little rock of her hips, each little breathy moan, sending him closer to the edge. He reached down, closed one hand over his cock, and stroked. Long. Hard. Fuck, he needed her. Needed to feel hot flesh wrapped around him, needed to feel her muscles squeezing him as she came.

And fuck, if he didn't stop, he'd come before he even had the chance to drive into her.

He moved his hand, focused on the sweet taste of her against his mouth. Fingers suddenly tangled with his tongue and he looked up. His heart slammed into his ribs and his cock jumped at the look in her eyes. She pushed up on one elbow as her free hand dipped lower. One long finger, the nail painted a pale pink, slid along her clit. Lower, dipping inside, pressing, moving back out to slide the wet tip against her clit again.

His hungry gaze snapped to hers, his lungs freezing at the need in her eyes. "Don't stop. Let me watch you."

Holy shit. Holy *fuck*. Did she mean—? Her gaze dropped to the hard length of his cock, jutting up in proud desperation. Then she looked back at him, her meaning clear in her eyes. "Don't stop."

He slid closer, sat back on his heels and draped her legs over his thighs. Watching as she touched herself, pleasured herself. Then he reached between them and folded his hand around his cock, stroking. Long. Slow. Hard. Watching as Shannon fingered her clit, always watching. Knowing she was watching him.

"*Fuck*. Shannon. That is so fucking hot." His words were barely more than a growl, lost in each harsh breath as he tried to fill his lungs with air. And fuck, if he wasn't careful, he'd come right now.

He closed his eyes, tossed his head back and clenched his jaw against an image of him leaning over Shannon as he came. On her stomach, her chest, her hot pussy. And fuck, he needed to stop. *Now*. He was so fucking close, his balls pulling tight, his cock throbbing with each hard stroke.

He stilled his hand, opened his eyes and looked down at Shannon. At the shimmering hair tangled around her face. At the sharp points of her nipples, rising and falling with each harsh breath. At the creamy flesh of her thighs draped over his own darker ones.

At the long finger sliding along her clit, each movement faster.

Her hips surged forward, her back arching as her head tossed from side-to-side. She nibbled on her lower lip, her free hand lifting, blindly reaching.

He grabbed her hand, felt her fingers tighten around his as her hips rocked once, twice. A low cry escaped her mouth then she called his name.

Begging for him. Now.

He grabbed a foil packet, ripped it open and quickly sheathed himself. Then he was there, driving into her, hot flesh clamping around his cock as her climax washed over her. Strong, powerful.

And fuck. *Fuck*. He was so close, it would be so easy—

No, not yet. Not now.

He held himself still, fought for control, struggled for the last scrap of his willpower until her clenching muscles eased. Then he moved forward, rocking into her. Deep. Hard. Slow, not stopping until her nails dug into the flesh of his arms, not until she screamed his name one more time.

Harder. Deeper. Fast now. Faster. Deeper still, until he couldn't tell where his body ended and hers began. It didn't matter, they were one. Her. Him. *Them*. Together.

Harder. Faster. Faster, until the world exploded around them, sending them both over the edge. Soaring. Flying.

Together.

chapter
NINETEEN

Something wasn't right.

In that hazy mist between sleep and awake, something niggled at her. Annoying little pokes in her subconscious, telling her something wasn't right.

Something was *different*.

She frowned and tried to brush the pokes away, rolled over and buried her head under the pillow. The room was too cold, she never kept it this cold. She didn't have to look to know her flesh was pebbled from the chill—she could *feel* her skin prickling as a draft moved over her body.

She mumbled under her breath and reached for the covers. Just a few more minutes of sleep, that's all she wanted. A few more blissful minutes cloaked in the darkness of sleep, where she didn't have to worry about anything.

And where the *hell* was the comforter?

Her hand swept along the bed beside her, finally

closing over the thick comforter. It felt different but it didn't matter, not when she pulled it over her bare skin and burrowed deeper, searching for warmth, for sleep.

And dammit, something poked her again. Harder this time, in the shoulder. She tried to brush it away, waving her hand through the chilly air. "G'way."

A quiet chuckle sounded somewhere just beyond her reach. No, that wasn't right, she must be dreaming. Except she could still hear the laughter, deep and rich, oddly familiar.

She swore under her breath, telling the laughter where to go. Why wouldn't it shut up? All she wanted was sleep, just a few more minutes—

"G'way."

"Rise and shine, sleepy head."

The voice wasn't in her head, in her dreams. She knew that voice—

Shannon bolted upright, swearing when her hand hit the edge of the nightstand. She blinked against the bright light coming in through the curtains then slowly turned her head—

And nearly screamed. Would have screamed if she was fully awake.

Caleb was stretched across the bed, leaning on one elbow, watching her. She blinked, forced her bleary eyes to focus on him for a long minute. Tousled hair, eyes glittering with silent laughter, that damn dimple deepening in his cheek as his mouth spread into a wide smile. No shirt—she blinked again, taking an extra few seconds to appreciate the expanse of skin pulled tight over his broad chest and ridged abdomen. Her gaze followed the thin trail of dark hair that disappeared into the open waistband of his dress pants. She blinked one more time, sending him a sleepy scowl.

"Go. Away."

She fell back onto the bed and pulled the covers over her head, only to have them yanked off her a second later. Shannon grabbed a pillow and tossed it at him, then swore under her breath when he caught it and leaned over her.

Too awake. Too aware.

And too damn sexy for this early in the morning. Too damn sexy, period.

"Someone here isn't a morning person."

"You think?" She tried to push him away but it was like moving a concrete wall, solid and immovable. He leaned closer, his mouth only inches from hers. She quickly turned her head to the side and his kiss landed on her cheek. Oh God, how could even stand being this close to her? She probably had morning breath. And bed head. And smeared make-up.

But he didn't seem to care because his mouth trailed a path across her jaw and over to that sensitive spot just below her ear. She sighed, her body melting under his as he nibbled her neck. Then he sat up, still leaning over her, his eyes still glittering with his soft laughter.

"I brought coffee."

She pushed against him again, finally sitting up and glancing around the room in desperation. "Where?"

"On the dresser. I wasn't sure how you took it—"
"Black. Strong. Now."

He laughed again, the bed dipping as he rolled off and moved toward the coffee. He handed her the cup, barely large enough for three long swallows. She didn't care, she'd take what she could for now.

"Careful, it's hot."

She grunted then peeled back the top, blew on it, then took the first sip. Liquid heat slid down her throat and settled into her stomach, nudging her toward full consciousness. Another sip, then one more before the last threads of sleep finally fell from her hazy mind.

She glanced around the room and mentally cringed at the disaster meeting her gaze. Clothes were strewn everywhere. One of her heels was tossed on the small chair in the corner of the room, the other was resting on the floor beneath the curtains. Her dress was tossed over the television—how the hell had it ended up there?—and the scrappy lace of her underwear was beside the bed, tangled with his red boxer briefs. A handful of foil wrappers, torn and empty, rested on the nightstand. And the bed...she glanced down at it, frowning at the way the covers were twisted and tangled, half on the bed and half on the floor. No wonder she had been cold.

She wasn't cold now, not with the embarrassment heating her from the inside. She took another sip of the awful coffee and hoped Caleb would think her red face was from the steam.

Yeah, right. Not with the way he was looking at her, like he was ready to eat her up. How was that even possible? She had to look like shit, like death warmed over.

Or like someone who had been kept up all night, deep in the throes of wild sex.

She swallowed back a groan and placed the coffee on the nightstand, trying to ignore all those wrappers sitting there, trying not to count them. She kicked her feet free from the tangled sheets and swung her legs over the side of the bed. She hesitated, wondering if she should grab the sheet and wrap it around her before heading to the bathroom.

Was she really worried about modesty *now?* After everything they'd done last night? Yes, she was. There was a huge difference between the dark hours of last night—even if the light *had* been on most of the time—and now.

She tugged the sheet free and yanked it around her, then shot Caleb a dirty look when he chuckled. She swept past him, tripped, caught herself at the last minute, then headed into the bathroom and closed the door.

And holy shit, she really did look like death warmed over. Her hair was a tangled mess around her face, sticking out here and there. Mascara was smeared under her eyes, making her look like a raccoon—

Or like a hooker who had spent the last ten hours alternating between her back and her knees.

Which probably wasn't too far from the truth.

She swallowed back a groan, dropped the sheet, then stared at her reflection with wide eyes. Red marks marred the skin of her chest. Not just red marks. She leaned closer, frowning at the small bruise just above her left breast.

No, not a bruise. A small bite mark.

Holy shit.

She turned away from the mirror then leaned into the shower and turned the water on, twisted the knob to the hottest setting. Then she took care of personal business and stepped into the tub, pulled the curtain closed—

And remembered that her small overnight bag was still in the other room.

Dammit.

She stepped out of the shower and grabbed a

towel, wrapping herself in it before opening the door. Then she nearly screamed. Caleb was leaning in the doorway, a devilish grin on his face, her bag held in one hand.

"Forget something?"

She growled at him, yanked the bag from his hand, then slammed the door in his face.

And damn if he didn't start laughing.

"You really aren't a morning person, are you?"

"Not when I don't get any sleep, I'm not."

"Are you complaining?"

She wanted to say *yes*, just to throw him off. Just to tease him. But she couldn't force the lie from her mouth so she settled for another growl instead.

Which only made him laugh again.

Damn him.

She grabbed the small toiletry bag from the duffel, pulling out her shampoo and conditioner before climbing back into the shower. The water was too hot now, nearly scalding her. She adjusted the temperature then stood under the stream, closing her eyes as water washed over her. Blissful, hot water. Relaxing her, waking her.

She waited for the morning-after regret, expecting it to wash over her as fully as the water streaming from the showerhead. What they'd done last night—what *she* had done. That wasn't like her, to be so brazen and wild. To sleep with someone even knowing nothing would come of it. But there was no regret. How could she regret it, when she had wanted it? *All* of it. When she had wanted Caleb?

She had no idea what they were doing, where they would go from here. Were they dating? Maybe. Were they a couple? No, she couldn't let herself think that.

She couldn't read into anything they'd done, couldn't make more of it than what it was.

Sex. That was it.

Pure, raw, blissful sex.

Everything else had to be one-day-at-a-time. God help her if she tried to make more of it than it was. God help her if she let her heart get in the way.

The shower curtain whipped open, startling her. She wiped the water from her eyes and glowered at Caleb. At least, she tried to. It was hard to glower when all she could do was stare at the hard length of his cock.

She forced her gaze to his and tried to frown. "What are you doing?"

"What's it look like I'm doing?" He climbed into the shower and pulled the curtain back. "You're using all the hot water."

"Am not."

He didn't say anything, just watched her with smoldering green eyes. He reached behind her and grabbed the small bar of soap, moving it between his hands until a bubbly lather formed.

"Turn around."

The intensity in his eyes scorched her, knocked all thought from her mind. She turned, the stream of water falling across her chest as Caleb's hands slid along her back. Warm, strong, fingers digging into the muscles of her shoulders, her lower back. Lower, teasing the round curve of her ass before sliding into the cleft.

She sucked in a breath, her head falling back as Caleb's mouth traced a line of fire along her neck. Heat raced through her, pooling low in her belly, between her legs. She reached behind her, draped one arm behind his neck as his hands slid around her waist. Up, to cup the fullness of her breasts. Squeezing, teasing, his thumbs scraping the hard points of each nipple.

Lower, down across the flat of her stomach, one hand cupping between her legs. His mouth nibbled the sensitive flesh of her skin, tugged on the lobe of one ear.

"Spread your legs for me."

She sucked in a deep breath, braced one hand against the tile wall, and did as he asked, helpless to tell him no.

Helpless to do anything but *feel*.

Her breath left her in a hiss as one slick finger slid across her clit. Back and forth, harder and faster as her hips bucked against his hand. She pulled her lower lip between her teeth, biting down as that solitary finger slid inside her.

"Christ, Shannon. You are so fucking wet. So fucking hot." His voice, hoarse with need, made her knees buckles. He draped one steely arm around her waist, supporting her as he slid his finger in and out, up across her clit, back inside. Over and over until her vision swam, until her breath came in short gasps, until her muscles clenched and her body shuddered with release. But it wasn't enough, not nearly enough. She wanted more. Needed more.

Needed *him*. Caleb. All of him.

Deep inside her.

She rocked her hips backward, bent over and braced her hands against the wall. She heard him groan, felt his hands rub her ass, squeezing, pinching.

Shannon glanced at him over her shoulder, captured his gaze, held it with a desperation she didn't know possible. "Now, Caleb. Fuck me. Now."

He leaned to the side, grabbed something from

the edge of the tub and ripped it open with his teeth. She watched, her glazed eyes focused on the way he sheathed the hard length of his cock, the way his hands closed over its thickness and stroked. Once. Twice. Then he leaned forward, guiding the tip of his cock into her from behind. Stretching. Filling.

She closed her eyes, sucked in a deep breath as he drove into her. Hard and deep, fast. Heat spiraled through her, scorching her as muscles tensed. Clenching, gripping, tightening.

Tightening even more, until there was nothing but sensation. The heat of his cock driving into her, the tug of his hand as it twisted in her wet hair, the glide of his fingers as they rubbed her clit.

Over and over.

Fast.

Deep.

Hard.

Driving her over the edge. Tumbling. Falling.

Trusting Caleb to catch her.

chapter
TWENTY

Caleb yanked the tie from around his neck and threw it across the room. It hit the bed, slid off and landed in a wrinkled heap on the floor. He thought about kicking it but what the fuck good would that do?

It sure as hell wouldn't do anything to relieve the anger and frustration boiling inside him.

Tonight's game had been a fucking fiasco. The Banners had been annihilated by Vegas, to the point where he wondered why the fuck they had even bothered playing. Eight to one? Seriously? That wasn't a fucking hockey game. Not even close. It had been so damn bad, he had honestly thought Coach Donovan was going to have a fucking heart attack right there on the bench.

Neither of their goalies had performed worth a shit. Then again, neither had any of the players—including himself. Their single goal had been nothing more than a fluke, a crazy-ass loose puck tipped in by

Lucas Sacco. And the only reason he had scored was because Vegas's goalie had thought he had stopped the play and was waiting for the fucking whistle to blow.

And now, to make things even worse, Shannon was telling him she probably wouldn't be able to see him on Thursday night.

Caleb dropped to the bed and swallowed back his frustrated sigh. "Just a few hours. I can meet you at your place right after we land."

He heard noise in the background, the sound of running water and something banging, a low voice followed by a muffled grunt. From the television? Probably. It was already past eleven, Shannon was usually asleep by now.

"I have practice Thursday night, you know that."

"It'll be after practice. We probably won't be getting in until close to midnight anyway."

"Which means you won't get here until at least one. That's not going to work, not when I have to get up at six for work."

"Then call in sick." He winced as soon as the words left his mouth. Fuck. Did he have to sound so desperate?

Yeah, because he *was* desperate. He hadn't seen her since Sunday evening, when he finally took her home after spending all day with her. They'd had lunch after leaving the hotel, went back to his place to watch movies—and barely made it through the door before falling all over each other with a hunger that still left him breathless. He was addicted to her, pure and simple. Couldn't get her out of his system. Didn't *want* to get her out of his system.

It was only Tuesday, just over forty-eight hours since he had seen her, and he was already going through withdrawal. The team had flown out early this morning for tonight's game and would fly out early tomorrow for Thursday's game in New York. Then they were back home for a few off days, an unusual weekend with no games before an extended home stretch next week.

Unless you counted the exhibition game on Saturday afternoon.

Caleb didn't want to wait that long to see her. Didn't know if he *could* wait that long.

He blew out another frustrated sigh and readjusted his grip on the phone. "No comment to that, huh?"

"No, because I'm pretending I didn't hear you say that. You know I can't call out sick."

He opened his mouth to ask her why, snapped it closed before the words left his mouth. He *knew* why, knew she had bills to pay, knew that she didn't make shit playing for the Blades.

"How about if you leave your door unlocked and I'll just sneak into bed with you? I won't even wake you up." And yeah, that sounded as pathetic as he thought it did because Shannon actually snorted her laughter.

"Yeah, right. Like that's realistic."

"I've seen you sleep, remember? I think a bomb could go off next to you and you wouldn't notice it."

"Probably not, but somehow I think I'd notice *you* in my bed. Which means neither one of us would get any sleep."

"Then how about Friday?"

"Hang on." He heard some more muttering, a small click, then Shannon's voice again, the sound just a little different. "That's not going to work, either. Inventory is Friday so I'm working late, picking up some extra hours."

"Is it mandatory?"

"No but I already committed to it."

"Can't you tell them you changed your mind?"

"Yeah, I could." She paused and Caleb could hear her stifling a yawn. "Except it's overtime and I need the money."

"You could always move in with me." And whoa. What the fuck? Had he just said that? What the hell was wrong with him? His mouth opened and closed, like a fish drowning on air, as he struggled to say something—anything—in an effort to brush the words off. To turn them into a joke. To—

Shannon snorted, her laughter bright and maybe just a little forced as it came through the phone. "Did you get hit in the head tonight? Get boarded or something?"

"What? No, of course not."

"Really? Because I know I didn't hear what I just thought I heard. Don't be an ass."

Caleb pulled the phone away from his ear, frowned at it, then moved it back. "An ass? Why does that make me an ass?"

"You're kidding, right? You just asked me to move in with you."

Yeah, he had. It was just a slip of the tongue, words leaving his mouth before his brain could engage. He hadn't meant it. At least, he didn't think he'd meant it. But did she have to sound so cynical about it? Did she have to make it sound like the world's worst idea?

It was, but that didn't matter.

"It, uh, it was just an idea."

"A stupid one. Moving in." She laughed, the sound breathy, still a little forced, filled with disbelief.

"Not happening, Caleb."

He ground his teeth together and drew in a quick breath through his nose. Time to change the subject. "So how about Friday night when you get home from inventory?"

"That's not happening, either."

"You're killing me, Shannon." He fell back onto the bed, his gaze studying the rough surface of the ceiling. "I need to see you."

"Yeah. Me, too." Her voice lowered, turned a little husky. Was she in bed, pretending he was with her? Touching herself, pretending it was *his* hands on her, pretending it was *his* finger sliding in and out of her wet heat?

He squeezed his eyes closed, pressed the palm of his hand against the aching length of his cock. Fuck, he had to stop thinking like that, had to stop picturing her that way. Not when he was here, hundreds of miles away and unable to do anything about it.

Especially when Logan could decide he'd had enough down in the bar and come back to the room at any minute.

Fuck it. The door was locked, the security latch in place. Nobody was coming inside.

He fumbled with the button of his pants, yanked down the zipper and freed his aching cock with a sharp sigh. Long strokes, up and down, his thumb grazing the tip, spreading the bead of moisture over soft skin stretched tight. Picturing Shannon on her knees between his spread legs, her long hair tickling the skin of his inner thigh. Her mouth, hot and wet, closing over him.

Christ, he wanted her, needed her. With a fever he didn't understand, a fever that threatened to fry the last molecule in his brain. "What, um, what are you doing?"

"Right now?"

"Yeah. Tell me." He stroked harder, a little faster, imagining Shannon in her bed, her legs spread wide, her fingers sliding over her slick clit.

"Trying to unclog this damn garbage disposal. Why?"

Caleb's eyes shot open as disappointment shot through him. He released his cock with a growl. "Just, um, just wondering."

"Everything okay? You sound...I don't know. Weird."

"Yeah, fine. Good to go."

"You sure about that?"

"Yeah. I was just hoping—never mind."

"Hoping, what?"

"Nothing."

"Caleb, out with it."

"I was just sitting here, picturing you next to me. Naked. Hot. Wet. Fingering that sweet wet pussy—"

Something like a crash echoed in his ear, followed by a muttered curse. The sound grew muffled, dull and distant. More noises, like hurried footsteps, followed by what sounded like a door slamming shut.

He pushed up on his elbow, frowning. "Shannon? You there?"

"Uh, yeah. I'm here."

"Everything okay?"

"Uh, yeah."

"What was that noise?"

"Um...that would have been the phone flying off the counter."

Caleb smiled, a spurt of male pride shooting through him. "Got you a little worked up, huh?"

"Um, no."

No? Really? So much for the male pride. He reached down, readjusted his pants, then pushed himself to a sitting position. "Then why was your phone flying off the counter?"

"Because I was trying to get it off speaker phone."

Caleb leaned forward and pinched the bridge of his nose then pulled in a deep breath. He didn't want to know, didn't want to ask. Couldn't ask.

He didn't need to, because Shannon kept talking, her voice just a little choked. From embarrassment? Laughter? Something else?

"My, um, my brother's here."

"Your brother?"

"Yeah. You know, the one who's letting me live in the studio above his garage?"

"He's there now."

"Yeah."

"Did he, uh, did he hear?"

"Um, yeah. Pretty much."

Fuck. "I'm sorry, I didn't think—"

"Yeah, neither did I."

"Did he, um, did he say anything?"

"Not really but I'm pretty sure he wants to meet you now."

Great, just fucking great. What the fuck had he been thinking? He hadn't been, not with his brain, at any rate. "I didn't mean—"

"I know you didn't. I should have warned you."

How could she have warned him? It wasn't like she knew what he was thinking, what he was doing...what he was hoping she *would* do. Hell, even he hadn't known, hadn't planned on it.

He ran a hand over his face, released a deep sigh.

"So, how about Friday night? When you get off work?"

"Caleb, I can't." He heard the regret in her voice, but he also heard the determination and knew nothing he said would change her mind.

"Then how about Saturday?"

"We're already seeing each other Saturday. You know—when we kick your ass on the ice."

Caleb didn't even laugh. How could he, after tonight's slaughter? "I was thinking more along the lines of after the game."

"After the game, I'm all yours."

"I'm going to hold you to that."

"After the game, you can hold whatever you want."

"Is that a promise?"

"That's a promise."

Caleb smiled, some of the tension easing from his shoulders. He apologized again, finally said goodbye, and disconnected the call.

Four days. He could last four days.

Couldn't he?

chapter
TWENTY-ONE

Breathe.
Focus.
Breathe.

Shannon rolled her head from side-to-side, shrugged the tension from her shoulders. This was just a game, like every other game she had ever played in since she was six years old. Nothing in her routine should change. It *couldn't* change, not if she wanted to be ready.

She could do this.

They could do this.

She opened her eyes, looked down at the small rubber balls cupped in her hand. One more deep breath then she tossed the first one against the wall. The second. The third. Watching as they bounced off the painted concrete, arcing through the air toward her.

One. Two. Three.

She batted each one as it moved closer, fast.

Faster. Over and over, her gaze focused on the movement of each rubber ball, anticipating, breathing, focusing. Finding her zone, settling into it.

Faster still, until each swipe of her hand came automatically, all thought gone, trusting only her instinct.

Thwap. Thwap. Thwap.
Thwapthwapthwap.

Deep breaths, her heart rate slowing as she changed the rhythm of each swipe. High. Low. Stepping away from the wall, then moving closer. Always watching. Always anticipating.

Slower now, nice and steady. Slower still until she caught each ball with her hand. One. Two. Three.

She closed her eyes, inhaled deeply, let her head hang down. Relaxed. Free of the tension that had been gripping her since this morning.

Free of all thought except for the game that was due to start in fifteen minutes.

Just another game. Just like every other game she had ever played in.

She pressed a hand against her stomach, pushing away the tangle of nerves that wanted to resurface, just like she pushed away the negative thoughts threatening to surface.

She tossed the balls into her small duffel then sat cross-legged on the floor, hands resting, palm up, on her knees. A few more minutes to meditate, to focus, to go deeper into the zone. Just a few more minutes...

Footsteps echoed along the tile floor, hesitated then moved closer. Shannon blew out a heavy breath then opened her eyes, raised her brows in Taylor's direction.

"Yeah?"

"It's about time."

A burst of nerves fluttered in her stomach. Dammit. She didn't need the nerves, not now. None of them did.

She swore again then pushed to her feet. "How crowded is it?"

That question had been on her mind all morning. Hell, it had been on her mind all week. She wasn't the only one wondering about it, either. Yes, this exhibition game was a great opportunity for the Blades, for the entire league—but only if people actually showed up.

Taylor shrugged. "I haven't looked."

"What? Why not?"

"I'm afraid to." Taylor made the admission with a small grin, like she was trying to play it off. But Shannon knew her too well, could feel the tension and worry radiating from her. Taylor was nervous? She wasn't sure what to make of that, wasn't sure if that was a good thing or not.

"Well, fuck them then. They don't know what they're missing."

Taylor laughed then clapped her on the shoulder. "You're right."

"Damn straight, I'm right."

"You ready?"

Shannon opened her mouth, ready to say *as ready as I'll ever be*. But she couldn't say that—she *never* said that. It wasn't her, wasn't who she was. So she forced a confident smile she didn't quite feel and nodded. "Abso-fucking-lutely."

Then it was time to head to the locker room, time to finish gearing up. Coach Reynolds came in, gave them her usual rah-rah speech, pumping them up. And they *were* pumped up, every single one of them, despite the tension and nervousness that hovered around them.

They moved out to the hall and into the tunnel, listening to the heavy beat of rock music as the announcer introduced the Banners. Loud cheers greeted each name, echoing off the ice.

Shannon exchanged a surprised glance with Taylor at the noise level. How many people were out there?

Definitely more than the Blades usually played in front of.

Sammie groaned and grabbed Shannon's shoulder, dropping her head against the pads. "OhmyGod. Holy crappola. I think I need to pee." It was what Sammie said before every game, part of a ritual that had become ingrained in them since their very first game.

Shannon tapped her on the leg with the flat of her stick and grinned, just like she always did. The familiar words fell from her mouth, filled with a hint of laughter—just like always.

"It's a little late for that."

And it was, because the announcer's voice boomed through the arena. "Ladies and gentleman, the...Chesapeake...Blades!"

Holy shit, the applause was nearly as loud for them as it had been for the Banners. Shannon closed her eyes and took a deep breath, willing her stomach to settle as each player was introduced.

Taylor. Dani. Maddison.

Sammie. Rachel.

One by one, until Shannon was next in line.

"And in net, number thirty-seven, Shannon

Wiley!"

Shannon pushed through, hit the ice with a smooth stride, the stick raised over her head in greeting as she moved toward the net. And holy shit, the place was packed. Not completely filled, but still more crowded than she had anticipated.

More crowded than she had hoped.

She moved into position, crouching low, bouncing on her skates as she slid her stick across the ice in a wide arc, tapping each post twice. Her gaze moved over to the players' benches then slid toward center ice. Dani was taking the face off, lined up against Hunter Billings from the Banners. Even from here, she could see the grin on the man's face—on the faces of all the Banners. This was nothing to them but a light-hearted game. All of them probably thought it would be child's play, that they'd win without even trying.

Was Caleb thinking the same thing?

She sought him out with her gaze, noticed the way he was positioned on the ice. Standing straight up, his weight on his right leg. Casual. Relaxed.

Yes, even Caleb thought this was going to be an easy win, no matter how many times she had told him otherwise.

Fine, let him think that. Let all of them think that. They were about to find out otherwise.

Would the Blades win? Maybe. Maybe not. But they sure as hell were going to try.

The puck finally dropped. Hunter reached out with his stick, the move almost nonchalant, like it was a given that the Banners would win the face off. But the puck was already sliding across the ice, hitting Taylor's tape dead-center before she spun around and moved toward the Banners' net.

Shannon almost laughed at the expressions on the men's faces. Had they really thought the Blades were going to make this easy for them?

Aw, hell no.

Shannon relaxed, just a for a second, as she watched the play unfold as they had planned. Taylor slowed down, turned and made a big show of looking around, like she was searching for someone to pass the puck to. Jordyn slid in closer, stumbled, nearly fell. The Banner who had been following her reached out like he was going to catch her, like he was afraid she might actually fall.

Instead, Jordyn casually slid the blade of her stick in front of his left skate, sending him flying to his knees—just as Taylor passed the puck on her direction.

Shannon glanced over at the Banners' bench, saw the surprise on half a dozen faces as Jordyn skated behind the net for a beautiful wrap-around. Connelly wasn't even looking, his gaze directed on the spot where Jordyn had been a few seconds before.

A second later, the red light flashed above the net and the horn blared. Twenty-eight seconds in, and the Blades had scored their first goal. Shannon almost wished they had waited, that they'd taken more time to lull the guys into a false sense of security. Then again, maybe they'd think it was just a fluke and continue to underestimate them.

Shannon's gaze moved across the ice, finally resting on Caleb. He turned toward her, his green eyes flashing with an intensity she could feel even from this distance. Was he surprised? Maybe. Did he think it was a fluke?

Probably.

Did she care?

Abso-fucking-lutely not.

Caleb reached out and snagged Jaxon Miller's sleeve, leaned in to say something. Both men looked over at her, then Caleb finally raised his stick, waist-level, and pointed it at her with a crooked smile.

Was that supposed to worry her? Not even close. And if that's what he thought, then shame on him.

Shannon tipped her helmet back, her gaze never leaving his. Then she nodded and pointed her stick right back at him.

Game on.

chapter
TWENTY-TWO

Fuck!

They were losing. How the fuck was that even possible?

Caleb clenched his jaw and stared up at the scoreboard. Giant red numbers stared back at him, taunting him. Two-to-one. How? How the *fuck* had that even happened?

Yeah, that first goal was a fluke, coming at twenty-eight seconds into the game. They hadn't been ready for it. Hell, they hadn't been *looking* for it. This was an exhibition game, nothing more than a casual, relaxing, friendly game.

Yeah. Sure. It may have started that way for the Banners...for the first twenty-eight seconds. Something told him it had never been that way for the Blades, though. And Christ, he still couldn't believe it. They were actually giving them a run for their money—and winning. Skating fast, shooting hard. Playing hard.

Like they had every intention of winning.

Caleb glanced at the scoreboard again, his eye on the clock. Fuck. If they didn't do something soon, the Blades would win. And how fucking embarrassing would that be? To be bested by a women's hockey team. A brand-*new* women's hockey team.

Fuck.

He wasn't the only one sitting there in disbelief, the only one feeling the pressure. They all were: Shane, Logan, Hunter. Even poor Ilya Semenov, who had made the mistake of reaching for Jordyn Knott to keep her from falling on the ice, only to faceplant himself when she tripped him during that first play.

This wasn't supposed to be a physical game. No hitting, no boarding, no cross-checking or tripping. Somebody must have forgotten to give that memo to the Blades because damn if they weren't doing exactly that. Not blatant, not enough to draw any penalties. Either that, or the refs were simply turning a blind eye to it. And their fucking hands were tied. No way in hell could the Banners pull half the shit the ladies were pulling. The arena had erupted in a chorus of *boos* the one time Christian Harper had bumped into Taylor. It really had been an accident—one look at the mortification on Christian's face was enough for everyone to see that. But Taylor had played it for all it was worth and dropped to the ice. And damn if the whistle hadn't blown. Christian had been sent to the penalty box for two minutes on a tripping call, when it should have been Taylor sitting in the bin for embellishment.

That had been enough to give the Blades their second goal of the afternoon on the power play. Because fucking Connelly still wasn't paying attention, still didn't have his head in the fucking game.

Coach had finally pulled him, put Dan Lory in. And how the hell Coach wasn't having a fucking fit right now was beyond Caleb. He glanced over, wondering if maybe he was just missing the signs. No, he wasn't. Donavan was leaning against the glass partition separating the players' benches, looking relaxed and at ease, like he didn't have a care in the world. The Blades' coach leaned over, said something with a smile on her face, and damn if Donovan didn't start laughing.

What the fuck?

Caleb turned back to the ice just as Jacob Riley sent a hard shot toward the Blades' net. He leaned forward, holding his breath, waiting for the puck to go in. It had to go on, no way could it miss.

And *fuck*. Shannon stopped it with a quick twist to the left, catching the puck with her glove hand and pulling it into her chest. The whistle blew, signaling a stop in play.

"Holy shit. I wish to fuck she played for us." Logan muttered the words under his breath, low enough so Connelly wouldn't be able to hear him from his spot at the far end of the bench. Caleb grunted, unwilling to agree. If the Blades had been playing any other team, he would have said it himself. But they weren't playing any other team—they were playing the Banners. *His* team.

And fuck if he could get over the fact they were losing long enough to appreciate the saves Shannon had been making all afternoon.

Time for the face off, then more scrambling for the puck. Donovan leaned forward, motioning for a line change with a few quick hand signals. Caleb jumped the boards, his skates hitting the ice as he took Jacob's spot. Taylor whipped past him, chasing the puck as it cleared center ice. He didn't hesitate, just tore off after her, knowing he couldn't wait for an icing call.

Damn if he could let her score—none of them could. Ilya and Parker Gibson obviously realized the same thing because they were close behind her as well, moving in to defend the net.

And yes, finally! Ilya slid behind her, reaching with his stick and knocking the puck free. It slid straight toward Jaxon Miller, who took off with it. Taylor swore, her voice easily heard from where Caleb was, a few feet away. Let her get frustrated. It was time to show them who was the better team.

Calen spun around, doing a one-eighty as he followed Jaxon down the ice. There was no open shot, they'd have to set this one up. Cycle it. Wait for the right second then shoot toward Shannon's weak side.

But she didn't have a weak side, that was the fucking problem. She anticipated every shot, never moving until it was time. She had to be fucking tired by now, blocking as many shots as she had so far, just in the third period. It would have been funny, the way the Banners kept ripping them toward the net, almost like they were desperate to score.

Yeah, it would have been real fucking funny...if it wasn't the truth.

Caleb slid closer to the net, spraying snow on Shannon's legs as he turned, waiting for the pass. He heard her mutter something, ignored her as he watched Jaxon and Shane pass the puck back and forth. Closer, closer still.

He slid back, just a few inches, crowding Shannon. She said something again, her voice a little louder, the words still indistinguishable. But there was no mistaking her anger, her impatience.

Caleb clenched his jaw, ignoring her, focusing on the puck. Waiting...

Watching...

He leaned over, getting into position, let himself move back another few inches. Definitely crowding her, getting in her way, blocking her view.

"Get the fuck out of my crease!" He heard her words that time, low and angry. Something smacked him across the lower back and he stumbled forward, caught himself at the last minute. What the fuck? Had she just shoved him?

He shook his head, ignoring everything but the puck as Shane shot it toward him. Caleb caught it with the edge of his blade—barely—and spun around, flipping it toward the net. Once, twice. Once more, only to have Shannon block it each time. One more shot to her right, his breath held as she dove for it.

Close. So fucking close...

He didn't think, didn't stop to think, was only reacting. That's all he had time to do: rely on his instinct and react. He lunged forward, swiped at the puck with the flat of his stick just as Shannon moved to cover it—

And caught her in the wrist with the edge of his blade, hard.

He ignored the flashing light, the horn signaling the goal, the boos of the crowd filling the arena. He dropped his stick and bent over, reaching for her—

She jumped to her feet, brown eyes flashing in anger as she threw her helmet to the ice. "What the fuck do you think you're doing?"

"I didn't—"

She lunged forward, both of her hands pushing against his chest hard enough to cause him to stumble. "Don't ever fucking get in my crease like that again. What the fuck do you think you're doing?"

"Shannon, I—"

She wasn't listening. And holy shit, she looked like she was ready to tear him a new one. And if this had been a real game, he'd expect nothing less. If this was a real game, they'd be two seconds away from a major brawl.

And maybe they were because her teammates were suddenly surrounding her, pushing him away. Taylor was waving her arms at the ref, getting in his face and yelling about slashing and goalie interference.

Caleb moved closer, looked down when another hand shoved him in the chest. It was Sammie, the petite, quiet, newlywed. Only not so quiet as she jammed a finger in his face.

"Back off!"

Holy fucking shit, they were out for blood. Caleb opened his mouth, slammed it shut when he realized he had no idea what to say. This shit didn't happen in real games.

Yeah, because instead of all this verbal back-and-forth, they'd be fighting. And that so wasn't going to happen. Not here, not tonight.

Someone yanked on the sleeve of his jersey, tugging him back. He looked over his shoulder, frowned at the wide smile on Jaxon's face as he led him toward the bench. "Dude, they're out for your blood."

"It was an accident. I didn't mean—"

"Bullshit. You meant it. I just hope the fuck it was worth it."

"What the hell is that supposed to be mean?"

Jaxon stopped, right there at center ice, and leveled such a look of incredulity at him that Caleb actually considered skating away. "Was that goal so fucking important that you actually slashed your fucking girlfriend?"

"I didn't—"

"The hell you didn't." He nodded toward the giant screen hanging above them, at the larger-than-life slow-motion replay. Caleb watched, his stomach twisting each time they showed the play from different angles.

"I wasn't thinking—"

"No shit."

Caleb clenched his jaw, brushing off the guilt. "It's no different than what I'd do if we were playing anyone else. It's a game, that's how you play it."

"Hey, asshole. This is an *exhibition* game. It doesn't count. And there's something more important than what the fuck is showing on the scoreboard. Maybe if you weren't so fucking focused on winning all the time, you'd realize that."

"What are you talking about?"

"Just what I said." Jaxon shook his head in disgust and skated over to the bench. Caleb slowly followed, wondering what the fuck he meant.

Had he gone overboard? Yeah, probably. He'd lost his perspective for a split-second, had acted on intuition and instinct, like he would in any other game. Yeah, okay, maybe he'd gone a bit more than overboard, but he really hadn't been thinking, had forgotten it was Shannon in the net, had focused solely on tying the game.

And he had—the officials were letting the goal stand. Caleb nodded, climbed over the boards and dropped to the bench. But there was no congratulations, no pats on the back. Even the crowd seemed less than enthusiastic about the goal.

What the fuck was that all about?

Caleb reached for a water bottle, shot a stream into his mouth and started to spit off to the side when he noticed Shannon skating toward the bench. Her left arm was held loosely against her chest, her jaw tight with anger and frustration.

Fuck. Oh fuck. No, she wasn't hurt. She couldn't be hurt.

He jumped to his feet, pushed past his teammates to reach the glass partition dividing the two benches. He started to lean over the boards, to call out to her, but Donovan pulled him back.

It didn't matter, not when Shannon shot him a withering look laced with disgust. Regret churned in his stomach, twisting it inside out.

"Shannon—"

She simply turned away, ignoring him as she headed into the tunnel. The Blades' backup goalie, Karly Durant, headed to the net, taking Shannon's place. Caleb didn't care, all he cared about was seeing Shannon, making sure she was okay.

"Let it go, Johnson. Give her time to cool off." Coach Donovan's voice was low, meant for his ears only.

"I just want—"

"And I said let it go. She needs time to cool off. And you need time to think about what the hell you did out there."

"I didn't—"

"Johnson, do me a favor. Just sit the fuck down and think." Donovan turned away, effectively dismissing him. Caleb hesitated then moved back to the bench, trying to understand what the fuck Coach was talking about.

He was still trying to figure it out when the game ended, the Banners winning three-to-two. The handshake line was little more than a blur, the same with the quick meeting in the locker room, followed by a hasty shower. Everyone was talking about heading to the Maypole—not just the Banners, but a few of the Blades as well. Caleb brushed off the invitations. He already had plans, plans that included Shannon and nobody else.

He just needed to find her first.

That part was easy. She was just coming out of the locker room for the visiting team, her gear bag and a small duffle slung over her shoulder. He glanced at her wrist but couldn't tell if it was bandaged because the sleeve of her coat hung past it. She wasn't cradling it, though. That must be a good sign.

He hurried up to catch her, wondering where she was going when he knew she had seen him. Hadn't she? Maybe she hadn't, maybe she'd been too busy listening to Taylor to notice him. He moved in front of her, turning around and walking backward because she wasn't stopping.

"Hey. How's the wrist?"

"Fine." Her voice was short, the word clipped and a little frosty. He tossed a curious glance at Taylor then kept talking.

"So. Good game, huh?"

Shannon finally stopped, anger flashing in her eyes as she stared up at him. "Yeah. Fan-fucking-tastic. You won. Happy?"

"I—" He paused, frowning. "Are you actually

pissed we won?"

"No, Caleb. Not even close."

"Then what am I missing? Because you look pissed."

"You think?"

"I don't get it. Why are you angry?"

"*Why?* You really have to ask me why? After that fucking cheap shot—"

"It was an accident. I didn't mean—"

"Yeah. Sure you didn't." She tried to move past him but he blocked her.

"Shannon, it was an accident."

"Maybe you should watch the replay again. Really watch it."

Caleb swallowed, his gaze shooting to Taylor for assistance. She simply stared at him, saying nothing. He looked back at Shannon, not bothering to hide his confusion. "You don't honestly think I slashed you on purpose, do you? It was an accident, Shannon. I got carried away—"

"You were pissed."

"What the hell are you talking about? I wasn't pissed. I was just playing hockey, like I always do. It got physical. It wasn't deliberate."

"Really?" She stepped forward, anger flashing in her eyes. "Are you honestly saying you weren't pissed that we were beating you?"

"I wasn't *pissed*, no. A little frustrated maybe—"

"Like I said, you should watch the replay." She tried to step past him once more, but he blocked her again. Impatience and irritation—and yes, maybe even a little anger—were bubbling to the surface and he pushed them away, tamped them down.

"It's a game, Shannon. It gets physical. You know

that—"

"Is that why you think I'm angry? Because it got physical?"

"Aren't you?"

"No, I'm not." A muscle jumped in her clenched jaw, finally stopped when she took a deep breath and let it out—slow, like she was struggling for control. "It was the look on your face, Caleb. You were pissed we were winning and you were going to do anything to make sure that didn't happen."

"That's not true."

"Bullshit." The word came out in a sharp hiss, forced through clenched teeth.

"I can't believe we're even talking about this. Yeah, maybe I forgot myself for a second. That doesn't mean—"

"Tell me, Caleb. Why were you pissed? Because you were down by one? Or because you were being beaten by a bunch of women?"

"What the hell is that supposed to mean?"

"You heard me. I've seen you play, remember? How many times have you guys been down by one? By more than one? Especially this season. And not once—ever—have you gone after another player like you did out there. So tell me, Caleb: why? What were you so fucking pissed about?"

"I wasn't—" He snapped his mouth closed, shook his head and ran a hand over his face. *Had* he gone overboard? Yes, he'd been angry, filled with disbelief. But would that have pushed him to do something on purpose? To deliberately go after Shannon? No, he didn't believe it. *Couldn't* believe it.

His gaze darted to Taylor, wondering why she was still standing there, still listening to every single word.

Didn't she know he'd prefer some privacy? Yeah, probably. But this was Taylor so he shouldn't be surprised.

He turned to the side and leaned closer to Shannon, lowering his voice. "Listen, can we talk about this later? Grab some dinner and go back to my place like we planned?"

"Yeah, that's not happening."

"But—"

"Forget it, Caleb. I'm done." She started to push past him. He caught her arm, quickly dropped it at the withering expression on her face.

"I thought—"

"You thought wrong. I'm done. *We're* done. Over." She readjusted her grip on the bag then stormed off, not once looking back. Caleb watched as she disappeared around the corner, disbelief and anger mingling in his gut.

And below that, something else. Something that cut deep, deeper than he could have imagined: hurt. Confusion. A sense of loss he didn't quite understand. And none of it made sense. That was it? She was walking away, just like that? Calling it quits?

Because of a fucking *accident*?

He turned, nearly knocking Taylor over in his hurry to get away. She stepped back and he expected her to give him shit, too. To say something caustic and biting or sarcastic. What he didn't expect was the understanding in her eyes—or the pity.

"Sucks, doesn't it?"

Caleb shook his head, thought about pretending he had no idea what she was talking about then, for reasons he didn't understand, changed his mind. "I don't get it. I don't know what I did, Tay-Tay."

She watched him for a long minute, her whiskey-colored eyes sizing him up. Making him feel small. Inadequate. He expected her to walk away, to not say a word—and she almost did. But she must have changed her mind at the last second because she spun around, her gaze still filled with pity.

"You need to watch the replay, Caleb. And I mean *really* watch it. Watch your expression during the play. Hell, watch your expression throughout the entire game. And if that doesn't answer your question, then you don't deserve her."

Chapter
TWENTY-THREE

"You going to sit there and fucking mope all night?"

Caleb ignored Jaxon's question and kept staring into his untouched mug of beer. Why the fuck was he even here? He wasn't in the mood to hang out at the Maypole, wasn't in the mood to hang out with the team while they commiserated yet another loss. How many in a row was this now? Four? Five? He frowned, counting back. Yup, five. Five losses in a row—because he wasn't counting that clusterfuck of a game that they won against the Blades four days ago. Yeah, they had won the game. So fucking what?

He'd lost a lot more in the process.

Caleb had finally watched the game film, an exercise that had left him sick to his stomach. When the fuck had winning become the only thing that mattered? When the fuck had he become so consumed by winning that he'd willingly cross the line and do whatever he had to do in order to win?

Watching his face, his expressions, his *anger* staring back at him from the screen—it was like watching a totally different person. He hadn't recognized himself at first, had refused to believe that was *actually* him. Jaw clenched, anger and frustration flashing in his eyes as he swung his stick at Shannon.

Swung? No, not even close. He'd been *hacking* at her wrist with the blade of his stick. Not just once, like he'd first thought. Shannon had actually covered the puck; the play should have been stopped. But the furious stranger on the screen didn't seem to care, had just kept hacking at her wrist, over and over until she finally moved her hand and he shoved the puck across the line.

Why the fuck didn't he remember it that way? He had told himself, at the time, that he was simply acting on instinct. That he was doing what he'd do in any other game. That he was simply playing like usual. Why did it take actually watching the footage on the screen to see all the little details he had no memory of?

Talk about fucking up.

He started to raise the cold mug to his mouth for a long swallow, needing something to wash down the taste of bitterness filling his mouth. Beer sloshed over the thick rim, drenching his wrist when Jaxon elbowed him in the arm.

"Well? Are you?"

Caleb ignored the damp cuff of his shirt, ignored the small puddle of beer gathering on the polished bar in front of him. And he tried to ignore Jaxon as he finally took that first swallow—except the other man wasn't taking the hint.

"You need to come sit with us, stop hanging over

here by yourself."

"Not in the mood."

"Yeah, no shit. Ask me if I care."

"Doesn't matter if you do or don't. I'm not in the mood."

"You can mope over there just as well as you can over here. Come on." Jaxon tugged his arm, trying to get him to move. "Join the crowd. Get to know the new goalie."

Caleb swallowed back a sigh with more beer then looked over at the noisy crowd in the far corner. Luke Connelly was gone, traded to Columbus then immediately sent down to the minors, where he would no doubt disappear into oblivion. Corbin Gauthier had been picked up from Colorado in exchange for a draft pick and who knew what else, had flown in two days ago to join the team. Nobody knew what to make of that, what to make of *him*. He had played for the Banners once before, leaving when Vegas had picked him up in the expansion eight years ago. And there was some kind of history between him and Coach Donovan, some kind of tension nobody understood.

Not that Caleb cared. Right now, he didn't care about much of anything.

Jaxon swore under his breath then finally sat on the empty stool beside Caleb. He leaned forward, motioned for a beer, then settled in. Getting comfortable—like he was prepared to sit there all night and bug the living shit out of Caleb. Until Caleb gave in.

Or until he just got up and left.

"Why don't you just fucking call her and apologize and get it over with?"

Caleb grunted, the sound filled with every ounce

of disbelief he could muster. Apologize? It would take a hell of a lot more than an apology to fix this. He could apologize until he was blue in the face and it wouldn't help. Why the hell should Shannon forgive him, when he couldn't even forgive himself?

"You're not even going to try to call her, are you?"

"Why, when I know she won't answer the phone?"

"How do you know if you don't try?"

Caleb twisted on the stool, leveling a flat glare at Jaxon. "I did try." And he had—at least two dozen times. And every single time, his call had gone straight to voicemail. Had she blocked his number? Probably.

He'd even gone over to her place but she wasn't home. Her brother had come out while Caleb was standing in the driveway and made it very clear that he wasn't welcome there. That Shannon wanted nothing to do with him. That he should leave and not bother coming back.

Caleb didn't miss the silent *or else* tacked onto the end of that last suggestion.

"Then try one more time."

"What good would it do?"

Jaxon made a little humming noise then slowly nodded. "Fine. I'll call her myself."

And damn if the asshole didn't pull the phone from his pocket and pretend he was dialing a number. Except maybe he wasn't pretending, maybe he was really doing it—

Caleb reached for the phone, his fingers slipping off the sides as Jaxon held it out of his reach. "I don't need you intervening for me."

"Who the fuck said anything about intervening? I'm calling to ask her out. Shannon's hot, man. And funny. And—"

Caleb's hand shot out, closed around the other man's collar and twisted. "Do it and I will fuck you up."

Jaxon didn't even flinch. He simply stared at Caleb, his dark blue eyes totally void of emotion. Several seconds marched by, quiet and tense. Then he reached up and slowly, calmly, pushed Caleb's hand away.

"Don't ever grab me again." There was something in the other man's low voice, an eerie calmness that made Caleb sit back with a frown—and more than a little wariness. An apology hovered on the tip of his tongue but before he could get it out, Jaxon's demeanor changed. In the blink of an eye, he was the same man Caleb had known for two years: the laughing jokester, the one who always saw the silver lining.

Had Caleb imagined that lethal stillness? Had he read more into it than what had been there?

Fuck. Maybe he was just losing his mind. Maybe he was so caught up in the realization of how big an ass he really was that he was starting to see things.

"You can't have it both ways, Johnson. If you like her, if you really think there's something there, then fucking call her and apologize. Better yet, go see her and grovel. I've heard that works."

"Like she'd even take the time out to see me."

"See her. Don't see her. Apologize or don't apologize. Doesn't bother me one way or the other." Jaxon slid off the stool with a careless shrug. "But don't cry foul when someone else decides to move in and she moves on."

Caleb watched him as he walked away, wondering what the hell the words meant. Were they a warning? Was there someone else interested in Shannon? His gaze moved to the corner of the room, where loud conversation and laughter rang out. Had one of his teammates already asked her out? More than one of them had made a comment about Shannon's looks, about how they wouldn't mind getting to know her better. Like Shane, all those weeks ago. Like Jaxon, just now. Were there others?

Why the hell wouldn't there be? It wasn't just Shannon's looks, but her attitude, too. Her sense of humor. Her sarcasm. And yeah, even her talent in the net. Apparently, he wasn't the only one who appreciated that—even if he had been the only one having a meltdown on the ice during the exhibition game.

And hell, could he blame any one of them if they *did* ask her out? He had fucked up. Totally. Royally. Publicly. Shannon deserved better. She deserved to be with someone who wasn't so fucking insecure around her.

He looked over at his teammates once more, anger simmering inside him at the mere thought of anyone else being with Shannon. Not just his teammates...*anyone*. The image of Shannon laughing with anyone else—of spending time with anyone else, of *being* with anyone else—curled his stomach. The bitterness of loss filled him, churning his gut until he wanted to heave.

Fuck.

Fuck.

He had to make this right. Had to apologize.

What was it Jaxon had said?

Grovel.

The idea that he would *grovel* for anything would have made him laugh a few weeks ago. But not now. Not anymore.

And if that's what it took, then so be it. He'd grovel. Hell, he'd do more than grovel. He'd do whatever it took to win her back.

Caleb stared into the half-empty mug and frowned. Yes, he'd do whatever he had to do.

But something told him it wouldn't be enough. It would never be enough.

chapter
TWENTY-FOUR

As far as distractions went, Shannon had put up with worse.

When she was younger, playing on the same team as her brother, the guys—the *boys*—from the other team would taunt her. Call her names. Get in her face or deliberately get too close, crowding her. Trying to distract her, to make her lose focus enough to miss a save. The first few times, it had worked. Not because she had been upset—although she could reluctantly admit now that part of her was—but because she had been angry. Furious. All she wanted to do was play hockey, to be a goalie. They didn't torment the other goalies the way they did her. Why was she different? Why couldn't they just let her play?

The name-calling and taunting didn't stop, even when she got older. Instead, it became more personal, almost threatening. Not by everyone. For the most part, she wasn't treated any differently. She was just another goalie, except she had long hair and was starting to fill out in ways the other guys on her team weren't. She'd have a locker room all to herself because they weren't little kids anymore, because it wasn't appropriate for her to be in the same locker room with her teammates when they were changing. She was different—but she was still one of the guys.

For the most part.

As for the small-minded jocks who couldn't see past her looks—she'd simply smile at them, laughing when they got flustered, then put them in their places the only way she knew how: by beating them on the ice.

She thought the time for the juvenile tactics was over, that it had been over for years. That was just one of the reasons why Caleb's stunt last week hurt so much. Not because he was upset about losing—Shannon could understand that, could even relate to that.

What she couldn't understand was the anger etched so clearly on his face as he crowded her. Shoved her. As he slashed at her wrist, repeatedly. He had reminded her so much of all those boys who taunted her, teased her, convinced she couldn't play the game because she was a girl.

Who became angry and threatening when they learned not only could she play—but she just happened to be better than they were. She knew Caleb was competitive; what she didn't know, not until that exhibition game, was that he also happened to be just like those boys from years ago.

That he was insecure. That his ego couldn't let him accept that maybe, just maybe, they were on equal footing.

Someone yelled, catching her attention. Shannon blinked, her gaze darting to the action on the ice just ahead of her. Holy shit, what the hell was she doing? Standing here, getting lost in her thoughts when there was a fucking game going on right in front of her.

She exhaled, forced all thoughts and memories from her mind as she focused on the game. Her gaze darted to the puck, watched as one of the players from Philly dodged around Sammie, moving closer. There was something almost desperate about her actions, about the speed she was building as she approached the net.

Shannon narrowed her eyes, bracing herself for the collision even as she prepared to block the shot. They happened almost simultaneously—the puck hurtling toward her, hitting the pocket of her glove with a sharp thud just as the body drove into her chest.

Shannon tossed the puck to the side, away from the net, then crashed backward, arms and legs tangling together with the other woman's as the net slid into the boards behind her. The air rushed from her lungs, leaving her breathless for an agonizing few seconds. A shrill whistle split the air. Hands reached for her, pulling and yanking and tugging until she was finally resting on all fours, sucking frigid air into her struggling lungs.

More hands reached for her, pulling her to her feet. Voices, bombarding her with questions.

Are you okay?
Did you get hurt?
Can you breathe?

Shannon nodded, shook her head, shrugged. Yes. No.

Maybe.

She bent over at the waist and gulped, sucking in more air until finally, thank God, her lungs stopped seizing and started working on their own.

A hand gripped her elbow and she looked up. Taylor was watching her, concern etched on her frowning face. "Need a minute?"

Shannon shook her head and finally straightened, shrugged off Shannon's hold. "No. I'm good."

Taylor shifted, looking up in the stands, then turned back to Shannon. "Are you sure about that?"

"Yeah. Positive." Shannon reiterated her words with a sharp nod, doing her best not to look over.

Doing her best to ignore Caleb.

It had worked, for the most part. There had been a brief moment of confusion and surprise—of anger— when she first came out on the ice and saw him sitting in the stands with a few of his teammates. She felt his eyes on her, had to force herself not to look, even though she wanted to shout and scream and ask him why he was here. But only for the first few minutes. Once the game started, she put him from her mind. Ignoring him. Forgetting he was here.

Right up until a few minutes ago, when Caleb's presence had somehow mingled with unbidden memories of her childhood games. Distracting her, when she couldn't afford to be distracted.

She nodded at Taylor again, then nudged her in the side. "I'm good. Stop worrying."

"You sure?"

"Abso-fucking-lutely." Shannon adjusted her helmet. "Come on, we've got a power play. Let's finish this thing so we can go grab some food."

Taylor hesitated then finally nodded, a crooked smile on her face. "Sounds like a plan."

Five minutes later, the game was over and they were back in their musty locker room, celebrating another win. How long could they keep the streak going?

As soon as the thought entered her mind, Shannon pushed it away. One game at a time. They couldn't think in terms of streaks—if they did, they might jinx it.

Coach Reynolds finished up her post-game speech then caught Shannon's attention. "Wiley, don't forget your interview after cleaning up."

Shannon's excitement immediately dimmed. Shit. How had she forgotten? TR was out in the stands somewhere, waiting for her.

Maybe she could postpone it again, come up with some excuse. Tell TR she wasn't feeling good, or that she had other plans. That wouldn't exactly be a lie—she did have other plans: food and drinks with the team. That counted, right?

Except Shannon had been blowing TR off ever since the exhibition game a week ago. She didn't want to finish the interview. Didn't want to answer any more questions. Didn't want to take a chance that TR might ask about—

No, TR wouldn't do that. Shannon was fairly sure of that. But she still didn't feel like finishing the interview. Maybe she could convince TR to pick someone else. Like Dani. Or Sydney. Maybe Maddison. Anyone but her.

That wasn't possible, though. Yes, she could probably get out of it if she wanted to—she had a feeling TR would understand. But the idea left a hollowness in the pit of her stomach. She wasn't a quitter, never had been. She couldn't start now.

Shannon hurried through the shower, drying off and getting dressed in simple black pants and a tailored blouse that didn't need to be tucked in. She didn't bother with her hair, just simply pulled the damp length back into a ponytail. Then she grabbed her bag and followed everyone else out of the locker room—

And froze when she saw Caleb standing there against the boards, waiting for her.

A dozen different emotions churned inside her, none of them good. She wanted to ask him why he was here. Wanted to ask him why he kept calling, why he showed up at her place the other day. She wanted to tell him to leave her alone.

Most of all, she wanted to ask him why he had acted the way he had last week. Why? She still didn't understand. Or rather, she was afraid she understood too well.

She did none of those things. Instead, she turned away, ignoring him as she searched for TR. Caleb didn't take the hint because he followed her, his hand reaching for her. She shot him a withering look and his hand dropped to his side. But he kept staring at her, those deep green eyes filled with remorse. With loneliness. With sorrow.

She almost snorted. Yeah, she was definitely seeing things.

"Shannon, can we talk?"

"No."

Surprise flashed across his face and she almost laughed—except it wasn't funny. None of this was funny.

"Shannon—"

"Can you just leave me alone? I have nothing to say to you."

"Fine. Don't say anything. I'm just asking you to listen."

She hesitated, feeling herself giving in. And how totally stupid would that be? "I'm busy. I'm meeting TR—"

"She had to step out for a phone call. She said to tell you she'd be a few minutes."

Was he telling the truth? She didn't know. And she wouldn't put it past him to ask TR to disappear for a few minutes, not if it would help him get what he wanted.

Shannon looked around, not quite willing to believe him. There was no sign of TR, not up in the bleachers, not by the benches near the front doors. But she did see Mac, leaning against the wall, arms crossed in front of his broad chest, a scowl on his face. The man seemed to be everywhere TR was lately, always hovering in the background, always watching.

Shannon swallowed back a sigh and readjusted the grip on her gear bag. She could either walk over to Mac and wait with him, or she could give Caleb the few minutes he asked for.

If Mac wasn't so freaking intimidating, if he didn't scare her just the tiniest bit...

As an excuse, it was fairly lame—even if it was mostly true. But if she was going to be honest with herself, she had to admit she was curious to hear whatever Caleb had to say. What excuse would he give her? Or would he try to spin it somehow, to defend his actions—his *attitude*?

She clenched her jaw and turned to face him, meeting his gaze with her own direct one. "Fine. You have until TR comes back."

Relief flashed across his face as he moved toward

her, reaching for her once more. He stopped, hesitating, then pointed to the bleachers to their right. "Can we sit down and—"

"No. If you have something to say, just say it."

He nodded. Jammed his hands into the back pockets of his jeans. Nodded again and glanced around. He finally let out a heavy sigh and met her impatient gaze. "You're okay after that hit? It looked like you had the wind knocked out of you."

"Seriously? That's what you wanted to say?" Shannon shook her head and took a step back, throwing his words from last week back at him. "Yeah, Caleb. I'm fine. It's a tough sport. It gets physical sometimes. I'm a big girl, I can handle it."

Was it her imagination, or did he actually flinch in discomfort?

"That's not—I know you can. You're a damn good player. A great goalie."

"For a woman, you mean."

Emotion flashed in his eyes. Anger. Impatience. Regret. All swirling together in those deep green depths, threatening to draw her in. Caleb stepped closer, looking down at her. Was he trying to use his height to deliberately intimidate her? Yeah, like that would work. She squared her shoulders and tilted her chin up, refusing to give even an inch.

"No, not *for a woman*. For anyone." There was a steely determination in his voice, almost a hint of a bite that she didn't understand. Was he pissed because he had to finally admit it? She wanted to ask him, opened her mouth to do just that when he finally sighed and stepped back, his shoulders slumping. "And I'm sorry."

"Fine. You're sorry." She slung the bag over her other shoulder and started to walk away but he reached for her, closed his hand around hers and tugged.

"Shannon—"

She pulled her hand from his, ignoring the scalding heat of his touch, ignoring the pleading in his eyes. "What is it, Caleb? What? You said you were sorry. Fine. Your conscience is clear. Now leave."

"I don't want to leave. Not until we talk."

"What else is there to talk about?"

"I—" He took a deep breath, ran one hand down his face and along the back of his neck as he stared up at the dusty steel beams above them. He exhaled, lowered his head and stared at her. "I'm an ass. And you were right. I was pissed that we were losing. Not just losing, but losing to *you*. To all of you. I didn't want to believe you guys were better than us. *Couldn't* believe it. And when you blocked that shot—"

He paused, exhaled deeply and looked around. Shannon followed his gaze but there was nothing around them. Her teammates were gone and there was no sign of the two guys who had been in the stands with Caleb earlier. Not even a sign of TR. The rink was empty now, except for Mac, who hadn't moved from his spot by the door.

Shannon looked back at Caleb. His discomfort was obvious, from the way he kept shifting his weight from foot-to-foot, to the way his gaze darted from hers to the floor and back again.

"I kept telling myself I was pissed because you guys were a new team. That you didn't have the experience we have. That you hadn't been playing as long as we have. But that wasn't it. You were right: I was pissed that we were losing to a bunch of women. And I'm sorry. Sorrier than you'll ever know."

Did she believe him? Yes, she did. His discomfort

was too real, the edge to his voice too rugged to be fake. And she had a feeling that the admission cost him more than she could ever know.

But it didn't change anything. It didn't change her anger, her frustration and disappointment.

Her hurt.

Because what he'd done *had* hurt. Not physically—her wrist was fine; the collision tonight had actually hurt worse. The pain she felt was emotional, not physical.

Because Caleb was no different than some of those boys she had played with growing up. No different than any other man who turned tail and ran because they were intimidated by her. Because their egos couldn't handle it. She thought he was different and had foolishly let herself get too close, had opened up in a way she never had before. She didn't think she'd be this hurt if it had turned out he was playing her, like she had first suspected.

She swallowed against the lump of emotion forming in her throat and forced herself to nod. She couldn't manage a smile, not even close. "Thank you for the apology. Now I have to go—"

"Go? But I thought—"

"Thought what, Caleb? That you'd apologize and that would be it?"

"No, but—" He hesitated, glanced over her shoulder then met her eyes. "So that's it? You just walk away, like we never happened?"

"Caleb—"

"I don't get it. I was an ass. I know that. But can't we talk about it? Can't we at least try?"

"Try?" She cleared her throat, hoping he didn't hear the emotion in her voice. "You mean until the next time your ego takes a hit from something I do? Because it will, Caleb. I am who I am. I can't help that, and I'm not going to change just to make you feel better."

"I'm not asking you to."

"Not yet, no. But you will." Because they did. They always did.

"You don't know that."

"Don't I?"

He stepped closer, his eyes flashing with a hint of hurt. No, not hurt—disappointment. But why? What did he have to be disappointed about?

"No, Shannon, you don't know that. I'm not like those guys you've scared off in the past."

"Scared off?" She laughed, the sound brittle and forced. "Oh, you mean the ones I intimidated? The ones with the fragile egos?"

"I'm not like them."

"But you are, Caleb." She blinked, silently cursing the unwanted moisture burning her eyes. "You just did a better job of hiding it than most."

chapter
TWENTY-FIVE

Shannon spun on her heels and walked away, her steps hurried.

She couldn't believe it—she was walking away, even though part of her screamed to stop. To let Caleb talk. To trust his words and believe he really did want to try. But she couldn't. She was afraid to, could admit that to herself at least. Afraid of what he made her feel. Afraid that the hurt she felt now would be a hundred times worse the next time.

And there *would* be a next time, she had no doubt about that. No matter how much he insisted otherwise, Caleb was just like all those other guys: the boys who didn't know what to make of her and the men who couldn't handle a strong woman.

So she walked away, no matter how hard it was to do.

Caleb called after her, started following her—she

could hear him behind her. But Mac was suddenly there, his scarred face grim and foreboding as he stepped around her, using his hulking body as a shield.

TR approached her, sympathy and understanding etched on her face. "Are you okay? Do you want to do this another time?"

Shannon pulled in a shaky breath and wiped one hand across her eyes. "No, I'm good. Let's get this done and over with."

"Are you sure?"

"Yeah. Positive." She glanced over her shoulder, saw Mac still standing at her back, making sure Caleb didn't come after her. "He's, uh, he's pretty handy to have around, huh?"

TR frowned, impatience flashing in her pale blue eyes. "He has his moments. When he's not being a pain in my ass."

"Relationships suck, don't they?"

"Relationships?" TR's eyes widened, then she shook her head on a soft laugh. "There is no relationship. Not with us."

"But—I thought you guys were dating."

"Nope." TR glanced over at Mac and Shannon didn't miss the disappointment that flashed in her eyes. "Just friends. Or something. I guess."

Shannon had no idea what to say to that so, for once, she kept her mouth shut. TR led the way back to the bleachers and took a seat. Shannon dropped her gear bag and sat next to her, watching as the other woman pulled a notepad and several pens from her tote bag.

"No tape recorder?" Shannon regretted the question as soon as it left her mouth.

"Not yet, no." TR shifted on the bench, crossed

one long leg over the other, then balanced the notepad on her knee. And then she just sat there, her head tilted to the side, watching.

And watching some more.

Shannon shifted, glanced over her shoulder, then looked down at herself, wondering if her shirt was buttoned the wrong way or if she had somehow spilled something all down the front.

"Is, um, is something wrong?"

"Can I ask you a question?"

"Isn't that what you're supposed to do?"

"This one's personal."

Shannon sat back, suddenly eager to put more distance between them. "How personal?"

"It probably crosses some boundaries."

"Okaaaaay. Do I have to answer?"

The barest hint of a smile curled TR's full mouth. "Of course not."

"Then ask away."

"What's really going on with you and Caleb?"

Shannon didn't even hesitate, just simply waved her hand like she was shooing away an annoying gnat. "Next question."

"I was just curious because you two seemed to really be into each other at Sammie's wedding."

"Yeah, well, things changed."

"Like?"

Shannon dropped her gaze, suddenly preoccupied with a piece of invisible lint on her pants leg. She toyed with the material, rubbing her finger against it. Back and forth, back and forth. Then she exhaled, loudly, and looked back up.

Not quite able to meet TR's direct gaze.

Not quite able to hide her disappointment.

"Turns out his ego was more fragile than I thought it was."

"Meaning?"

"You were at the exhibition game. You saw what happened."

"I did, yes. But I'm not sure what that has to do with his ego."

"He got pissed because they were losing to a bunch of girls. Embarrassed. Couldn't handle it. He even admitted that tonight. To me. Out loud."

TR nodded but she didn't exactly look convinced. "I guess that will make next week's little show at the Banners' game awkward, huh?"

And shit. Shannon had completely forgotten about that. The Blades were scheduled to do another mini-scrimmage during the first intermission of the game. She had no idea why—this was their fourth one, at least. And it was a weeknight game, which meant she'd have to leave work early.

Maybe there was a way to get out of it. They didn't need her *and* Karly there, not really.

Except they kind of did because they didn't have a third back-up.

Shit.

She must have said the word out loud because TR leaned forward, her smile a little uncertain. "Does that mean it *won't* be awkward? Or it will?"

"It means it doesn't matter because I won't even see him. Which is fine by me."

"Because you want someone you don't intimidate."

"Yeah."

"Someone who supports what you do?"

"Of course."

"You're not really into social media, are you?"

Shannon frowned at the sudden change of topic. Maybe TR was starting the interview now and that was one of the questions. "Not really, no. I mean, I have accounts but I'm not on them much. Actually, I pretty much ignore them. It's too much of a time-suck and..." Her voice trailed off, her gaze moving to the phone TR was playing with. Oh God, it was the recorder. Shannon hated that recorder, hated knowing that every word she said would be stored somewhere forever.

TR turned the phone around so Shannon could see the screen. "Then you haven't seen this."

It was a statement, not a question. Shannon shook her head, frowning as she leaned closer to the screen. It was footage from one of their games. They were playing Richmond, which meant it was from at least two weeks ago. And the footage was taken from the stands, not from behind the net, where the team had the video set up for the live streaming.

Shannon watched as the camera zoomed in on Taylor, speeding toward the net. A second later, she scored. The camera angle went a little crazy for a few seconds, as if whoever was filming had jumped up with everyone else to celebrate. Then Caleb's face filled the screen, the dimple flashing in his cheek as he grinned.

"Did you guys see that? Now that's how you shoot a puck. You guys have no idea what you're missing by not being here."

There was a break in the footage, then another shot, this one of Shannon making a save. Caleb's face filled the screen again, that broad smile still on his face.

"That is one of the best goalies I have ever seen play. And I would kill to have her play for us because she runs circles around Luke and Dan. Sorry guys, you know it's true. And everyone else, hands-off. She's mine."

Shannon's jaw dropped. When had this even happened? She remembered the game, remembered Caleb being there, but she had no idea he had been filming anything.

She snapped her mouth closed and shook her head. "So what? That was before Sammie's wedding, before the exhibition game. It doesn't mean anything—"

"He posted this, too. Actually, he reposted it. From the Blades' media page." TR tapped something on the screen then flipped the phone back to her. It was the shot of that crazy-ass save she made more than a month ago, when Sammie had jokingly called her the limbo queen. Above the video link was a short post, just five quick words: *Save of the decade! Wow!*

The post had thousands of likes and shares.

"How come I never saw any of this?"

"Caleb is great at posting stuff, but he doesn't tag anyone. Unless you actually follow him, you'd never see it."

"That still doesn't mean anything. Two posts, big deal. And they were from before the exhibition game so—"

"There's more than two. There are dozens. He even posted right after the exhibition game. And tonight, too, talking about...well, you should probably just watch for yourself." TR grinned and shoved the phone back in her bag. "And speaking of the exhibition game, I want to hear all about it. What you were thinking. How it felt. How you came up with the strategy—"

"Stop." Shannon held her hand up, interrupting TR's sudden stream of questions. "Wait. You can't do that."

"Do what?"

"Start telling me something then stop and change the subject and tell me to look at it later. You can't do that."

"But I thought you didn't care."

"I—" Shannon snapped her mouth closed, frowning when she noticed the other woman's knowing smile. "Did Caleb put you up to this?"

"No."

"Taylor?"

"No."

"Sammie?"

TR laughed and shook her head. A few strands of her long, dark hair fell in her face and she brushed them away. "No. Nobody put me up to anything. I just thought you might want to see them."

"Why?"

"I just thought you would, that's all." TR leaned forward and placed one slender hand on Shannon's arm. "You're right, Caleb did act like an ass that night. But at least he realized it and apologized."

"That doesn't mean it won't happen again."

"Doesn't mean it will, either."

Shannon sighed and turned away, her gaze skimming across the empty rink. The deserted seats. The scratched glass and freshly-painted boards. She didn't know what to think, how to feel, what to make of anything. Was she being too hard on Caleb? Expecting too much? Making more of it than it really was?

Sammie thought she was, thought she should talk to Caleb and work things out. But Sammie was a newlywed, still riding the emotional high from remarrying her husband. She thought *everyone* should be in love.

But even Taylor thought she should try talking to Caleb and couldn't understand why Shannon was ignoring his calls. Taylor, of all people. Taylor, who had been convinced Caleb was simply trying to play her. Taylor, who had tried to warn Shannon away from Caleb in the first place. Shannon had even thrown that in her face, accusing her of being a hypocrite. Taylor had simply laughed and said she was wrong.

But she wasn't. Not really. No, Caleb hadn't been playing her, but the end result was the same so that didn't matter.

Did it?

Shannon sighed and turned back to TR, not surprised to see the other woman watching her. Studying her. Probably seeing too much.

"Let me guess: you think I'm being too hard on him, too, just like everyone else."

"I'm not saying that, not exactly."

"Then what are you saying?"

"I saw you two together at the wedding. I watched how you were with each other. I just think you'd regret it if you didn't at least talk to him more. That's all."

That's all.

TR said it like it was no big deal, like talking to Caleb wouldn't open her up to even more hurt. And that was the problem: she hadn't expected what he'd done to hurt, but it did. That's what scared her the most. If she didn't care, she wouldn't hurt. The fact that she hurt meant she cared.

More than she wanted to admit.

And that terrified her.

chapter
TWENTY-SIX

Shannon stood in the empty hallway, staring at the door and telling herself, once again, that she needed her head examined.

The impulse that had seized her more than two hours ago was suddenly gone, replaced by an even stronger urge to turn and run. How stupid was that? It was because of the strength of that stupid impulse that she was even here. How long had she tried to ignore it as she lay in bed, tossing and turning? Ten minutes? Twenty? No, longer than that.

It was a stupid idea, no matter how she looked at it. That apparently didn't matter because here she was, dressed in a sweatshirt and track pants and her freaking slippers because the impulse had actually driven her from her bed and out of her small apartment above her brother's garage before she realized that wearing slippers with track pants probably wasn't a very smart fashion choice.

Giving in to that impulse wasn't a very smart choice, either, but here she was.

And all she wanted to do was turn around and run back home.

Shannon ran a hand through her hair, frowning when her fingers encountered a few tangles. Holy hell, she hadn't even thought to run a brush through her hair. What had she been thinking?

She hadn't been, that was the problem.

Which was why she was standing in a deserted hallway in front of Caleb's door after midnight, when she should be home in bed. Asleep. Alone. She had to get up in five hours to go to work. She didn't need to be here, staring at a stupid door.

But she couldn't quite make herself turn around to leave. TR's words kept replaying in her mind: *I just think you'd regret it if you didn't at least talk to him more. That's all.* Shannon didn't want to think the other woman was right, didn't want to admit that maybe she had a point. But what if she did? What if Shannon *was* overreacting? What if she didn't at least try and talk to Caleb some more? What if...

Too many *what ifs*.

That was why she finally rolled out of bed and got dressed in the first thing her hands had wrapped around. *That* was why she hurried from her place so fast, she forgot to put shoes on.

And that was why she was still standing here like some kind of idiot, afraid to turn around and leave, but afraid to knock on that door.

A wave of frustration washed over her—frustration at herself, for being so indecisive. So uncertain. That wasn't like her. Why now? Why was she standing here, arguing with herself *now*?

Because she was afraid. Afraid of giving Caleb a second chance. Afraid of being hurt. Afraid of *not* taking a chance. Because what if she didn't, and it turned out there really could be something between them?

What if she *did*, and he turned out to be just like everyone else? What if he tried to change her then walked away when he realized he couldn't?

A little voice piped up inside her head. *But what if he's not like that?*

And that was the problem. That stupid little voice inside her head kept reminding her of all the fun they'd had the last two months. Taunting her with the memories. Reminding her that Caleb had never given any indication of wanting to change her. At all.

Except for the exhibition game, when he got so pissed that the Banners were losing to a bunch of *women*.

Wouldn't you be pissed, too, if you were losing?

Shannon told that stupid voice to shut up but it was too late. Would she be pissed? Yeah. She hated losing. Who didn't? But it wasn't the fact that the Banners had been losing that pissed Caleb off—it was *who* they had been losing to.

And she was abso-fucking-lutely losing her mind because she was still standing out in the hallway, arguing with herself.

Fine. She'd knock on the door, wait ten seconds. If he didn't answer, she'd turn around and go home.

She raised her hand, dropped it. Raised it again.

Dropped it again.

This was ridiculous. Caleb was probably asleep. His huge bedroom was on the second level of the sprawling waterfront condo, no way would he hear her knocking on the door. She'd just go home, come back later.

Maybe in a week or two, after she had time to really think this through. Or maybe she'd just call him. That would probably be better than just showing up unannounced. Safer.

No. She'd send a text. *That* would be the safest thing to do.

She nodded and turned around, willing her feet to carry her to the elevator. One foot in front of the other.

Except her feet weren't moving.

She swore under her breath, turned back to face the door. Paused, turned back around and actually managed to move. Just a few inches, but it was progress.

Then she stopped. Hesitated. Was she really going to just *quit*? She wasn't a quitter.

But this wasn't quitting. This was just being smart. Regrouping so she could come back later.

Or text him later.

Something.

Coward.

Shannon paused, her head tilted to the side. She really *was* losing it because she could have sworn she just heard that in stereo. It was the little voice inside her head, piping up once again.

But it was also deeper than usual. A little gruff, a little sleepy.

And it didn't just come from inside her head, it came from behind her.

Shannon spun around, surprise and embarrassment filling her at the same time. Caleb was leaning just inside the doorway, one bare shoulder propped against the frame. Tousled hair fell into deep green eyes. Those same eyes watched her, sleepy but still intense. Freezing her in place when all she wanted to do was run for cover.

She raised her chin a notch, forcing bravado into her voice. "I'm not a coward."

"Then why haven't you knocked yet?"

"Because I thought you'd be sleeping and I didn't want to disturb you."

"I *was* sleeping—"

"See? All the more reason for me to leave—"

"—Until they called me to let me know someone was coming up."

"Oh." Shit. She hadn't thought of that. Hadn't given the guy at the lobby desk any thought at all when she hurried past him with a wave, telling him she was going to see Caleb and wouldn't be long.

"They asked if they should come up and escort you back down."

"Oh." That made sense, if she stopped to think about it. Probably one of the perks of living here. "Did you tell them yes?"

"No." He stepped to the side and opened the door a little wider. "You coming in? Or are you going to run away?"

Shannon narrowed her eyes, told herself not to take the bait. "I wasn't running away."

"Looked like it to me."

"I told you, I figured you were sleeping and didn't want to bother you. I was going to come back later." She wasn't, but she wasn't about to admit that to him.

"I'm not, and you aren't. And you're here now so you might as well come in."

Dammit. Dammit, dammit, shit. She was stuck now. There was no way she could leave without looking like a coward.

But it was tempting. So tempting.

Shannon hesitated, but only for a second. Then she squared her shoulders and marched right past him, trying not to brush up against, trying to ignore the sleepy determination in his eyes, trying to ignore the expanse of flushed skin that heated her as she walked by. Why couldn't he have put on some clothes, instead of answering the door in nothing but a pair of loose gym shorts that were in danger of falling off his lean hips?

The door closed behind her with a soft click, plunging them into gray shadows broken only by the dim light spilling out from the kitchen. Caleb brushed past her, turning into that very kitchen. She heard another click and bright light spilled into the hallway.

She slowly followed him, heading straight for one of the stools sitting at the granite-topped island in the middle of the gleaming room. She pulled the stool out, climbed up, then propped her arms on the cold granite.

A bottle of water appeared at her elbow. Unfortunately, a hand was wrapped around the bottle. And that hand was attached to Caleb, who stood entirely too close to her.

"Nice shoes."

She didn't bother looking down, barely bothered looking at him. She simply smiled and nodded, like she always wore her slippers out when she visited people after midnight. "Thanks."

Caleb lowered himself onto the stool next to her. Too close. Crowding her. His bare leg brushed against hers and she wanted to move to the side, away from him. Away from his heat. But she couldn't, not without looking like she was trying to avoid him.

He propped his elbow on the counter and leaned forward, his face entering her peripheral vision. Again, too close. "So what brings you out this time of night?"

Shannon twisted the cap off the bottle, took a quick sip, then shrugged. "Oh, you know. Just driving around."

"Shannon." He leaned even closer, crowding her, and this time she did move. Just a few inches, so they weren't touching. It didn't work because he simply moved with her, closing the distance she had just put between them. He cupped her chin in his warm palm and eased her head to the side so she was facing him. Dark green eyes pierced hers, holding her in place, silently willing her not to look away. Not that she could, even if she wanted to. "Talk to me."

"I just..." Her voice trailed off, her mind dangerously blank. What had she come here to say? She didn't know, hadn't thought that far ahead. Not when the impulse to come see him had finally pushed her from her bed and out the door. Not during the drive over here. Not even when she had been standing outside his door, arguing with herself.

She took a deep breath and yanked her gaze from his, focusing on the granite countertop. Polished black, with swirling veins of white and gray. Soft, smooth. Cool beneath her fingers.

She pressed her hand flat against the surface, spread her fingers wide then drew them together. Again and again, until Caleb's hand closed over hers. Warm, heavy. He turned her hand over, cradling it in his before slowly threaded their fingers together. Then he gently squeezed, silently encouraging her.

Shannon kept staring at their joined hands. If she focused on them instead of the man sitting next to her, maybe she'd be able to get the words out. "I was always the oddball growing up. I never fit in with the girls, never understood why they wanted to play with dolls or dress-up when it was more fun running and climbing and getting dirty. But I never really fit in with the boys, either."

"Shannon—"

"It wasn't so bad when I was younger. We were just little kids, you know? But when I got older, the boys realized I was *different*. And *different* wasn't good." Shannon paused, raised the bottle to her mouth and took a long swallow. Caleb didn't say anything, just sat there holding her hand. Waiting.

"My best friend growing up was Russell Matthews. He lived a few doors down and we were always hanging out together, doing stupid stuff. Building forts, climbing trees, that kind of thing. We played hockey together, too. Until I turned thirteen."

"What happened then?"

"Puberty." Shannon laughed, the hollow sound just a little too loud. "Well, that, and Russell decided he wanted to be a goalie. It was a new travel team so we had to try out, not like the previous years, when we were just playing rec."

"Let me guess: you kicked Russell's ass."

Shannon laughed again, the sound sad and bitter, devoid of all humor. "Yeah. And my best friend, the one I had done everything with for the last six years, turned on me. He told me there was something wrong with me, that I wasn't normal. That girls shouldn't play hockey and that I scared all the boys. And then he never spoke to me again."

The room fell quiet, filled with nothing more than the sound of their soft breathing and the low hum of the shiny black refrigerator standing in the corner. Caleb finally squeezed her hand, his heavy sigh echoing around them.

"Russell was an ass."

"True."

"So am I."

Shannon laughed again, the sound surprising her. "True, too."

"But I'm not Russell. And you don't scare me, Shannon."

She turned her head and their gazes met, held. She didn't look away, didn't try to hide the doubt and worry she knew he could see. "Maybe not, but I pissed you off. Is that really any different?"

He opened his mouth and Shannon held her breath, *knowing* he was going to say it was. *Knowing* he was going to make an excuse or blow it off. But he surprised her instead.

"No, it's not."

"Oh. I thought—"

He squeezed her hand, silencing her. "The difference is that I know I was wrong and I'm willing to admit it."

"What if it happens again? I meant it when I said I can't change, Caleb. I don't *want* to change."

"Nobody is asking you to."

"But what about next time?"

"*If* there's a next time—and I don't think there will be because I don't think I'm really as bad as Russell—you'll just have to sit me down and lecture me."

"And if that doesn't work?"

"Then you can take me outside and beat me up." And damn if he didn't smile when he said that, the devilishly crooked smile that deepened that damned dimple in his cheek.

"I think you'd enjoy that too much."

His smile widened, danced in his eyes. "Maybe." The smile faded and he leaned closer, reaching out with his free hand to tuck the hair behind her ear. He caressed her cheek, traced the line of her jaw, ran his thumb along the fullness of her lower lip. "What we've got going here, Shannon...I'm not sure what it is, but I'd like to see where it goes."

Her heart pounded in her chest, a steady *thump-thump-thump* that echoed in her ears. This was it, the chance she had been so afraid of. She could either take it...or she could walk away and always wonder *what if*.

She didn't want to wonder. And if it didn't work—well, that was a chance she'd have to take. A chance she *wanted* to take.

She leaned in, brushed her mouth against his, felt her body soften and melt as his arms folded around her and pulled her closer.

"Me, too."

chapter
TWENTY-SEVEN

"What the fuck do you mean, he's not available? Where the fuck is he?"

Coach Donovan's desperate voice echoed down the hallway, bouncing off the concrete walls and spilling through the open door of the locker room. Caleb rested his arms on his knees, trying to pretend he couldn't hear every single word.

Just like the rest of the team.

His gaze slid across the room, stopping to rest on Corbin Gauthier. His eyes were closed, his head tilted back and resting against the wall. His chest rose with each deep breath, fell with each silent exhalation. If Caleb didn't know better, he'd think the goalie was sleeping. But he *did* know better, knew the man was simply meditating, or doing whatever the hell that whole breathing thing was to mentally prepare. He'd done the same thing before every game since he'd been back. The only thing that surprised Caleb was the fact that he was doing it *here*, instead of the spare room down the hall where Dan Lory usually went before games. Gauthier was going to be in net tonight, not playing backup like he had been, so there was no reason he couldn't use that room now.

Because Dan certainly wasn't using it, not when he was in the bathroom, throwing his guts up.

Another loud retch drifted in from the bathroom. Ryan Grant paled just the tiniest bit and looked away, a damp sheen breaking out on his forehead. He noticed Caleb watching him and forced a brittle smile. "I wish he'd just go home before he gets us all sick."

Caleb was pretty sure that Ryan was more concerned about puking his own guts up instead of catching whatever the hell Lory had, but he didn't say anything. And Christ, how many times could one man hurl? He'd been at it for the last hour, ever since he finally made it to the arena. Pale, sweating, shuffling like a condemned man taking his final steps to the gallows.

Donovan had taken one look at him and swore—then swore some more when Lory admitted he'd been throwing up since this morning and had just barely made it through game-day skate.

"Why the fuck didn't he tell anyone?" Logan asked the question to nobody in particular, his voice pitched low so it wouldn't be overheard by anyone except those around him. Caleb wondered the same thing. Only Dan could answer that, though—and he was in no position to talk, not with his head in the toilet bowl.

Ryan winced when more loud retching drifted from the bathroom. He got up and moved to the door, slamming it closed just as Dan started dry heaving—but not quick enough to hide the sound of bowels exploding.

"Oh for fuck's sake, you have got to be kidding me." Ryan hurried to the other side of the room, his face paling even more. "There's something seriously fucking wrong with him."

"Food poisoning."

Everyone turned to look at Jaxon. He shrugged, his gaze focused on the blade of his stick as he wrapped it with tape. "Vomiting. The shits. Just saying it sounds like food poisoning, is all."

More yelling drifted in from the coach's office, the words unintelligible. Caleb didn't need to hear them to know they were in trouble—none of them did. They were down a goalie and they couldn't play without a backup. Normally they'd pull someone up from the Bombers but the Bombers were a few hundred miles away. No way could either of their goalies get here in time for the game, not when puck drop was in forty-five minutes. If Lory had come clean this morning...maybe. But even then, it would have been cutting it close.

And apparently the team's EBUG—emergency backup goalie—was MIA. Listening to Coach Donovan's desperate yelling was enough to clue everyone into that little newsflash.

Hunter leaned forward. "You think he'll use Mitch Halterman?"

"No idea. Wouldn't be the first time a goalie coach was used as backup."

"True. Of course, he could always use one of us. That's happened before."

Evan Leeds laughed, the sound short and sarcastic. "Yeah, but how long ago has that been? And who would he use? The only one of us who ever played in net was Ilya."

The other man's eyes widened and he shook his head. "*Da nyet.* Too many long ago. Not good."

Caleb wasn't sure if Ilya meant *not good* in that he wasn't any good, or *not good* in that the whole situation sucked. He didn't have a chance to ask because Coach Donovan barreled into the room, with the assistant coaches John Solon and Terry Dreistadt right behind him. John kept going, straight into the bathroom—probably to check on Lory. Hopefully to take the man to the hospital.

Or at least get him out of earshot before everyone else started hurling.

Donovan's fingers tightened around the papers curled in his hand as his gaze swept the room. He pulled in a deep breath then ran his free hand over his jaw, the rasp of his beard whispering in the silence surrounding them. "We need an EBUG."

Nobody said anything. And Caleb had to choke back a laugh when Ilya actually slid down on the bench, trying to hide behind Jacob. Did the big Russian think that would work, when Jacob was at least a head shorter and fifty pounds lighter?

The laughter Caleb had been choking back abruptly died. He started to speak, swallowed back the words, shook his head. No. It was ridiculous. There was no way—

"Got something to say, Johnson?"

He started to shake his head again, thought about joining Ilya in hiding behind Jacob. Then he stopped. Why not? The worst thing that could happen was everyone would laugh at him and think he'd lost his mind.

But he hadn't. And the more he thought about

it—

"Well, Johnson? Out with it."

"I just remembered that the Blades are here tonight. For that whole intermission thing they do."

Silence descended over the room, quick and complete. Heat filled his face but he refused to back down, refused to shrink under the weight of every single gaze focused on him.

Shane was the first one to speak up, his voice filled with surprised laughter. "You're out of your fucking mind. No fucking way."

A few more voices joined in, echoing Shane's words. But only a few, their tone not quite as disbelieving.

Coach Donovan wasn't one of them. In fact, the man said absolutely nothing. He just stood there, staring at Caleb, his expression carefully blank.

Then surprisingly thoughtful.

"They're here now?"

Caleb glanced at the clock hanging on the back wall then nodded. "Yeah, I think so."

Donovan ran a hand along his jaw again then shifted, turning back to exchange a look with Terry. "Are you coming up with anything else?"

"Not a fucking thing."

"Coach, you can't be serious." Disbelief filled Shane's voice as he started to stand, his hands waving frantically in front of him. Donovan leveled a dark glare in his direction and Shane quickly sat back down, not saying another word.

"Gauthier, how are you feeling tonight?"

Corbin opened his eyes, meeting Coach's direct gaze with his own. "Fine." The chilly tone in his voice matched the coach's and Caleb wondered once more what had caused the tension between the two men.

It didn't matter, not now. Not when Coach Donovan was watching him now. And why the hell was he looking at him that way, like he'd suddenly grown two heads? Caleb wanted to look away, to drop his gaze and pretend he hadn't said a fucking word. But he didn't, because Coach was suddenly talking to him, asking him a question he never thought he'd hear.

"You going to be okay with her sitting on the bench?"

Her. Shannon. Because holy shit, Coach was actually considering using her as the EBUG. He had to be, or he wouldn't ask.

"Yes, Coach." Caleb didn't try to hide his smile. "I'm more than okay with her being on the bench with us." Because unless something happened to Corbin, she wouldn't leave the bench. She'd be there as a backup only, just in case something *did* happen. And if something happened and she ended up in the net? He'd be fine with that, too. Shannon was a great goalie, he knew that from firsthand experience.

Donovan glanced around the room, his gaze resting on each player before moving to the next. "Anyone else have a problem with it?"

Nobody said a word, not even Shane.

Donovan finally nodded, almost like he was trying to convince himself, then turned toward Terry. "Find her and get the paperwork signed."

chapter
TWENTY-EIGHT

Seven minutes left in the game.

Seven minutes.

Her nerves had lasted this long. Surely they would last seven more minutes.

Shannon still couldn't believe it. The last two-plus hours were still fuzzy, cloaked in that dream-like quality that filtered everything in shades of wispy gray. But this wasn't a dream—not in that sense, anyway. This was reality...a reality she had never thought would happen.

She was playing in a real, professional hockey game. In an arena filled with close to twenty thousand people. On a bench surrounded by players who made millions of dollars a year.

Not in a quasi-semi-pro league that still struggled to sell tickets.

Not in a charity exhibition game that was supposed to have been played more for fun than anything else.

A *real* game.

Her. Shannon Wiley. Goalie for the Chesapeake Blades.

And now the emergency backup goalie for the Baltimore Banners.

She was wearing one of Dan Lory's jerseys, number thirty-seven—which just happened to be her own number. The nameplate from her Blades jersey now sewn over his—because they didn't have time to get her a jersey of her own. Everything had happened too fast. So fast, her head started spinning every time she thought of it.

She had been downstairs in the back hall of the arena, not doing much of anything except hanging out with Taylor and Sammie and Dani while they waited for everyone else to show up. TR was there, joking about doing a live broadcast from one of her social media accounts during the intermission—and teasing Shannon about her new mission to convert her into a social media junkie. Shannon had been ready to toss the soccer ball at TR when Coach Reynolds had come running up to them, followed by some man she didn't recognize.

Then Coach Reynolds looked at her, something glinting in her dark eyes, and told her to grab her gear, that she was going to be playing some hockey.

Like an idiot, Shannon had simply stared at her. Had almost said, "Duh." That was why they were here, right? To play some hockey during intermission.

Then the man stepped forward, explaining everything to her as he led her down a long hall. The Banners were short a goalie and their normal EBUG was out of town. They needed someone else to fill in.

And hey, by the way, sign this ATO and suit up because the Banners needed to be on the ice in twenty minutes.

Shannon had stared at the paperwork, completely baffled until Coach Reynolds leaned in and explained it was an amateur tryout contract. That, for one night, she'd be playing for the Banners.

Now. Tonight. *Here*.

Then she was whisked away to some office so she could change, while someone else—the equipment manager maybe, she wasn't sure—grabbed her jersey and disappeared with it. He came back a few minutes later with another jersey and pushed it toward her. She glanced down at the ball of blue material in her hands, frowning when she noticed her nameplate had been sewn over someone else's name.

Because that was all they had time for and she needed to hurry up, now, because it was time to hit the ice.

Then Caleb was there, his face close to hers, his brows pulled in a low frown as he watched her. His voice had been quiet, meant for her ears only when he spoke.

"Are you okay?"

And Shannon had looked at him, shook her head, and in a clear voice that still surprised her, told him she thought she was going to hurl.

Caleb had simply chuckled and said that was why she was here to begin with, then nudged her into line ahead of him.

And then she was on the ice, skating around for the pre-game warmups with everyone else. The Banners' new goalie, Corbin Gauthier, urged her into the net with quiet words of reassurance. There was something about him—his penetrating eyes and softly accented voice—that calmed her. And that was what she needed—calm reassurance.

After that, things settled a bit. At least, everything besides her nerves. She had time for some breathing exercises, time to relax just a bit during the first intermission as she sat in the locker room with everyone else—*the* locker room, not by herself in some small musty office with barely enough room to move.

Coach Donovan came in, talked about strategy and sticking to the script and keeping their heads in the game. Shannon almost laughed because Coach Reynolds did the same thing at every Blades' game, only with less colorful language.

The second intermission was a little more tense—which was odd, because Shannon's nerves had lessened just a little bit. They were going into the third period leading the game two-to-one, they needed to go out shooting hard to keep the lead. Instead of focusing on Coach Donovan's words, she let her mind drift, searching for her zone. She wouldn't need it—she was the backup in name only, there only if something horrendous happened and Gauthier couldn't play. She knew enough about these guys to know that wasn't going to happen, that they'd play through anything short of a heart attack or a sliced carotid artery.

And now the game was nearly over. Seven more minutes. She only had to last seven more minutes. And yeah, that was a long time in a hockey game, anything could happen. She hoped it didn't, at least not on Pittsburgh's part, because she didn't want the game to end in a tie and be forced to go to the three-on-three overtime and then, God forbid, to the shootout. She was fairly certain her nerves would finally snap and she *would* hurl if that happened.

She closed her eyes and took another cleansing breath, surprised she wasn't hyperventilating from taking so many. It was the only way she knew to make certain she looked calm on the outside. That, and frantically chomping down on the gum Coach Donovan had given her.

To help settle her nerves, he had explained with a quick wink.

Shannon reached up to adjust the Banners ballcap on her head then settled into her perch against the boards, watching as the play moved toward them.

As it moved closer to the net.

Two guys from Pittsburgh were passing the puck between them, getting closer and closer even though Ilya Semenov and Parker Gibson were right there, trying to stop them. They shot the puck, missed, moved in for the rebound and missed again. Shannon held her breath, leaning forward as she watched Gauthier make yet another save. Instead of covering the puck and killing the play, he whipped it to the side, toward Caleb. It hit the blade of his stick, bounced over, and slid toward the boards. Caleb spun around, pure poetic motion on ice, and passed the puck behind him.

The pass was intercepted by someone from Pittsburgh, who charged toward the net—

And barreled straight into Gauthier just as he'd been dropping into a butterfly position. Bodies collided, loud grunts echoing in the cold air as the net slid free. The officials were already there, pulling bodies apart, separating players before a brawl could start.

But Gauthier just lay there, not moving except for

the hands grabbing his upper thigh.

The bottom of Shannon's stomach dropped open and an icy blast of dread rushed in, numbing her as she looked on. The Banners' trainer hurried out to the ice, slipping and sliding before finally reaching the goalie. Minutes stretched around them, each passing one pulling tighter on Shannon's nerves.

Get up. Get up. Get up.

But the goalie still wasn't moving. Two more people from the Banners' bench made their way out to the ice. They were talking but Shannon couldn't hear. They were too far away. It didn't matter, she wouldn't have been able to hear even if they had been right next to her, shouting. The blood was pounding through her veins, the noise escalating until it was nothing more than the loud beat of a bass drum filling her ears.

Someone tapped on her shoulder, hard, making her think the tapping had been going on for a while. She swallowed, nearly choking on the gum, then turned to meet Coach Donovan's gaze.

"Get ready. You're going in." He nodded at something behind Shannon and she looked over her shoulder, trying not groan out loud when she saw Corbin Gauthier being helped back to the bench.

Oh shit. Holy fuck. Dammit. Dammit, dammit, *shit*.

This couldn't be happening.

This *was* happening.

She pushed the ballcap from her head, turned to reach for her helmet—and saw at least a dozen sets of eyes staring at her from the bench. Surprise. Disbelief. Disappointment. Encouragement. So many different emotions. Too many. She couldn't look, couldn't let them get to her. If she did, she'd collapse before she could make it past center ice.

She closed her eyes, breathed in, held it for a count of five. Then she dropped the helmet on her head and secured it, grabbed her stick, and started for the ice. A hand grabbed her arm and she turned around, surprised to see Coach Donovan leaning so close to her.

Surprised at the quiet encouragement in his eyes.

"I had other options for EBUG tonight but you were the best one. Just remember that."

Shannon nodded—at least, she tried to—then stepped onto the ice and skated toward the net. There would be no chance to warm up, no chance to settle in and get her legs under her. No chance to clear her head and get into her zone. This was it.

Six minutes and twelve seconds left to go in the game. And the faceoff would be right in front of her.

Talk about pressure.

She choked back a nervous laugh and got into position, ignoring the increasing noise level around her. She had to ignore it, couldn't get caught up in wondering if the crowd was cheering—or jeering.

Breathe.

Focus.

This was no different than any other game. No different than any other time she had played goalie for the last seventeen years. She could do this.

She *had* to do this.

Caleb slid up to her, his green eyes focused on hers from behind his mask.

"You okay?"

Shannon exhaled, forced a smile to her face. "Yeah. I think."

"You got this."

"Abso-fucking-lutely I have this."

"I know you do. And we've got your back." Caleb grinned then tipped his head toward her, tapping her helmet with his before skating off. Then, one by one, the other players did the same. Ilya and Parker. Marc Sanford. Even Shane Masters. All tapping their helmets against hers, all giving her words of encouragement.

And then the puck dropped and the game exploded into action. Shannon held her breath, trying to find the puck, trying to follow the game but holy fuck it was fast. Faster than she expected.

And shit, she needed to breathe. Breathe, dammit. Focus.

Shane cleared the puck and play moved away from her, giving her a chance to draw breath. What the fuck was her problem? She was fucking freaking out for no reason. She couldn't afford to do that. Couldn't afford to let the Banners down.

To let her team down.

Yes. *Her* team. For the next five minutes and eighteen seconds, the Banners were her team.

And she abso-fucking-lutely would *not* let them down.

The minutes seemed to drag on, though she knew that wasn't the case. There hadn't even been a line change yet, though she suspected one was coming soon. Maybe now—

No, not now, because dammit, Pittsburgh had the puck again and they were heading her way.

Shannon narrowed her eyes, focused on the puck hurtling toward her and nothing but the puck. Knees bent, arms relaxed, not moving, just watching. Watching...

The guy—she wasn't sure who it was, hadn't been paying attention—shot the puck, hard and fast, aiming top shelf. And oh please, was he trying to take it easy on her? Not even.

She snagged the puck midair, bringing her arm across her body and tossing it to the opposite side, right to Marc Sanford. And she couldn't help it, she was smiling. She *knew* she was smiling and figured that was probably bad form but what the hell.

She'd just made her first save in the big leagues.

Now if the Banners would actually score that insurance goal. Two would be better. Please let them score. But no, Pittsburgh's goalie blocked each shot, sending it back into play. How many minutes? How much longer before a line change? The guys had to be getting tired, she could see it on the strained lines of their faces, in the way their skates dug even harder into the ice, propelling them forward because shit, Pittsburgh was going to try to score again.

She blocked the shot again, then the rebound, then one more. She almost pulled it into her chest to stop the play. Almost—until she saw Caleb hovering near center ice, his stick at the ready, his gaze on hers.

And nobody else around him.

He tapped the stick against the ice, just once. She didn't stop to think, didn't hold her breath, didn't question the enormity of the risk she was taking. It would either work—

Or it wouldn't.

She dropped the puck right in front of her, saw a flash of white and gold and black dart toward her, like he couldn't believe she was actually giving him this sweet chance to score. And she wasn't, not even close. She gripped her stick and hit the puck, sending it flying straight toward Caleb just as something heavy bumped into her. She staggered, caught herself at the last minute, then turned to look into a pair of soft brown eyes.

And damn if the guy wasn't grinning.

"Ballsy move."

Then he took off, racing toward the other end of the ice, trying to catch Caleb. But it was too late because Caleb was already shooting the puck, fast and low, right past Pittsburgh's goalie.

And yes! Finally! The red light flashed, the horn blaring as close to twenty thousand people jumped to their feet.

Three-to-one. The Banners had that insurance goal. Now all Shannon had to do was keep blocking shots, keep Pittsburgh from scoring. For another...she glanced up, wondering how much time was left in the game. Two minutes and forty seconds.

Dread filled her. More than two minutes? And she'd be facing six players now instead of five, because she had no doubt that Pittsburgh would pull their goalie to give them an extra man.

She could do this. She *had* to do this.

She looked back at the clock, tried to tell herself that the last two minutes and forty seconds would fly by. Then she did a double-take because her name was flashing on the giant screen, just below Caleb's.

Holy shit, they were crediting her with the assist on Caleb's goal. No fucking way.

She looked around, finally hearing the cheers and applause, noticed people were actually looking at *her*. Shannon nodded before she could stop herself, realized she probably shouldn't have done that, then dropped back into position.

Breathe. Focus.

Again and again, her eyes following the puck, blocking each shot every time Pittsburgh made their way into the zone. Thankfully, it wasn't as often as she first feared because the Banners were playing aggressive hockey now, keeping the puck away from her, forcing Pittsburgh's goalie to stay in his net and even scoring that second insurance goal.

And then, finally—*finally*—the loud blare of a horn split the air, signaling the end of the game. Shannon sucked in a deep breath and leaned against the net, muttering a small prayer of thanks.

She'd done it. Her legs were shaking, her stomach was still in knots, and sweat poured from her, covering her from head to toe—but she'd done it.

Except it wasn't over yet because a tidal wave of blue and white was moving toward her then whoa, holy shit, she was sucked into the middle of it. Hands knocked her on the back, the shoulders. Heads butted against hers, helmets knocking together in congratulations. And then she was falling, buried under a sea of bodies and worried she might actually be crushed because holy hell, they were heavy.

The sea parted and someone was helping her to her feet. Steadying her. Supporting her. She adjusted her helmet, stumbled a little when her eyes met Caleb's. He opened his mouth, ready to say something, but was pushed to the side as more bodies came toward her.

The players from Pittsburgh. One by one, they skated toward her, stopping long enough to either tap her in the leg with their sticks or tap their helmet against hers. Congratulating her.

Her.

Then they were gone and it was just a few of the

Banners and her. She tugged the helmet from her head and ran her fingers through her sweaty hair, sighing in relief. Caleb was still standing next to her, his helmet cradled in the crook of one arm. And he was watching her with that crooked grin, the one that made her weak in the knees.

She dropped her hand and slid back an inch, suddenly self-conscious. "What?"

Caleb slid closer, his smile growing as he snaked an arm around her waist to keep her from skating away. "Awesome game, Wiley."

"Yeah? You think so?"

"Definitely. And that was a beautiful play. How did you even know to look for me?"

"I didn't. It was just instinct." Shannon leaned closer, her own smile growing a little wider. "Because I am *that* good."

"Yeah, you definitely are."

Then he leaned forward, his mouth capturing hers in a kiss that left no doubt about how he felt.

Nearly twenty thousand fans watched from the stands, cheering them on.

epilogue

Three Years Later

Shannon sat against the boards in her corner of the player's bench, watching the action come to a stop with the shrill blow of a whistle. She bit back a smile as a Caleb started arguing with one of the officials. It didn't matter, Caleb was being sent to the sin bin for the blatant slash against Colorado's goalie.

She had to force herself not to chuckle—Coach Donovan would tear her a new one if he caught her. Not to mention that it wouldn't look good if any of the cameras happened to be focused on her while she was laughing.

It still took more effort than it should have to keep the chuckle from breaking free. She couldn't help it, not when her husband had a really bad tendency to get pissed off whenever a goalie blocked his shot.

She should know: he still did it to her every once in a while. In practice. When they were simply playing around on the ice for fun.

And during the annual charity game between the

Banners and the Blades.

So much had happened these last three years. The Blades were still around. In fact, the league had gained enough in popularity that they had expanded to eight teams instead of the original four. The money had gotten a little better—but not good enough that any of them actually made a living from playing.

Most of the original Blades were still with the team, too, though the dynamics had changed just a bit. Taylor and Chuckie were married now, with a little girl who wasn't quite two-years old. It wouldn't be long before the little squirt was on the ice, learning everything she needed to know from her mom and all her aunts.

Shannon was the permanent EBUG for the Banners now, had been since that fluke of a game three years ago. She was sitting on the bench tonight because Corbin Gauthier left during the first period—apparently his wife had gone into labor unexpectantly so Shannon had been pulled into action for the rest of the game. Not that she expected to actually play—she'd only made it on the ice that one time. But at least she had her very own Banners jersey now: WILEY, number seventy-three.

Would she ever have a permanent position with the Banners? Not as EBUG, but as an actual paid player? Would there ever be a real contract with the Banners—or with any other team? She had hoped. Had thought that maybe, just maybe, things would have changed these last three years.

But not yet.

That didn't mean she stopped hoping. And if not for her, then maybe in plenty of time for Taylor's daughter.

Was it enough? Not really, but it was more than she had hoped for when she first started playing hockey all those years ago. When her best friend had turned on her and told her girls couldn't play; when he told her she scared all the boys.

Her gaze darted across the ice, stopped to rest on Caleb. And damn if he wasn't looking at her—she could feel the heat in his gaze, feel the love. The pride.

She wondered where Russell was now. If he still played hockey, or if he even followed the sport. She hoped he did. She hoped he could see her out here now, see all of them, and know how wrong he was.

And if she ever accidentally ran into him again, she'd look him straight in the eye and laugh in his face and tell him how wrong he'd been.

Maybe some *boys* were scared of her. Intimidated and threated.

But there was one man who believed in her. Who didn't run scared. Who loved her for who she was.

And that was abso-fucking-lutely the best feeling in the world.

###

PLAYING HARD

About the
AUTHOR

Lisa B. Kamps is the author of the best-selling series *The Baltimore Banners*, featuring "…hard-hitting, heart-melting hockey players…" [USA Today], on and off the ice. Her *Firehouse Fourteen* series features hot and heroic firefighters who put more than their lives on the line and she's introduced a whole new team of hot hockey players who play hard and love even harder in her newest series, *The York Bombers*. *The Chesapeake Blades*—a romance series featuring women's hockey—recently launched with WINNING HARD.

Lisa currently lives in Maryland with her husband and two sons (who are mostly sorta-kinda out of the house), one very spoiled Border Collie, two cats with major attitude, several head of cattle, and entirely too many chickens to count. When she's not busy writing or chasing animals, she's cheering loudly for her favorite hockey team, the Washington Capitals—or going through withdrawal and waiting for October to roll back around!

Website: www.LisaBKamps.com
Newsletter: http://www.lisabkamps.com/signup/
Email: LisaBKamps@gmail.com
Facebook:
https://www.facebook.com/authorLisaBKamps

Kamps Korner Facebook Group:
https://www.facebook.com/groups/1160217000707067/
BookBub:
https://www.bookbub.com/authors/lisa-b-kamps
Goodreads: https://www.goodreads.com/LBKamps
Instagram: https://www.instagram.com/lbkamps/
Twitter: https://twitter.com/LBKamps
Amazon Author Page:
http://www.amazon.com/author/lisabkamps

GAME MISCONDUCT
The Baltimore Banners Book 11

Corbin Gauthier never expected to play with the Baltimore Banners again, not when he'd been traded away in the league expansion eight years ago. Yet here he was, three teams and a lifetime later, back where he started as the hockey team's goalie. And back to the one woman he's never been able to forget—the one woman who is completely off-limits.

Lori Evans isn't the same young girl she'd been all those years ago when she first met the shy goalie. She's older now, more mature and confident, with her feet planted firmly on the ground. Or so she thinks until Corbin shows back up. He's not the same young man she's dreamt of all these years: a little harder, more jaded, more cynical…and more tempting than ever. And he's just as off-limits as before, maybe even more since her uncle is now the head coach for the Baltimore Banners.

At least, he's *supposed* to be off-limits. Lori has other ideas—and she knows exactly what she wants and isn't afraid to go after it. All she has to do is convince the straight-laced goalie that some things are worth drawing a penalty for—even if it means risking a chance of getting ejected from the biggest game of all.

Turn the page for an exciting peek at *GAME MISCONDUCT*, available now.

The memory hit him from out of nowhere, the pain as sharp and biting as taking a puck to the throat. He struggled to draw breath, raised his hand and clawed at the flesh of his neck as a dozen fragmented curses fell from his lips.

The woman standing several feet away blinked then slowly, carefully, raised her sculpted brows. In amusement? In silent question? He didn't know, didn't care, not when he was in danger of passing out from lack of oxygen.

Lori Evans. Was he imagining her? Was she nothing more than a hazy vision brought about from the sudden memory? No, it was her, the same girl he remembered from all those years ago.

The same, yet different. Not a *girl*—a *woman*. Her hair was a little longer now, the deep shades of honey blonde accented with lighter streaks that framed her smooth face. Her curves were a little fuller, a little softer where there had been dangerously lean muscle before. Gone were the scuffed leather boots he had always teased her about, replaced with shiny black heels that made her look taller than he remembered. Her mouth was the same, soft and full, the color a little darker thanks to the lipstick she wore. And her eyes...

She'd always had beautiful eyes, an unusual shade of amber that saw everything but could hide nothing. All emotion, all thought, had always been reflected in those deep eyes framed in sinfully long lashes. Those amber eyes watched him now—but he could no longer tell what she was thinking. Had she finally learned to hide her thoughts? Or was it simply because he hadn't seen her in so long? Because he no longer knew her?

Just as she no longer knew him.

He'd been dreading this moment for the last

several weeks, ever since he'd been traded back to the Banners. Dreading it...yet anticipating it at the same time. What kind of masochist did that make him? What did that say about his character, about the man he'd become?

Familiar amber eyes slowly raked him, from the top of his head down to the tips of his expensive black shoes, then back up again. Her gaze finally met his and he thought he saw a flash of regret in their depths. A flash of pain and betrayal. But then she blinked and the emotion was gone, maybe it had never been there, maybe it was nothing more than his imagination or his guilty conscience—

He finally sucked air into his starving lungs, a strangled grunt of relief falling from his lips in the process. Heat filled his face and he wanted to look away, wanted to turn around and dive headfirst into the elevator that would take him back upstairs.

But the doors were already closing behind him, the quiet hiss echoing off the concrete of the floor and ceiling of the parking garage. He cursed again, in French, then bit his tongue as her brows shot up once more.

Had she understood him? No, she couldn't have. He'd always had to translate for her, and even then—even knowing she didn't understand—he'd always been careful not to swear around her.

But that was eight years ago. A lot of things happened in eight years. A lot of things changed. *People* changed. Just because she hadn't understood the words and phrases back then didn't mean she didn't understand them now.

An apology hovered on the tip of his tongue, quickly dying as she moved toward him. Her eyes never left his as one hand reached out, reaching for him—

No, not *him*. The elevator. Her finger pressed the button then her arm dropped to her side as she took a step back. Still close enough that he could smell the faintest hint of her perfume, something light that reminded him of fresh air and bright sun. Close enough that he could feel the heat of her body through the tailored pantsuit she wore.

Corbin swallowed, his gaze dropping to the fit of the jacket and the way it accented her rounded chest and trim waist. More heat filled his face when he noticed her necklace, a simple silver chain with a four-leaf clover pendant resting oh-so-temptingly in the hint of cleavage peeking out from the bright blue blouse.

Corbin yanked his gaze away and swallowed again, tried to work up enough spit to loosen his tongue from the roof of his mouth. He needed to do something, say something, anything—

The elevator doors hissed open behind him. Lori hesitated, one sculpted brow darting up just a fraction of an inch as she watched him. Disappointment flared in her eyes and she shook her head, stepping around him to enter the elevator.

He should let her go. He hadn't wanted to see her, he wasn't ready, not yet. He'd been doing his best to make sure he didn't run into her—which should have been easy enough, considering she worked in one of the many offices in the building that housed the Banners' practice rink. How many people worked in that building? Sixty? A hundred? Maybe more, he didn't know. And he never saw any of them, none of the players did.

And he had never expected to run into her here, at the arena after a game.

In the *parking garage* of the arena.

If he was smart, he'd let her go. Let her walk away, the same way he'd done that humid morning eight years ago on the sidewalk of his old condo.

The doors started their silent slide closed. Another second, maybe two, and she'd be gone, back on her way upstairs to the arena. Gone, just like that morning—

He spun around and grabbed the door with his hand, pushed it back open with a flick of his wrist then stepped into the elevator. Lori's eyes widened for a fraction of a second then quickly narrowed as she watched him.

"Forget something?"

"I—" He swallowed, heat filling his face once more under her narrowed gaze. He cleared his throat and looked away, shaking his head. "No."

She didn't say anything for a few long seconds that felt like a lifetime. Was that a small chuckle he heard? He wasn't sure, was afraid to face her to find out, afraid that maybe she was laughing at him. He waited for her to push one of the buttons but she didn't. The doors closed...but the elevator didn't move.

Silence wrapped around them, suffocating him in the small space. His lungs seized again, threatening to stop working altogether as the space grew even smaller. Was he suddenly claustrophobic? Small spaces had never bothered him before, so why now?

Because he'd never been trapped with Lori before.

Trapped? No, he wasn't trapped—he'd followed her on here of his own free will. But why? What did he hope to accomplish? They hadn't seen each other for eight years, hadn't even talked in all that time. Yes, there had been a few brief calls when he first moved to

Vegas, but they were awkward, strained, filling him with remorse until he simply stopped answering.

Coward.

A fitting word, describing what he'd done. How he'd acted. It was easier to let the friendship die, easier to let his heart shrivel up instead of maintaining long-distance communication when he knew nothing would ever come of it.

When he knew nothing would ever come of *them*. There was no *them*—there could never be a *them*. Not all those years ago.

And not now, not after the things he'd done. Not after how he had treated her. He was a different man now—and not one the woman beside him would want to know.

"How's your leg?"

Her quiet question caught him off-guard, pulled him from the suffocating grip of a hundred different regrets. He darted a quick look at her, then glanced down at his leg. "My leg? It's fine. Why—"

"Must have been a quick recovery then." One corner of her mouth quirked in a quick smile before she schooled her face into a carefully blank mask.

Corbin frowned then shook his head. "Recovery? I wasn't hurt—"

He snapped his mouth closed with an audible click, remembering too late. How could he forget? The game had ended less than sixty minutes ago—the game where he had feigned an injury to his leg so their unusual EBUG—emergency back-up goalie—could play. The ruse had worked—even if Coach Donovan had given him a look that clearly said he wasn't buying the act for a second.

It didn't matter because Shannon Wiley—the

goalie for the Chesapeake Blades—had been put in during the third period. She had stopped all nine shots that Pittsburgh had sent her way while the Banners added two more to the scoreboard, winning the game four-to-one. But he couldn't admit what he'd done to anyone, especially not to the woman standing so close next to him.

He forced a grimace and reached down to rub his left thigh. "I'll be fine. Just a minor pull—"

"It was your other leg." She didn't hide her smile this time as she pointed to his right leg. "Nice try, though. And I'm impressed. By what you did, I mean."

Corbin straightened with a sigh, his gaze not quite meeting hers. "I did nothing. It was just a pull, eh? Nothing more—"

"We both know you're lying so don't deny it. What you did—" She tilted her head to the side, her thick hair falling over her shoulder with the movement. "That was really sweet of you. Honorable."

Corbin stiffened, her words slicing through him and leaving him chilled. He looked away, each word clipped when he spoke. "There is nothing sweet or honorable about me."

To his surprise, she laughed. Not a full laugh, just a whisper of a chuckle, but her amusement was clear. "Believing your own bad press, I see."

His head snapped to the side, his brows lowered in a frown as he stared at her. Why did a smile play around the corners of her mouth? Why did the same amusement he heard in her voice dance in the depths of those beautiful amber eyes? He shook his head, ready to deny whatever she thought she knew, ready to tell her she needed to look closer.

He wasn't the same man he'd been all those years

ago. Not man—*boy*. Twenty-two, yes, but still a boy. Filled with hopes and dreams. Still too innocent. Still wanting to believe—

He shook his head again and reached for the control panel to his left. His finger jammed a button near the bottom. Once, twice, the air growing thicker, suffocating him until the door finally eased open. He shoved his hand through the small space and pushed against the metal panel, forcing it to open faster until he finally stumbled out. Dank air, tinged with the mingled odors of must and gasoline, filled his lungs. He pulled in a deep breath and held it, then quickly turned to face Lori.

Corbin ignored the surprise on her face, ignored the flash of emotion in her eyes as she stared at him, her full lips slightly parted. He shook his head a final time, the movement sharp, adamant, filled with denial. "There's nothing sweet about me, *ma cocotte*. You'd do well to remember that. I'm not the same person I was all those years ago."

He spun on his heel, barely resisting the urge to run, to escape, to never look back. Her muted gasp stopped him and he turned around just as the elevator doors started sliding closed, their soft hiss nearly drowning out her words.

"Neither am I."

PLAYING THE GAME
The York Bombers Book 1

Harland Day knows what it's like to be on rock bottom: he was there once before, years ago when his mother walked out and left him behind. But he learned how to play the game and survived, crawling his way up with the help of a friend-turned-lover. This time is different: he has nobody to blame but himself for his trip to the bottom. His mouth, his attitude, his crappy play that landed him back in the minors instead of playing pro hockey with the Baltimore Banners. And this time, he doesn't have anyone to help him out, not when his own selfishness killed the most important relationship he ever had.

Courtney Williams' life isn't glamorous or full of fame and fortune but she doesn't need those things to be happy. She of all people knows there are more important things in life. And, for the most part, she's been able to forget what could have been—until Harland gets reassigned to the York Bombers and shows back up in town, full of attitude designed to hide the man underneath. But the arrogant hockey player can't hide from her, the one person who knows him better than anyone else. They had been friends. They had been lovers. And then they had been torn apart by misunderstanding and betrayal.

But some ties are hard to break. Can they look past what had been and move forward to what could be? Or will the sins of the past haunt them even now, all these years later?

Turn the page for a preview of PLAYING THE GAME, the launch title of The York Bombers, now available.

The third drink was still in his hand, virtually untouched. He glanced down at it, briefly wondered if he should just put it down and walk away. It was still early, not even eleven yet. Maybe if he stuck it out for another hour; maybe if he finished this drink and let the whiskey loosen him up. Or maybe if he just paid attention to the girl draped along his side—

Maybe.

He swirled the glass in his hand and brought it to his mouth, taking a long sip of mostly melted ice. The girl next to him—what the fuck was her name?—pushed her body even closer, the swell of her barely-covered breast warm against the bare flesh of his arm.

"So you're a hockey player, right? One of Zach's teammates?"

Her breath held a hint of red wine, too sweet. Harland tried not to grimace, pushed the memories at bay as his stomach lurched. He tightened his grip on the glass—if he was too busy holding something, he couldn't put his arm around her or push her away—and glanced down. The girl looked like she was barely old enough to be in this place. A sliver of fright shot through him. They did card here, right? He wasn't about to be busted picking up someone underage, was he?

She had a killer body, slim and lean with just enough muscle tone in her arms and legs to reassure him that she didn't starve herself and probably worked out. Long tanned legs that went on for miles and dainty feet shoved into shoes that had to have heels at least five inches tall. He grimaced and briefly wondered how the hell she was even standing in them.

Of course, she *was* leaning against him, her full breasts pushing against his arm and chest. Maybe that was because she couldn't stand in those ridiculous heels. Heels like that weren't meant for walking—they were fuck-me heels, meant for the bedroom.

He looked closer, at her platinum-streaked hair carefully crafted in a fuck-me style and held in place by what had to be a full can of hairspray—or whatever the fuck women used nowadays. Thick mascara coated her lashes, or maybe they weren't even her real lashes, now that he was actually looking. No, he doubted they were real. That was a shame because from what he could see, she had pretty eyes, kind of a smoky gray set off by the shimmery eyeshadow coloring her lids. Hell, maybe those eyes weren't even real, maybe they were just colored contacts.

Fuck. Wasn't anything real anymore? Wasn't anyone who they really claimed to be? And why the fuck was he even worried about it when all he had to do was nod and smile and take her by the hand and lead her out? Something told him he wouldn't even have to bother with taking her home—or in his case, to a motel. No, he was pretty sure all he had to do was show her the backseat of his Expedition and that would be it.

Her full lips turned down into a pout and Harland realized she was waiting for him to answer. Yeah, she had asked him a question. What the hell had she asked? Oh, yeah—

"Uh, yeah. Yeah, I play hockey." He took another sip of the watery drink and glanced around the crowded club. Several of his teammates were scattered around the bar, their faces alternately lit and shadowed by the colored lights pulsing in time to the music.

Jason pulled his tongue from some girl's throat long enough to motion to the mousy barmaid for a fresh drink. His gaze caught Harland's and a wide grin split his face when he nodded.

Harland got the message loud and clear. How could he miss it, when the nod was toward the girl hanging all over him? Jason was congratulating him on hooking up, encouraging him to take the next step.

Harland took another sip and looked away. Tension ran through him, as solid and real as the hand running along his chest. He looked down again, watched as slender fingers worked their way into his shirt. Nails scraped across the bare flesh of his chest, teasing him.

Annoying him.

He put the drink on the bar and reached for her hand, his fingers closing around her wrist to stop her. The girl looked up, a frown on her face. But she didn't move her hand away. No, she kept trying to reach for him instead.

"What'd you say your name was?"

"Does it matter?" Her lips tilted up into a seductive smile, full of heated promise as her fingers wiggled against his chest.

Did it matter? It shouldn't, not when all Harland had to do was smile back and release her hand and let her continue. Or take her hand and lead her outside. So why the fuck was he hesitating? Why didn't he do just that? That was why he came here, wasn't it? To let go. Loosen up. Hook up, get things out of his system.

No. That may be why Jason and Zach and the others were here and why they brought him along—but that wasn't why he was here. So yeah, her name mattered. Maybe not to him, not in that sense. He just wanted to know she was interested in *him* and not what he did. That he wasn't just a trophy for her, a conquest to be bragged about to her friends in the morning.

He gently tightened his hand around her wrist and pulled her arm away, out of reach of his chest. "Yeah. It matters."

Something flashed in her eyes—surprise? Impatience? Hell if he knew. He watched her struggle with a frown, almost like she didn't want him to see it. Then she pasted another bright smile on her face, this one a little too forced, and pulled her arm from his grasp.

"It's Shayla." She stepped even closer, running her hand along his chest and down, her finger tracing the waistband of his jeans.

He almost didn't stop her. Temptation seized him, fisting his gut, searing his blood. It would be easy, so easy.

Too easy.

Then a memory of warm brown eyes, wide with innocence, came to mind. Clear, sharp and almost painful. Harland closed his eyes, his breath hitching in his chest as the picture in his mind grew, encompassing soft brown hair and perfect lips, curled in a trembling smile.

"Fuck." His eyes shot open. He grabbed the girl's hand—Shayla's—just as she started to stroke him through the worn denim. Her own eyes narrowed and she made no attempt to hide her frown this time.

"What are you doing?" Her voice was sharp, biting.

"I could ask you the same thing."

Her hand twisted in his grip. Once, twice. "Zach told me you needed to loosen up. That you were looking for a little fun."

Zach had put her up to this? Harland should have

known. He narrowed his eyes, not surprised when the girl suddenly stiffened. Could she see his distaste? Sense his condemnation? He leaned forward, his mouth close to her ear, his voice flat and cold.

"Maybe you want me to whip my cock out right here so you can get on your knees and suck me off? Have everyone watch? Will that do it for you?"

She ripped her hand from his grasp and pushed him away, anger coloring her face. "You're a fucking asshole."

Harland straightened and fixed her with a flat smile. "You're right. I am."

She said something else, the words too low for him to hear, then spun around and walked away. Her steps were short, angry, and he had to bite back a smile when she teetered to the side and almost fell.

Loathing filled him, leaving him cold and empty. Not loathing of the girl—no, the loathing was all directed at himself. What the fuck was his problem?

The girl was right: he was a fucking asshole. A loathsome bastard.

Harland yanked the wallet from his back pocket and pulled out several bills, enough to cover whatever he'd had to drink and then some. He tossed down the watered whiskey, barely feeling the slight burn as it worked its way down his throat. Then he turned and stormed toward the door, ignoring the sound of his name being called.

He should have gone home, back to the three-bedroom condo he was now forced to share with the sorry excuse that passed for his father. But he wasn't in the mood to deal with his father's bullshit, not in the mood to deal with anything. So he drove, with no destination in mind, needing distance.

Distance from the spectacle he had just made of himself.

Distance from what he had become.

Distance from who he was turning into.

But how in the hell was he supposed to distance himself...from himself?

Harland turned into a residential neighborhood, driving blindly, his mind on autopilot. He finally stopped, eased the SUV against the curb, and cut the engine.

Silence greeted him. Heavy, almost accusing. He rested his head against the steering wheel and squeezed his eyes shut. He didn't need to look around to know where he was, didn't need to view the quiet street filled with small houses that showed years of wear. Years of life and happiness and grief and torment.

"Fuck." The word came out in a strangled whisper and he straightened in the seat, running one hand down his face. Why did he keep coming here? Why did he keep tormenting himself?

She didn't want to see him, would probably shove him off the small porch if he ever dared to knock on the door. He knew that, as sure as he knew his own name.

As sure as he knew that she'd be sickened by what he had become. Three years had gone by. Three years where he'd never bothered to even contact her. Hell, maybe he was being generous. Maybe he was giving himself more importance than he deserved. Maybe she didn't even remember him.

He rubbed one hand across his eyes and took in a ragged breath, then turned his head to the side. The house was dark, just like almost every other house on the block. But he didn't need light to see it, not when it was so clear in his mind.

A simple cottage style home, with plain white siding that was always one season away from needing a new coat of paint. Flowerbeds filled with exploding color that hid the age of the house. A small backyard filled with more flowers and a picnic table next to the old grill, where something was always being fixed during the warmer months.

An image of each room filled his mind, one after the other, like a choppy movie playing on an old screen. Middle class, blue collar—but full of laughter and warm memories. He knew the house, better than his own.

He should. He'd spent more time here growing up than he had at his own run-down house the next street over. He had come here to escape, stayed because it was an oasis in his own personal desert of despair.

Until he had ruined even that.

He closed his eyes against the memories, shutting them out with a small whimper of pain. Then he started the truck and pulled away, trying to put distance between himself and the past.

A past that was suddenly more real than the present.

Made in the USA
Middletown, DE
30 August 2019